F
You
or

ABOUT THE AUTHOR

Michael Coleman was born in Forest Gate,
East London. In his life journey from aspiring footballer
to full-time writer he has variously been employed as
a waiter, a computer programmer, a university lecturer,
a software quality assurance consultant and a charity
worker. He is married, with four children
and one grandchild.

Michael has written many novels, including the
Carnegie-shortlisted *Weirdo's War*. His website can
be found at www.michael-coleman.com

Acclaim for *Weirdo's War*:

'Tense, psychological and instructive.' *The Times*

'As thought-provoking as it is exciting...addresses
fundamental truths about human character
and behaviour.' *Booktrusted News*

For my wife, Theresa

ORCHARD BOOKS
338 Euston Road, London NW1 3BH
Orchard Books Australia
Level 17, 207 Kent Street, Sydney, NSW 2000, Australia

Hardback ISBN: 978 1 84616 344 9
Paperback ISBN: 978 1 84616 345 6

First published in 2007 by Orchard Books

3 5 7 9 10 8 6 4
Printed in Great Britain

Orchard Books is a division of Hachette Children's Books,
an Hachette Livre UK company

www.orchardbooks.co.uk

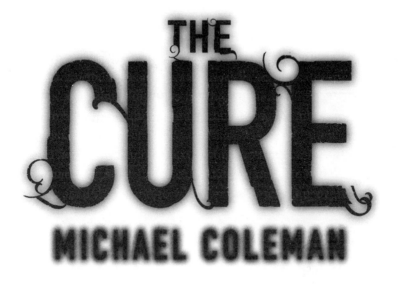

THE CURE

MICHAEL COLEMAN

ORCHARD BOOKS

'Where wast thou when I laid the foundations of the earth?
Declare, if thou hast understanding.'

The Book of Job, 38:4

Book One

The day was Thursday, 25th December. The year, 274 AD. The time, according to the silent clock on the dormitory wall, just before 6.30am.

Raul lay awake for a few moments, listening to the sounds punctuating the chill air: Nahmet's dry and rasping cough, which always miraculously vanished the moment he woke up; Odam's snuffling, boar-like snores; Kohn's creaking bed-spring, almost metronomic so regularly did he turn during the night. Each familiar sound told Raul that the three boys who shared the nurture-house dormitory with him were dead to the world, in no hurry to greet another anonymous day.

Holding his covers tight around his shoulders, Raul eased himself from his lumpy bed and stood up. He gasped as his feet landed on the cold floor. Dabbing blindly for his shoes, he thrust his feet inside. A couple of noiseless steps later he was inching open the heavy dormitory door.

Outside, a short, dimly-lit corridor led to a dormer window. Raul crept to the padded bench seat beneath it and sat down. He smiled. The windowsill, scarred by the carved initials of previous residents, was littered with breadcrumbs. Odam, it had to be! Only he was ever hungry enough to risk the loss of a day's pay for breaking the Guardian's house rule – one of many – which forbade the removal of food from the eating table.

Sweeping the crumbs into one hand, Raul gently opened the window and cast them out onto the icy breath of the morning. He felt a flutter of excitement. Perhaps the first snowfall of winter was on its way! That at least would make this a December day to remember.

Closing the window, Raul hoisted his feet up onto the seat and tucked his knees beneath his chin – his 'dreaming position' his sister Arym called it, always with a roll of her eyes. Raul didn't care. This short period at the dawn of the day was precious. All too soon the Guardian's alarm call would be stirring the nurture-house like a stick thrust into a hornet's nest. Peace would give way to commands and noise, and thought to a day filled with dull classes and monotonous Industry. This was his one chance to be still.

Even in the short time since Raul had got up, the sky had lightened from charcoal grey to pewter. Familiar landmarks were becoming visible.

Against the horizon the bulky outline of Parens Island was taking shape. The island stood some three miles offshore, beyond the chill waters of Craston Sound. It was a regular topic of debate. Exactly what went on there, nobody seemed to know. Into this vacuum nurture-house residents had flooded tales of their own invention. Odam insisted the place was an asylum. Nahmet had been told on good authority that it was a squalid prison. Arym simply *knew* it was a disease-infested children's hospital and that Orb Island – the tiny island beyond it, as unseen as the dark side of the moon – was nothing less than a graveyard for the hospital's wretched young patients. Arym claimed to have seen one once, on a free Sunday afternoon.

'A boy!' she'd said. 'Looked like a walking ghost, he did. Sitting in the cargo boat, he was, like he was going to his execution!'

No one had believed her. It seemed that everybody but Arym knew that the master of the daily cargo boat to Parens Island occasionally took his drippy son with him.

Closer to home, Raul noticed other tall dwellings – many of them nurture-houses like his own – beginning to show signs of life. Windows glowed. A doorway would flare briefly into light as it was opened, then close again. Soon it would be possible to discern the pinks, blues and creams of the pastel-washed stucco walls.

And then, as if it were a magnet, one building in particular drew Raul's gaze. Almost equidistant between his nurture-house and the harbour, its blunted spire stood tall amongst the grey-tiled rooftops like an adult surrounded by infants. The Celebreon of Our Saviour.

Raul felt his stomach tighten, his body grow tense. There was so much about the Celebreon that attracted him, that appealed to his senses. Its aged stone walls virtually seeped with history. Inside, at those inexplicable moments when the teeming hordes of pilgrims would simultaneously fall silent, feelings of peace and warmth seemed to penetrate his heart.

And yet, Raul's feelings of unease still remained. If anything, they'd grown stronger of late. Why was the Celebreon such a contradiction? Why, when it was so old, was it so much a symbol of the new and ever-changing? Why was it so wrong to question the doctrines and

7

dogmas that it represented? Were they really as infallible as they'd always been taught...?

'Couldn't you sleep, either?'

The whisper made Raul start. Then, quickly realising who had crept up behind him, his stab of fear turned into mild irritation.

'What do you want, Arym?' he hissed, glaring at the arrival even as he made room for her on the bench seat.

'Oh, that's a nice way to greet your sister,' said the tousled-haired girl.

'*Half*-sister,' corrected Raul.

'The *better* half,' responded Arym, with a poke of her tongue. 'Elder and better.'

It was a cheerful exchange, regularly made. And yet, beneath it, the banter carried a shared understanding which it would have pained them both to admit.

Raul and Arym had been born of the same mother. Their respective fathers, unknowing and unknown, were a complete mystery to them. They both accepted this and cared little. That was the way of the world and of every resident in the nurture-house. But as for their nameless mothers, that was different. They all carried the same hope in their hearts: that their mothers had suffered some misfortune, had been carried away by accident or illness – anything but the savage truth that Raul and Arym had recently discovered.

The Guardian had spoken without ceremony a few weeks previously, on Arym's fifteenth birthday.

'Arym and Raul, the law requires that you be told the known facts of your origins. They are these.' She'd begun to read from a formal-looking document with a crest at the

8

head. 'Your mother transferred you both into the care of the Republic...'

'That's not true!' Raul had shouted instantly, more in hope than from the few memories he had, which were as thin as mist.

The Guardian had continued without pause, 'Arym, you were born on 17th Quarmon 259 AD. Raul, you were born just over fifteen months later, on 22nd September 260 AD. Your birth-mother, with the Republic's assistance, continued to care for you for two further years. She then transferred you both into the care of the Republic.'

'What was her name?' was all Arym had been able to ask.

'That I am not empowered to divulge,' the Guardian had said.

'She means she can't tell us,' Raul had snapped, quick-tempered. 'Or won't.'

The Guardian had glared at him, her small eyes glittering in the subdued light of her panelled study. 'Entrusting you both to the care of the Republic was your mother's right. So, also, is her right not to be named.'

And, with that, the Guardian had brought the brief meeting to a close. Even before they'd left her room she had swept aside their early lives and was busying herself with other papers.

'So what are you doing awake this early?' Raul now asked his sister. Given the choice, Arym would retire with the owl rather than rise with the lark.

'You're not telling me you've forgotten?'

'Forgotten what?'

Head shaking, Arym pointed out through the window

towards the spire of the Celebreon. 'The Enshrinement, of course!'

Raul hadn't forgotten. He'd remembered, but only in the detached way he would remember the class work he should have completed or the house duties he'd been allocated. For him, the Enshrinement of yet another Blessed gave rise to none of the exhilaration and anticipation that it did for Arym. It was, he knew, just one of the ways in which they were different.

There were obvious similarities, of course. Raul only had to look at himself in a mirror to be left in no doubt that he and Arym were of the same flesh. They shared virtually identical warm brown eyes. Likewise their dense curls of hair, however much Arym tried to straighten hers. And each possessed a smile which, whenever it broke through their instinctive frowns of suspicion, would gladden the receiver's heart.

They both had a temper, too. Arym's was akin to a smouldering fire. It might take some time to reach flashpoint, but when it did the object of her rage would know about it for some time. Raul, by contrast, was a firecracker. For him an outburst against injustice was like a short sleep to a cat: essential, quick – and then forgotten.

All these, and more, Raul recognised and appreciated. They were the bonds which united them, as if he and Arym were in some way reflections of their mother to each other. Must they then have inherited their differences from their fathers? Differences which Raul was finding it as difficult to express as he was to ignore. Differences which went far deeper than appearance or temper...

'I just love Enshrinements!' whispered Arym, her face

aglow. 'Everything about them is so exciting! The music and the dancing, the pilgrims with their strange voices and smells... Why, even the traders seem livelier and friendlier.'

'Well, of course they are!' snapped Raul, more loudly than he'd intended. 'They know there's nothing to beat an Enshrinement for making a fat profit.'

Arym glanced nervously behind, as if worried that the shadows in the dim corridor might have heard. 'Don't say that kind of thing, Raul!'

Raul wanted to ask why not. He wanted to say what he thought, really thought, about Enshrinements and the doctrines that supported them. He wanted to assault Arym's unquestioning acceptance, make her think about it, have her defend it against his growing doubts. But now was not the time.

Instead he asked lamely, 'Who is it anyway?'

'Who is it?' echoed Arym. 'Raul, do you live on this planet or do you simply call in occasionally on your way home to Venus? It's the Blessed Dyna, of course!'

'A singer,' scoffed Raul.

'She's far more than that! She was actually *born* near Craston... In our *own* Region, Raul! And don't tell me you haven't heard what the Enshrinement Judgement said. Nobody can be that ignorant.'

Arym began to quote softly, as if the words were engraved upon her heart. '"Through her words and music Dyna has brought great joy to people of the Republic. She has also performed many acts of charity. Now her many followers have made their voices heard. Our decision is that Dyna be accorded the state of Blessedness."'

'So her songs are popular,' Raul argued. 'She's also covered her face and held her nose and gone to visit some of the poor living on the edge of the Wasteland. Great! And that's all it takes to become a Blessed?'

'No, of course it isn't! You have to be elected by the faithful, like Dyna was.'

'Yes, and in a couple of months the faithful will have forgotten about her. They'll be worshipping somebody else by then.'

Arym sounded almost tearful. 'That's not true!'

'Of course it's true. Sure, I know some of the early Blesseds still have their followers but nowadays we get a new one every five minutes. And why? Because they're worthy of worship? No – because they make money for the Celebreons!'

Now Arym did more than glance behind. She lunged for her brother, her hand trying to reach his mouth to shut him up.

'Are you mad, Raul? Don't even *think* that sort of thing!'

Raul leapt to his feet, evading her angry fingers. But her reaction was enough to calm him. She was right. Such thoughts weren't only disturbing; they could be very dangerous. He turned back to his sister. Arym was the only person he could really confide in. He had to tell somebody about the doubts that were increasingly filling his head and his heart. Arym wouldn't like it one bit – but there was nobody else.

The shrill jangle of the nurture-house alarm put paid to whatever opportunity there might have been. Both of them knew better than to get on the wrong side of the Guardian at any time, let alone first thing in the morning.

Quickly sliding out from the seat, Arym gathered up her shapeless gown and hurried away down the stairs to her own dormitory. Raul took one last glance out of the window before hastening back to the attic room at the end of the corridor. The three other occupants of Raul's dormitory were already on the move.

'Enshrinement day, Kohn!' cried Odam as he lumbered past. 'Shift yourself! If we miss time off because your powdered butt is late for breakfast the whole house will tear you apart!'

The threat snapped Kohn awake. Moments later he was scurrying towards the washroom, Raul beside him.

'You think the Guardian will give us some time off this afternoon?' he asked.

Raul shrugged. It was on the tip of his tongue to joke that if they were given work respite every time there was an Enshrinement they'd never earn a penny. He resisted the temptation. 'Maybe,' was all he said.

After washing they hurried back to the dormitory. There, each slid into their day clothes, made their beds, then spent just long enough tidying their respective quarters of the cramped room so as to pass any unscheduled inspection. That done, they hurried as noiselessly as possible down the main stairs where, like tributaries flowing into a river, other corridors disgorged their own outflows of residents.

There were eighteen of them at present: ten boys and eight girls. The number fluctuated as residents departed and others arrived. Newcomers were always twelve years of age, often shrewd and feral after spending their early years in the undisciplined atmosphere of a primary home.

The Guardian's regime came as a shock. For some it remained so until they left the nurture-house four years later. No resident was over sixteen years old. At that age the Republic officially ceased to raise them.

Reaching the ground floor, they shuffled silently into a large, square room that served at different times for dining, learning and Industry. After breakfast, the tables would be cleared and books taken from one of the room's many cupboards. After lunch a different cupboard would provide protective clothing for whatever that day's menial task might be.

Three long tables dominated the room. At one of them, Raul slid in to his regular place amongst the standing boys. Arym was already standing with the girls at the second table, her back to him. The third table was positioned at right angles to the other two, a discrete distance away. At this were seated the Guardian and the nurture-house staff.

The Guardian was writing on a vellum pad. Nobody moved until she finally put down her pen, looked up and said, 'Good morning, Daughters and Sons.'

'Good morning, Guardian,' came the sing-song reply.

'You may begin.'

Raul sat down hurriedly. He made short work of the bowl of tasteless cereal already laid in front of him. He gulped down the large glass of flavoured drink, then joined the queue for the servery hatch. There, unappetising though the food was, Raul always loaded his plate. Even if he couldn't force it all down he knew that Odam would usually be willing to part with a few pennies to satisfy his bottomless stomach.

They ate in suppressed silence until the Guardian rapped

on the table with the handle of her knife. It was the signal that they were allowed ten minutes for conversation. Immediately, Odam stretched a pudgy fist out into the centre of the table. In his palm nestled a black-dotted dice.

'One throw each,' he said. 'Lowest asks. Right?'

From the way the others nodded in agreement, Raul knew he'd missed something. An arrangement, perhaps made while he was in the corridor talking with Arym.

'Ask who, what?'

He didn't get an answer for a moment, not until Odam had thrown a five and, opposite, Kohn a four. Only when he'd moved the dice on to Nahmet did Kohn lean forward and hiss, 'Ask the Guardian if we can start Industry period late to watch the Enshrinement procession.'

Nahmet, groaning, had cast a two. On went the dice. Another six, a four, a couple of threes. It came to Raul. He let it lie where it was.

'I'm not doing this,' he said.

'I'll do it for you, then,' said Odam. Reaching forward he scooped up the dice and sent it tumbling against a mug. It bounced back and settled, just a single dot uppermost. 'One. Raul it is.'

Raul flicked the dice away with the back of his hand. 'Forget it.'

'Come on, Raul,' said Nahmet. 'The Guardian likes you. Everybody knows that.'

Raul wasn't so sure. True, he was one of the few residents who hadn't been caught thieving or fighting or begging at some time or other. But that wasn't to say the Guardian liked him. The stern, sour woman didn't give the impression of liking any of them.

'I don't care. I'm not doing it.'

'He's scared,' snorted Kohn. 'Got no balls.'

Nahmet sniggered. 'Like his mother!'

The jibe exploded in Raul's head. Lunging across the table he grabbed the front of Nahmet's frayed shirt and yanked him forward. 'I won't ask because I'm not interested in any stinking Enshrinement!'

From the head table came the loud crack of a knife handle on solid wood. The silence was instant, but as Raul slumped back onto the seat it seemed as if his words still hung in the air. He turned. The Guardian's eyes were trained on him, making him feel alone in the crowded room.

'Do you and Nahmet have a problem, Raul?'

'No, Ma'am.'

'Why did I just see you acting aggressively, then?'

'I lost my temper, Ma'am.' Raul quickly enacted the prescribed ritual, holding out his hand for Nahmet to shake and saying, 'I'm sorry, Nahmet, I ask for your forgiveness.' Then he fell silent, hoping that that was where it would end. But the Guardian immediately spoke again.

'Did I hear you mention the Enshrinement, Raul?'

There was no point in denying it. The Guardian never asked a question to which she didn't know the answer. 'Yes, Ma'am.'

'What about it? Exactly.'

'The boys wanted me to ask you if we could watch the Enshrinement procession this afternoon.'

The Guardian's features softened with a beneficent smile. 'A worthy request – and one I will consider. Paying homage to the Blesseds is our duty.' Her smile suddenly disappeared. 'But that was not what you said, was it Raul?'

'No, Ma'am.'

'Then what did you say?'

Raul stiffened. He'd seen her do this to others: subject them to an inquisition, emphasise her authority by making them wilt in front of everybody. Well he wasn't going to give her that pleasure.

'I said, Ma'am…that I'd prefer to do something else.'

'Such as?'

The Guardian was smiling again. But this smile was different. It was a mocking smile, inviting imitation by everybody else in the room. Raul's temper flared like ignited brushwood.

'Such as *anything*!' he snapped.

From all around came involuntary gasps. But the silence quickly returned, dense enough to feel. The Guardian was not smiling now, mockingly or otherwise.

'Explain yourself,' she said.

'There are too many Blesseds!' shouted Raul. 'Once they were great world teachers like the Saviour. But now you can have local Blesseds. It's as if anybody can become one. If you ask me, the only reason Dyna's being enshrined is because she was born near here!'

'That does not invalidate her worth, Raul,' said the Guardian icily. 'The highest state one can achieve in this world is to become a Blessed. Do not despise Dyna because she's made it.'

'I don't despise her, Ma'am,' Raul retorted. 'I just don't think she's done anything special.'

'She was elected by common consent. By the people.'

'That doesn't mean she's worthy, does it?'

'Yes, it does, Raul. The election procedure involved the whole community. Therefore the result is infallible. And what that means is that once a person has been deemed a Blessed we cannot – we must not – question that decision. It is binding.'

'Even when we know it's just a way of bringing the pilgrims into town with their money? Especially at this time of year,' snapped Raul.

The Guardian's eyes narrowed. 'That is an interesting theory. Please explain yourself.'

From behind, Raul felt a panicky tugging at his shirt. Arym, he knew, trying to shut him up. But he'd passed the point of no return. The Guardian's superior tone had only fanned the flames of his anger.

'It's obvious, isn't it?' he shouted. 'During spring and summer Craston gets plenty of visitors. But in the winter it's quiet – *too* quiet for the traders. So what better way of bringing in business than the Enshrinement of a new Blessed!'

The Guardian paused, as if in thought. Then, she addressed not Raul, but the others in the hushed room. 'Does anybody else here share Raul's, what can I call it? – *original* viewpoint?'

Heads turned downwards. Fingers fiddled with smeared plates or pushed crumbs back and forth. But nobody spoke. What point was there? Questioning such as Raul's could only lead to trouble, they all knew that.

The Guardian broke the hush herself. 'Arym,' she said sharply. 'Do you share your brother's opinion?'

Arym, startled and annoyed, shook her head violently.

'No, Ma'am. No I don't. I wish I could do more than watch the procession. I wish I could go to the Enshrinement itself!'

'I'm sure you do, Arym. But only invited guests are allowed into the ceremony.'

A smile of practised sympathy landed on the Guardian's face, but they all heard the unspoken words that lay behind it. Dignitaries would be there. Important people. But for those whose very survival depended on the charity of the Republic – people like Arym – there would never be a place.

'Neither, I have decided, will you be allowed to watch this afternoon's procession. There is far too much work to be done.' The Guardian paused, waiting with uncharacteristic patience for the groans to subside. Only then did she impart her good news:

'However, the Council of Guardians have arranged with the Celebreon authorities for a short Enshrinement celebration service for nurture-house residents to take place this coming Sunday afternoon. You will all be allowed to attend that.'

All around him, Raul heard the squeals of delight. They were swiftly quelled by the Guardian's raised hand.

'Do you wish to go, Raul?'

He felt a sharp dig in his side – from Arym, he didn't doubt. Her prompting was unnecessary. Raul knew full well what was expected of him. 'Yes, Ma'am. I do wish to go.'

'Do you have anything else to say?'

The Act of Contrition, of course. Raul stood, the words already forming on his lips.

'Oh my Guardian, representative of the Republic,

because you are so good I am sorry I have offended you. I firmly resolve, with your help, to amend my ways and never to do so again.'

The Guardian inclined her head in acceptance. 'Thank you, Raul. For your penance you will spend an extra hour in Industry this evening. Everybody stand.'

And that was it, the announcement of Raul's penance being almost submerged beneath the scraping of chairs. Only the sight of the Guardian adding a short note to her pad suggested to him that while his sin might have been forgiven, it was not going to be forgotten. Then she was putting her pen aside and placing that same writing hand solemnly across her breast.

'The Lyrene Promise,' she commanded.

The familiar litany came easily, mechanically, each of them reciting the words it seemed they'd always known:

'We promise this day to be cheerful and kind and curious and brave and patient, to study and think and work hard, all of us in our different ways.'

The promise said, breakfast-time was officially concluded. The residents all knew better than to move before the Guardian, but as soon as she and the rest of her staff had left, they all huddled together in excited groups, talking about what was to come.

This sense of anticipation lasted throughout the morning's study periods. Today's included Science and Computation, Raul's favourites. He found them endlessly fascinating, his mind buzzing with questions. How did Computation work? How could a formula describe a curve or a pattern or a chemical reaction? Why could all perimeters of all circles be described by exactly the same formula, whatever their diameter?

He'd found that fact quite staggering – even though Mr Sprague, their teacher for that day, had mentioned it with all the enthusiasm of a man commenting on the likelihood of rain:

'The circumference of a circle is given by the formula πd, where d is the diameter and π the universal constant.'

Did that mean that circles were governed by exactly the same formula wherever they were to be found? Would a circle on one of the distant stars be subject to exactly the same formula? And were there other universal constants? He'd asked Mr Sprague this question one morning.

'Dozens of them,' he'd replied curtly.

'Such as?'

'Velocity of light. Absolute zero of temperature. Universal constant of gravitation...nothing you'd understand.'

'I might. One day.'

Sprague had shaken his head – whether in disbelief or because it ached, Raul hadn't been sure. He'd simply added, 'Well if that day ever does come they'll not have changed. That's what a universal constant is: something that's been the same since the beginning of time.' And with that he'd lumbered off, fumbling for his hip-flask as he went.

Since then, Raul had studied *The Writings* carefully. In the book he'd found plenty of clues about how things came to be. He'd realised that in mysterious ways all sorts of things were connected. Equations and universal constants enabled the passage of the stars and planets to be

21

computed; they even had something to do with how the times of the tides in Craston Sound could be predicted to the minute.

The world he knew rested upon unseen scientific laws, laws that had operated since the dawn of time. *The Writings* said as much. But there was so much that it *didn't* say. Important things – infinitely more important than the Enshrinement of a new Blessed!

A giggling from the rear desks jolted Raul back into the here-and-now. Arym and her friend Shaani were head-to-head as usual. His sister interrupted her conversation for no longer than it took to give Raul a silent, withering look that told him his embarrassing outburst that morning hadn't been forgotten.

Raul returned to the exercises Mr Sprague had given them to complete. He enjoyed them, would even do some of his own devising – unlike Arym, whose only computational interest was in working out how to spend the miserly sums of pocket money they were handed by the Bursar every Saturday evening as scant reward for the Industry they'd completed during the week.

The Bursar was responsible for the Industry periods which filled every afternoon in the nurture-house. He was a small, punctilious man who regarded a resident's physical and moral welfare as being nothing to do with him: that was the role of the Guardian. His job was simply to make sure they generated income for the nurture-house coffers and, in so doing, paid back at least some of the outlay expended on them by the Republic.

And so, after a short lunch break, the study room became the Industry room. Bulging boxes and packages were unloaded from the cupboards. Normally the whole group of residents would be working on the same task, whatever it might be. Folding and collating circulars was common, as were various packaging tasks. Whatever the activity it was always mindless and repetitive; the only requirement was for the residents to work quickly and accurately. But on this afternoon there was a change to the usual pattern.

The Bursar drew Raul, Kohn, Arym and Shaani to one side. 'You four come with me,' he said curtly.

He led them to a separate room holding four chairs grouped around a large, square table. In the centre of this table sat two huge boxes, their tops already prised open. Beside each chair was another box – smaller, and empty.

The Bursar motioned the four of them to sit down. 'This task requires a certain neatness,' he said. 'But not at the expense of speed.'

Raul took his place, mentally interpreting the Bursar's words. 'Be careful, but get a move on. The more you do the more the nurture-house earns.'

One of the boxes in the centre of the table was packed with gold-coloured medallions. They were glittering now but the layer of gilt was wafer-thin. It would rub off within weeks, if not days. The edge of each medallion was crenellated, giving it a passing resemblance to the sun. Its centre, however, was flat and blank.

Raul could guess what the second box contained, even before the Bursar lifted it up and tipped a cascade before him: icons of the newly Blessed Dyna, round and smiling, perfectly sized to fit in the centre of the all-purpose medallion. That was their job. To peel one of the icons from

23

its backing, then press it into position in the centre of a blank medallion. Result: one instant Enshrinement memento to be placed in the box at their side, before they did the same task again. And again, and again, until the jangling alarm would bring the Industry period to an end.

Once satisfied that they were up to the complications of the task, the Bursar soon drifted away to check on the residents he'd left behind in the main room. As each medallion and each icon passed through Raul's hands, his mind began to wander once again. Different sized circles – and yet both governed by the same universal constant, π. Who discovered it? How did they discover it? How would things have been different if the value of π had been different? What had caused π to be? Why did π exist at all? Could it be that his world and all the stars beyond depended, in some inexplicable way, on the very existence of such universal constants?

Slowly the chatter of the other three seeped into Raul's thoughts. While the Bursar had been around they'd stayed quiet. He was the Guardian's second-in-command, after all. But with him gone, talk was possible. Now, opposite him at the table, Kohn and Shaani were looking at their piles of finished work and grinning.

'Rich pickings on Sunday I'd say,' said Kohn, emphasising the second word.

Shaani laughed, softly and open-mouthed. 'Reckon I'd better take a big bag, then!'

'Ssh!' hissed Arym from beside Raul. She glanced back towards the door. 'If he hears you…'

'He won't. He'll be with the others for a good time yet. He *trusts* us…' Kohn grinned again, then leaned

24

across to Arym. 'Well, are you in with us or not?'

These few words were all Raul needed to work out what they'd been talking about during his reverie. Thieving. Stealing from the trader's stalls while their backs were turned. Lifting goods from the bags of unwary pilgrims – from their very pockets, sometimes. And, when they were done, taking their gains to one of the many unscrupulous traders who would pay for them, no questions asked. With the crowds in and around the Celebreon there would be rich pickings indeed for the likes of Kohn and Shaani.

Arym shook her head. 'Not this time, Kohn. I want to get to the Celebreon early. I don't want to miss anything. Dyna's my favourite Blessed!'

Shaani tossed a completed medallion into the box beside her and turned her doe-like eyes towards Raul. 'How about your brave little brother, then? Would you like to earn yourself something extra, Raul? Something more than the Bursar's stinking handout?'

Raul shook his head. 'Not this time, Shaani.'

Perhaps never again, thought Raul. He'd stolen before, of course, they all had. He'd justified it by telling himself that the Lyrene Promise said nothing about it – unless theft was against the commandment to 'be kind'. But in his heart he'd known it was wrong.

Kohn and Shaani simply shrugged at each other and grinned. 'All the more for us, then,' grinned Kohn.

The subject wasn't raised again, partly because the Bursar came and went at surprisingly short intervals – a sure sign that the task must be paying a good sum. Every visit was marked by a sour-faced grumble about how little they'd done. Full boxes were removed and replaced by empty ones. Finally the alarm called an end to their Industry for another day.

'Not you,' snapped the Bursar as Raul went to rise from his seat. 'An extra hour for you, remember?'

Raul sank back, to work out his penance. By the time the hour had ended, he had to go straight to join the queue pushing into the main room for supper.

He slipped upstairs the moment they'd been dismissed, back to the window seat at the end of the attic corridor. In the distance the Celebreon spire was now illuminated, in honour of the newly-enshrined Blessed. Raul sat, alone with his thoughts, until the alarm sounded for day's end. Returning to the dormitory, he undressed and slipped beneath the covers of his bed. At precisely 10pm the nurture-house lights were extinguished.

Raul fell asleep, to dream of the Blessed Dyna smiling out at him from the hearts of countless cheap medallions.

Sundays in the nurture-house were 'days of rest'. There were no morning classes and no afternoon Industry. Instead, residents were expected to thoroughly clean the dormitories and communal rooms. If completed satisfactorily, they were then allowed into Craston for the afternoon. But these outings were by no means guaranteed. The Guardian was very particular and her inspections thorough.

She had been known to peer beneath mattresses and under rugs, between sheets and on the tops of the highest shelves. A hastily disposed-of item, a sweeping that should have been consigned to the collection bins, a surface that had been skimped or ignored – the Guardian regularly used these as reasons to deny the culprit an afternoon out.

Knowing this, Raul, like every other resident, would conduct his own equally (he hoped) detailed inspection beforehand. It was while doing this that he realised his belongings had been tampered with.

The Guardian's doing, without a doubt. There was no shortage of thieves in the nurture-house but Raul was certain none of the residents was to blame. In the nurture-house they each had identical beds and tiny wooden cupboards. Each wore the uniform overalls for daily use, a separate – but standard – set of outwear for use on Sundays, and was allocated an identically-sized share of a wardrobe in which to store them. It was only through their small caches of private possessions that each of them could retain some shred of individuality. Stealing from those outside the house was seen as nothing more than a redistribution of wealth; but to steal from a fellow resident – even to touch their belongings without permission – was unforgivable.

Over the past weeks and months Raul had garnered together what he could to fuel his growing curiosity about the world around him. Writing materials; charts of the night sky; books to guide him on what to look for; and, his treasured possession, a cheap telescope to help his studies. None was missing, but they had undoubtedly been examined. One of the charts that he treated with so much care now had a crease. Someone had inserted a marker in a book at a different page to the one he'd last read. His handwritten notes were in a slightly different order.

Had the Guardian been looking for anything in

particular? If so, she obviously hadn't found it. He'd have heard soon enough if she had. During the occasional clamp-down on thieving from town, any residents stupid enough to have left a suspicious item amongst their worldly goods would be summoned immediately to the Guardian's office to explain how they had come by it. No, whatever she'd suspected he might have, she'd not found it.

Raul thought no more about it. He made his bed, put his dirty clothing in a sack and carried it downstairs to the store where the Bursar exchanged it for a freshly laundered set. He then spent the rest of the morning on his cleaning duties in the communal rooms. After a bland lunch of soup and a bread roll, the Guardian granted them permission to leave for the celebration service.

'Brother, I am *so* excited!'

It was Arym, attaching herself beside him before he'd even left the room. This was unusual. Shaani was his sister's usual town-partner. Raul then remembered: today Shaani had an 'arrangement' with Kohn. The pair of them were already heading for the door, holding folded bags they intended to fill without spending even a penny.

It wasn't a long walk to the Celebreon. Even a stranger to the town could have found the way: the route followed by the Enshrinement procession was unmistakable. Discarded bunting still lay in the gutters and home-made icons hung limply from branches, the remains of the celebration slowly being turned to mash by trampling feet and overnight sleet. At the bottom of the hill, the northernmost bastion of what remained of the old town wall was covered with now peeling pictures of the Blessed Dyna.

Raul and Arym walked beside it until they reached the ancient west gate. It was the only one of the original four left standing, and Raul marvelled at the workmanship of those who'd built it. The structure was not so much a gate as an open-roofed tower, complete with a vaulted gallery. He looked up, appreciating the intricacy of the work. That was what a proper human industry was all about, not sticking images of a Blessed onto cheap medallions.

'Look!' cried Arym. 'They've renamed the street!'

Through the gate, a new post had been mounted at the start of the block-laid thoroughfare. It bore the legend, *Blessed Dyna Way.*

'Let's see how long *that* lasts,' murmured Raul. 'Come on, let's move.'

They'd been walking in the relative warmth of the wintry sunshine, but in the shade of the gate it was bitterly cold. Even so, a clutch of hardy traders had set up their stalls out there, suffering the cold in the hope of catching customers before they reached the traders who'd paid the exorbitant fee to sell within the Celebreon itself.

Arym had slowed, her path arcing towards the stalls. She stopped as Raul took hold of her arm and pointed. Kohn and Shaani were on the fringe of a small crowd surrounding the stall of a burly, unshaven trader selling flimsy icons. They were shoulder-to-shoulder, Kohn idly turning different samples over in his fingers while Shaani watched the trader. It was simple. The moment his attention was distracted by a customer, Kohn would slip something inside his coat.

Not this time, though. As he caught sight of their nurture-house uniforms, the trader swung round. He pointed angrily at a scribbled sign hanging from the canopy above the stall.

'Hey! Can't you read? No nurture-kids!'

Kohn and Shaani shrugged and turned away, unconcerned. There would be plenty more opportunities before their afternoon was out. Raul saw them hurry past, heading with the swelling crowd towards the octagonal Celebreon spire now not far ahead. A standard fluttered from its blunt top in honour of the new Blessed.

And not only there. In front of the Celebreon, the Saviour's Square was flooded with smaller versions, all being waved by excited youngsters waiting to pile through the Celebreon's heavy oaken doors. Of course, thought Raul. No trader worth their name would have missed an opportunity like that.

Suddenly racing ahead of him, Arym bounded up the wide steps leading to the crowded entrance and forged on inside. Raul was about to follow when he was distracted by a commotion nearby. A group of adults had encircled a figure on the ground, shouting and gesticulating at whoever it was.

Raul moved closer. The person on the ground was a woman. At first he thought she must have fallen accidentally – until she managed to struggle to her feet and Raul saw the blue triangle stitched to the sleeve of her torn, black coat. That explained it all. The crowd had been taunting her, for the woman was a ghetto-dweller who had ventured out from the clutch of ramshackle homes on the Town Mount promontory overlooking the harbour. Begging probably, or scavenging for food. Why the ghetto-dwellers were so hated, Raul didn't know, but they

30

were and always had been. He'd lobbed bricks over the wire fence that surrounded the ghetto himself in the past, just because that's what everybody did. But as the woman hurried away, as fast as her frail legs would carry her, he felt pleased. Nurture-house children weren't popular, but he couldn't begin to imagine what it must be like to be hated like a ghetto-dweller.

After this, it took him a good ten minutes of searching before he found Arym in the Celebreon. She was at the front of a stall laden with gaudily-painted statuettes. The one which the fat woman stallholder was about to hand to Arym was just about the most sugary of all, an image of the new Blessed Dyna standing on a pedestal of roses.

'Look lovely beside your bed this one will,' the woman was cooing. 'You'd see her last thing at night and first thing in the morning!'

Squeezing through a gap between two other customers, Raul made it to Arym's side. The statuette, now in his sister's hands, looked even more tawdry close up. Then he saw the price dangling from its over-pink neck.

'You can't afford that!'

Arym spun round, clearly surprised that he should have found her, and angry that he had. 'Go away! Mind your own business!'

'But look at the price!' hissed Raul.

'So?' Arym handed the statuette back to the fat, sweating stallholder. 'I'll take it.'

'You must be mad. It's more than we earn for two months' Industry!'

'So? It's my money.'

Something about the way she said it, an indefinable

change to the timbre of her voice, gave Raul the spark of understanding. He looked quickly beyond Arym, searching the crowd around the stall. Raul spotted Kohn and Shaani almost at once. They were standing to one side, just beyond the stall, and looking their way.

'Where did you get it from, then?' hissed Raul.

'I've been saving hard,' sneered Arym.

'You're lying. You lifted it, didn't you?'

Arym opened her eyes in wide and mocking innocence. 'Not *me!*'

Raul glanced Kohn and Shaani's way once more. There his question was answered. Sliding a hand into his jacket, Kohn withdrew a shiny leather purse just far enough for Raul to see it. Then, grinning broadly, he slid it back out of sight.

Raul almost yanked Arym off her feet as he spun her round.

'You agreed to go stealing with them, didn't you?' He was finding it hard to keep his voice low enough for only Arym to hear. 'Are you stupid? The Celebreon guards are probably looking for that purse right now!'

The fat stallholder had finished wrapping the statuette in tissue paper, an extra pretence that the thing had a value which justified its price. She was about to slip it into a box for good measure when Raul pushed in front of Arym.

'Sorry. She doesn't want it any more.'

The woman instantly stopped what she was doing, looking for all the world like a larger and flabbier version of one of her own statuettes.

'I *do* want it!' Arym was holding the money out even as she tried to lever Raul to one side. 'She's my favourite Blessed!'

Temper flaring, Raul snatched the banknote from her fingers. 'This month, Arym!' he shouted. 'Next month there'll be another!'

'That's not true!' screamed his sister. 'Dyna's different to all the others. I want to be just like her!'

'So how's that thing going to help? It's a lump of plaster, that's all.'

'Hey, you watch your tongue!' the fat stallholder snapped at Raul. 'These are devotional images.' She returned the figurine to Arym's hands with an overdone reverence. 'It'll remind you of the Blessed Dyna every time you look at it, love,' she said in tone that was as oily as her face. 'It'll inspire you.'

Arym took it. 'I want it, Raul – and I'm having it.' She looked up at him, her eyes flashing with mockery. 'Now give the lady the money – *little brother.*'

As the jibe struck home, Raul felt an uncontrollable flash of rage.

'Give her your *own* money, then!' he yelled. Holding the note in front of Arym's eyes, Raul ripped it into shreds.

Considering her bulk, the stallholder's reactions were surprisingly swift. Seeing her sale about to disappear, she bounded forward, arms outstretched, to snatch the statuette from Arym. She was just beaten to it by Raul.

'Give me that back!' screeched the woman.

'Have it!'

Blood boiling, Raul hurled the statuette at the woman's feet. As it landed on the flagstones it shattered into a cascade of gaudy pieces.

'See!' shouted Raul. 'Hollow! As hollow as your precious Dyna!'

Their raised voices had been stifling the surrounding gossip, but the sound of the shattering figurine stopped it completely. Into this silence the fat stallholder cast a single, condemning shriek:

'Blasphemer!'

Within moments the cry had been taken up by those close by. Raul felt rough hands grab at him, pinning his arms to his side. He could hear the fateful word being spread, racing through the crowd like a contagious disease.

'Blasphemer! Guards! Blasphemer!'

Then came more shouting, harsh and guttural. 'Let us through! Make way!'

The crowd surrounding Raul parted. Two uniformed Celebreon guards strode into the divide, their feet resounding on the flagstones. Raul's arms were released by the bystanders, only for him to be gripped even more tightly by the guards as they restarted their litany: 'Let us through! Make way!'

They kept it up until Raul was marched through the crowds of open-mouthed and nudging pilgrims, and up to a small, studded oak door at the far end of the Celebreon. There he was released and thrust into a tiny, wood-panelled room. The door slammed shut, muffling the rising babble outside.

All he could hear clearly were the sounds of his own

laboured breathing and the cries of 'Blasphemer!' still echoing in his head.

Raul's temper cooled slowly. He tried the door but, to no great surprise, found it locked. What were they doing? And where was Arym?

The room contained no more than a small desk and a chair. A welcome trickle of cool air was seeping through a tiny grille in the end wall. Unable to do much else, Raul sat down to wait.

Now different sounds began to filter in from the other side of the heavy door. A loud cheer. Then a voice, strongly amplified, prompting a greater burst of cheering and whistling – a voice which could only be that of the celebrant conducting the service. The celebrant spoke again, stridently and loud, but the amplification distorted her voice so much that Raul couldn't make out what she said. More cheering and whistling. This same see-saw pattern continued, with each staccato shout from the celebrant whipping up even more fervent responses from the congregation until, finally, it was all swamped by a pulsating, throbbing burst of familiar music. The service of thanksgiving was about to begin.

Raul wasn't unhappy to be missing the service. But, as his temper subsided like a kettle coming off the boil, he began to feel increasingly anxious about what was going to happen to him.

Outside, the noise of the congregation had faded but would never completely die. Every so often the celebrant's amplified voice was punctuated by cries of joy or shouts of praise which only stopped when the throbbing, hypnotic music began again. Then the congregation would respond with fervour, singing as if their hearts were overflowing.

Familiar snatches of the liturgy seeped through to Raul – 'Praise and honour! Blessed is the name!' – until, with a final song of praise which sounded as if the congregation were singing with a single, tumultuous voice, the service ended.

The celebrant's amplified voice, to a background of muffled cries and ecstatic weeping, spoke the words of dismissal:

'This celebration is ended. Go in peace!'

Immediately Raul could hear the excited babble of people passing the locked door on their way out of the Celebreon. As he waited for a guard – anybody – to open the door, the uneasy thought came to him that perhaps in all the tumult he'd been forgotten. He considered hammering to attract somebody's attention then decided against it. The furious reaction of the crowd wasn't something he wanted to experience again. Besides, Arym would remind the guards. Furious as she must have been, she wouldn't simply leave him.

Slowly the hubbub subsided, leaving behind an empty silence. Close by, a heavy door swung shut. Raul heard the thump of iron bolts being driven home.

Stomach churning, Raul placed his ear against the gap between the door and the architrave. He was relieved to hear the sound of murmuring.

'Hello!' he shouted. 'I'm sorry! Let me out!'

The murmuring continued. Either he hadn't been heard – or he was being ignored. Raul was about to cry out again, perhaps thump on the door for good measure, when he heard the sound of clackety footsteps echoing on flagstones. He stepped back, knowing even before the door was opened who it was that had come to fetch him.

The Guardian wasn't alone. Arym was with her, following her into the room like a maidservant behind her mistress. Others were hovering outside, too. Raul caught the merest glimpse of the Celebreon guards in subdued conversation with a pair of dark-clad figures before the Guardian shut the door again. 'Tell me what happened, Raul.'

Raul glanced Arym's way, hoping for some clues in his sister's face as to what the Guardian might already know. He found none. And so, omitting any mention of how Arym had come by her money, he limited the story to his altercation with the stallholder. Even that was sufficient to get him simmering again.

'I'll pay her what that statuette cost to make,' he ended, defiantly. 'And I bet you it was a lot less than she was trying to charge Arym.'

'I'm not here about the damage, Raul,' said the Guardian absently.

Throughout his explanation she'd been making notes on her vellum pad. Now, as if her thoughts were elsewhere, she began to flip back over the earlier pages: to what she'd written when he'd let fly in the dining room, Raul knew at once.

'I'm sorry,' he said. 'It was…'

The Guardian wasn't listening. She was already turning away from him, to reopen the door and beckon to whoever was waiting outside. As the two dark-clad figures swung round at the Guardian's behest, Raul caught sight of their glittering buttons and shoulder flashes. Fear gripped him.

'Regulators? Why are they here? I haven't broken any Directives!'

'You have, Raul,' said the Guardian, only to add, 'but they're not here to take you into custody. They're here to ensure that the correct procedures are followed. And to escort you.'

'Escort me? Where? I don't understand.'

The two regulators had come closer, but still not entered the room. Now one of them, a tall man with knife-edge creases in the trousers of his uniform, produced two official-looking sheets of paper. He held them both out for the Guardian to check. She did so, quickly signing each at the bottom. Only then did she answer Raul's question.

'I've decided to send you away for a little while, Raul.'

'Why?'

The cry had come from Arym, the first sound she'd made since arriving with the Guardian. Raul took comfort in the fact that she appeared upset.

'Because...' the Guardian glanced at Arym but then turned her full attention back to him. 'I'm not sure about your health, Raul. Some of the things you've been saying lately suggest that you might be...unwell.'

'That's ridiculous! There's nothing wrong with me!' shouted Raul.

He made to run past her, but saw at once that it would be no more than a futile gesture. Not only had the tall regulator stepped quickly forward to bar his way, but so too had his companion – a powerful-looking female. Behind them, the two Celebreon guards were also on full alert.

'I truly hope there *is* nothing wrong with you, Raul,' said the Guardian. 'But your recent outbursts and violent actions leave me with no alternative.'

She nodded at the regulator by her side. He held up the sheet of paper for Raul to see. It had the lion-and-unicorn crest of the Republic at the top. Various blank sections had been inked in, some with his name. The Guardian's firm signature was at the bottom.

'Raul of Nurture-House Eleven,' intoned the regulator, 'your Guardian has cause to believe that you may be a source of harm to yourself and others in contravention of the Directive on Mental Uniformity, 269 AD.'

'That is why you have to go away, Raul,' said the Guardian. 'It is my duty under the law to send you for assessment by those who are experts in these matters. If, as we all hope, there is nothing wrong with you, then you'll be back with us in no time.'

'This way.'

The muscular female regulator was standing outside the doorway, with two hessian sacks in her hands. As Raul left the room she gave one of the sacks to him and grunted, 'Your belongings are in there.'

The sack felt light. Too light. 'Where are my books?' he demanded.

'They have been...retained,' said the Guardian, choosing her word carefully. Raul suspected she'd been going to say 'confiscated'. 'Don't worry. You'll be supplied with plenty of reading material on Parens Island.'

'You're sending him to the hospital!' cried Arym. She'd followed them out of the room, the male regulator following close behind. 'With the diseased kids?'

The Guardian sighed. 'Arym, really. I thought you were more sensible than to believe silly stories like that…'

'They're not silly. I've seen one! A boy, on the cargo boat…'

'Nonsense! The Parens Sanitarium is a special place. It does wonderful work in helping young people overcome their problems.'

'Time's getting on, Ma'am,' interrupted the male regulator. 'They'll miss the tide if we don't get going soon.'

Parens Island? Raul felt numb. Part of his mind was telling him to scream in protest, but his senses seemed to have shut down. As the female regulator approached him with the second sack he meekly reached out to take it. But it wasn't for him. The regulator was handing the second sack to a stunned Arym.

'Your possessions, Arym,' said the Guardian. 'You're going too.'

'Me?' cried Arym, her eyes searching for an explanation. 'You can't mean it, Ma'am. It's Raul that's been acting weird, not me. I'm fine!'

The Guardian was impassive. 'That may well be so, Arym, but Raul's mother was also your mother and this particular illness is often transmitted from parent to child. Until recently it was assumed that this happened through word and deed…'

'That's ridiculous!' shouted the distraught Arym. 'Neither of us can even remember what our mother looked like. How could we remember what she said or did?'

'…but there is growing evidence,' continued the Guardian, undeterred, 'to suggest that there might be a third possibility: namely that the illness can be acquired in the womb. As your mother's medical records have long since been destroyed – that was her right – the regulations require that both of you be assessed.'

The two regulators were closing in, trying by their sheer physical presence to bring the debate to a close. The male took Raul by the arm, urging him forward. The female tried to do the same to Arym but she resisted, wildly throwing her off and backing quickly against the Celebreon wall.

'I'm not going!' she screamed. 'Not until you tell me what's happening. I don't even know what illness you're talking about!'

'Why the illness of unbelief, of course,' said the Guardian calmly. 'That is the function of the sanitarium on Parens Island. To cure unbelievers.'

The regulators transported Raul and Arym quickly from the Celebreon to the harbour. The cargo boat was waiting, berthed beside the sloping stone jetty, its rear section already loaded with boxes, packages and sacks. Raul was led down a short flight of steps to the boat's near gunwale. From there he stepped into the well of the craft, feeling the gentle bob of water beneath his feet. The male regulator followed him down.

'There,' he said curtly, pointing to a slatted seat which ran around the inside of the craft and up into the prow.

Raul sat, watching as the female regulator guided an unresisting Arym to his side. She hadn't said a word since the Guardian had told them why they were being taken to the island.

Their work done, the two regulators climbed back up onto the jetty. A quick nod to the boat's master and they were gone, striding back up the sloping pathway to the main thoroughfare. The master leaned out from the shelter of his small wheelhouse.

'Crossing takes about twenty minutes,' he said. 'They'll be waiting for you when we get there. Regulators have told 'em you're coming.'

They were the first and last words he spoke to them. An urchin helper on the jetty cast off the ropes holding the boat fast, lobbing them aboard and pushing them away from the slimy brickwork in one practised move. The boat shuddered as its engine roared. Water churned and slapped beneath them. Minutes later they were threading their way through the mouth of the harbour and out into Craston Sound.

The boat immediately began to buck and dip, its prow see-sawing upwards then down into the foaming water. A chill wind whipped, stinging salt spray into Raul's eyes. Inside his oblong cocoon, the master spun the boat's wheel with practised ease. They began to change direction, slowly at first then more quickly. From due west, they began to head south-west. The change to the boat's speed was dramatic. Until then it had been labouring, as if unseen hands had been pulling at its keel to hold it back. Now it spurted forward, as if those same hands had switched to pushing them on.

Parens Island loomed larger and, with it, Raul's fears. While he'd never believed the rumours about the place, didn't every rumour contain a grain of truth? He shuddered at the thought of what unknown horrors might

42

await them. Yet, at the same time, he felt a strange calm. Hadn't the Guardian said the place did wonderful work in helping young people overcome their problems? That was definitely what he had – a problem with belief. He *was* doubting what had once seemed unquestionably true. Perhaps he *was* ill? Perhaps he did need to be cured?

Arym was his real regret. She couldn't be an unbeliever, that simply wasn't possible. She was here solely because of him. Somehow he would have to repair the damage he'd caused.

'I'm sorry, Arym,' he said yet again.

Arym's face was pinched tight with tension, her eyes shadowed with a mix of fear and anger. Her hands were trembling. She didn't reply.

Some features of Parens Island were becoming more distinct. To the west, bare-branched trees dotted the perimeters of square green fields. At its eastern tip, a scarred cliff face dropped vertically to an apron of yellow sand. At the edge of the sand sat a small jetty, waves slapping hard against it. Hurrying towards it from the woodland beyond were two figures.

The boat had slowed perceptibly. The boat master was taking care, clearly conscious that one rash move could result in his vessel being dashed against the unforgiving stone of the jetty. Reducing power to a minimum, he allowed the wind and current to do most of the work.

By the time the boat was nearly alongside the jetty, the two hurrying figures – both young, probably in their early twenties, Raul could now see – were in position. But when the boat master leaned out from his wheelhouse and shouted, it was at Raul and Arym.

'You pair! Throw those ropes across to them!'

Raul stumbled into the bow of the boat. Puddles of sea water lapped about his feet. He reached down, gripped the sodden end of the mooring rope, and heaved it on to the jetty. Arym reluctantly did likewise with the rope in the stern.

The ropes were quickly wound around a pair of rusting bollards positioned fore and aft. While this was happening the master expertly held his boat steady until the gentle scrunch of its cork fenders against concrete told him the manoeuvre was complete.

'And the water brought forth good things!'

The cheery cry had come from one of the two figures on the jetty – a fresh-faced young man wearing a pair of well-cut black trousers and a maroon sweater. He was waving a small black book with scarlet and blue ribbon markers dangling between its gold-edged pages. Raul didn't need to be told that it was a copy of *The Writings*.

'Doron! Stop quoting and start helping, eh?'

It was the young man's companion, a girl of similar age. Her lips were reddened and her fair hair tied back from her brow. Already clambering aboard, she too was dressed in the same black and maroon outfit.

'Welcome, Raul. Welcome, Arym. My name is Jenna.'

Arym, trembling and hesitant, had no choice but to go first. Taking the hand Doron offered, she climbed over the gunwale and on to the firm surface of the jetty. Raul followed. Not wanting to accept help, but wary of the nasty gap between the swaying boat and the jetty, he too gripped Doron's smooth fingers as he jumped across. Even after the mere twenty minutes they'd been afloat the solid stone felt good beneath his feet.

In the stern, the boat master was busying himself unloading the crates and boxes. The two hessian sacks had already been tossed out.

'A duty group will be down for today's cargo soon,' Jenna told him. 'We'll just take Raul and Arym's belongings with us. I'm sure they'd prefer not to be separated from them.'

As if in agreement, Raul quickly snatched up his sack and hugged it to his chest. Arym was about to pick up hers but Doron beat her to it, scooping it up one-handed and hoisting it over his shoulder. His other hand still held *The Writings*. He used it to point vaguely forward.

'It's this way. A bit of an uphill walk, but not too far.'

'Nothing is too far on the island,' added Jenna, now following behind, side-by-side with Arym. 'It's only a half-mile wide, and less than that from top to bottom.'

Both she and Doron had sing-song voices; it told Raul that they were local to his part of the Region.

Doron strode up the slight incline from the jetty to the beginnings of a wide pathway. From here the beach ran away to their left in an arc of gold before ending, like some single-coloured rainbow, at the foot of a sheer rock face. A group had appeared there and were milling about at the far end. They seemed to be collecting things, dropping them into baskets looped over their arms.

Raul was given no time to study them further. Doron marched quickly on, to a point at which the pathway was enveloped by trees on both sides. There he slowed, half-turning to point *The Writings* up at the canopy of branches way above their heads.

'"And the earth brought forth the green herb and the tree that beareth fruit!"' he quoted, adding, 'Chapter One, verse twelve.'

'I don't suppose either of you have been on many visits to the green areas,' said Jenna, from behind them. 'What with living in a nurture-house…'

'We can still recognise a tree when we see one!' snapped Arym.

Raul smiled thinly. At least his sister had found her voice again – and had decided to fight her fear with anger, by the sound of it.

'You're going be amazed at how many different kinds of tree grow on the island,' said Doron calmly, smiling at Raul. 'Every one of them far older than any of us. They've lived through what to us is history and they'll still be here when we've gone. Unless they're cut down, of course.' His smile faded. 'No other creature poses such a threat to them as the human animal. I sometimes think that there should be a Directive against cutting down any tree.'

'Then you wouldn't have room for paths like this one, would you?' said Raul tartly and – like Arym – found that it helped lessen the nervousness he was feeling. 'Or buildings. I suppose this place you're taking us to *is* a building?'

'Of course.'

Raul stopped. 'And what do you do there?' he asked bluntly. He turned to Jenna. 'And you?'

It was if the act of landing on Parens Island had broken a link with what the Guardian had said about him. If he *was* ill, let them prove it. And so he'd said what he'd said in as hostile a manner as possible, deliberately trying to provoke. He failed. Jenna simply smiled, her brown eyes showing nothing but amusement.

'The description we were sent was accurate, Raul! It said you were spirited!'

Raul was in no mood to be placated. 'Answer the question, eh?'

Doron did so, but with an edge to his voice that suggested he was not quite as resistant to insult as Jenna.

'We're healers.'

'We work under the direction of Doctor Tomas, who you'll meet later,' said Jenna.

'But we're all healers,' said Doron firmly. 'Every one of us. That is our calling, Raul. To heal you.'

'Even if there's nothing wrong with me?'

'And we don't want to be here!' shouted Arym. Raul gave her a look of support, hoping she'd see that whatever their differences, they were at least united against this common enemy.

Jenna's answer was calm and not a little surprising. 'And we don't want to keep you here, Arym. This is not a prison. It's a sanitarium, a place of healing. You're here to recover, to be cured of what ails you. When you are better, you will leave.'

'But there's nothing wrong with us!' shouted Raul.

'This is becoming a circular conversation, Raul,' said Doron, the mildness of his tone belied by the set of his face. 'I suggest we continue it later. For now, our task is to get you settled in.'

He turned on his heel and walked quickly. Raul had no choice but to follow. Jenna briefly left Arym's side to join him. 'There'll be plenty of time to talk about anything you want, Raul. There's no hurry here. Just peace and quiet and the time to reflect on what is important.' She half-turned, so that her smile embraced Arym as well. 'Who knows, you may both come to enjoy it so much that you won't want to leave. That's what happened to me...'

She didn't explain further. They were clearly getting closer. Ahead, Doron had stopped beside a blue-framed signboard with long grass nibbling at the base of its white posts. It conveyed the briefest of messages.

Parens Island Sanitarium
Here we care. Here we cure.

Beyond it, the trees gradually gave way to a large oval of grassed open ground. A blasted tree stump lay in one corner, testimony to the power of nature. Arced around part of the perimeter were a set of weathered, low stone benches. The whole area formed a kind of plateau, a pause for breath in the steady incline they'd been climbing since they'd left the jetty. Behind it the ground rose steeply for one final time, so that the sanitarium building at its summit appeared to be gazing down upon them.

It looked to Raul neither welcoming nor forbidding. Certainly not the epicentre of Arym's gruesome tales. It seemed – neutral. Made of rough grey limestone blocks topped by a roof of slate, it had an air of solidity rather than menace. So, too, did the row of upper casement windows – the only ones visible from down where they were – running the width of the building. In the nurture-house the Guardian had always ruled that windows were to remain closed, as if she thought her

48

charges might be allergic to fresh air. Here, many were open. Raul felt a tiny shaft of reassurance.

The pathway continued its climb around the western end, skirting a towering drystone wall. Doron led them in a different direction. Taking a small tributary of the path, he led them around the grass oval to the foot of a steep bank of steps. They climbed up, brushing aside the bare stems of wild fuchsia which drooped from both sides.

They were almost at the top when a bell began to toll mournfully. Raul wondered why. Back on the mainland, the great bell of the Celebreon of Our Saviour had pealed out across the town for the Enshrinement of the Blessed Dyna, as it did for every Enshrinement, but apart from that – and the Festival of Darmas, of course – it remained silent.

The same thought must have occurred to Arym. 'What's the bell for?' she asked.

'It's the Call to the Gathering,' answered Jenna. 'You'll soon get to know it.'

'The Gathering?' echoed Raul.

'A meeting of healers and guests,' said Doron.

'Guests?' Raul didn't try to disguise his sarcasm. 'So that's what we are, is it?'

Doron sighed, perhaps over-dramatically. 'Raul, we've told you. This is not a prison, it is a place of healing. The Gathering plays a central role in that.' He tapped *The Writings* with his index finger. 'Have you never read, "Where two or three are gathered together in the name of the Saviour, there will his teachings be"?'

Jenna leaned close, resting her hand fleetingly on Raul's arm. 'We like our guests to think of themselves as

49

members of a healing community. Yourself, Arym, the other guests – you're all here to help each other overcome your weaknesses and to rebuild the strength that the disease of unbelief has sapped.'

The steps had brought them up to a square, gravelled courtyard. Directly opposite, and clearly the main entrance, was a solid oak door set in an arched opening of dressed stone. Doron quickly led the way across to it. Pressing down on its fat, iron latch, he pushed the door open with the aid of his shoulder. Ushered forward by Jenna, Raul and Arym slowly crossed the threshold.

They found themselves in a quiet, almost tranquil, vestibule. Vases of dried flowers sat on a long side-table. The sweet odour of incense filled the air. Shafts of light slanted down from two clerestory windows set high above an arch in the end wall, illuminating and emphasising the herringbone pattern of the polished wood-block flooring.

Having rushed them across, however, Doron was now standing stock still. 'Wait,' he whispered. 'And be silent.'

The bell stopped. As its final triple faded away another sound took its place: that of soft, shuffling footsteps. To their right the vestibule gave way to a flight of stone stairs hollowed with wear. It was from here that figures now began to emerge in pairs.

Whether male or female it wasn't always possible to say. Each of them wore a long brown hooded garment, tied at the waist with white cord. Wide sleeves hid their arms from view and sometimes their hands as well. Each wore their hood over their head, some pulled down so low that little of their face could be seen. Only a few looked up, smiling serenely at them as they passed. Most simply ignored them, seemingly lost in thought. With no hint of hurry the pairs filed out through the archway opposite, where one turned to the left and the other to the right. Raul counted twenty-six. All were about his age. A small number might have been as young as twelve or thirteen, but certainly none were much older than Arym's fifteen.

'Now, did they look unhappy?' asked Doron quietly as the last of them disappeared.

Raul shook his head. 'No.'

'That's because they're not,' said Jenna. 'They're content. At peace with the world.'

'In full control of their emotions, Raul,' said Doron. 'In harmony with themselves and with each other, Arym.' He smiled righteously, clearly content that he'd won a small victory. 'Now, let's get you both settled in!'

Doron began to move again, up the stairway from which the procession had come. At a wooden-boarded landing, Arym was led off by Jenna. Doron motioned to Raul to follow him on up the hollowed stairs to the floor above. As he climbed, Raul tried to begin piecing together an image of the sanitarium's layout. He reasoned that they were now reaching the level of the casement windows he'd seen from down on the pathway.

Reaching another wooden-boarded landing, Doron turned off the stairway. Raul glanced upwards, wondering briefly where the remaining stairs led to. Then he remembered that there'd been a row of dormer windows set into the slate roof. Perhaps that was where the healers had their quarters? He'd seen no other separate buildings on their walk up from the jetty.

Following Doron, Raul found himself in an anonymous

corridor. Beneath a dark-raftered ceiling a row of doors were spaced uniformly along the length of one side. The other was a wall of bare plaster, once white but now an aged grey. Spectral oblong outlines, like shadows from the past, showed where picture frames had once hung. About halfway along the corridor, Doron stopped at a door. A small square of card had already been slotted into the brass holder screwed to its central panel: *Raul.* Doron turned the round door knob and stood back for Raul to step past him and into the tiny room.

It was simply furnished, not unlike his dormitory in the nurture-house except that it was for one person rather than four. The bed comprised a mattress on an oakwood pallet. It had storage space beneath – not much, but more than sufficient for the few belongings in the sack he was still clutching.

At the foot of the bed a china sink was attached to the wall. The bowl was stained, a dark line curving down from the dripping tap that had caused the damage.

'Be grateful you have a room with a sea view,' said Doron cheerfully. 'Arym's will be nothing like as good.'

Raul's mental mapping had been accurate. At the end of the room was a window which did indeed look down on the grassy oval. More than that, though, above the tops of the trees that enveloped the pathway to the jetty he could see the foam-flecked waters of Craston Sound and the flickering lights of the mainland beyond.

Beneath the window, a desk and chair completed the furnishings. A sheet of paper lay on the desk's scored wooden surface. Doron leaned across and tapped it with *The Writings.*

'This is the timetable we work to, Raul. It will mean very little for now, but look at it anyway. I'll be back when you've had a chance to settle in.' He left then, closing the door firmly behind him.

Raul tossed his sack on the bed and picked up the timetable. Doron had been quite right. Apart from the times he was expected to rise, eat and sleep, it told him hardly anything about what awaited him.

6.00 am	*Gathering of Lauds*
7.00 am	*Breakfast and Allocation of Duties*
7.30 am	*Duties / Assessment / Treatment*
12.30 pm	*Gathering of Sext*
12.45 pm	*Lunch*
1.30 pm	*Duties / Assessment / Treatment*
6.00 pm	*Gathering of Vespers*
6.30 pm	*Supper*
7.00 pm	*Community Time*
8.30 pm	*Gathering of Compline*
9.00 pm	*Retire*

There was also a tray of food and a pitcher of water on the desk. The timetabled *supper*, Raul assumed. It was nothing fancy, just hunks of bread and a selection of fruits and spreads, but like a gourmet meal to a boy who'd suddenly realised how ravenous he'd become. He ate quickly, washing every mouthful down with gulps of the clearest spring water he'd ever tasted.

Hunger satisfied, Raul lay on the bed. Above him the room light flicked on unaided, bathing the walls in a soft yellow light. They were in a similar state of repair to those in the corridor outside, for here too there were shadows on the paintwork: another oblong on the long wall to his right and, above his head, the barest outline of a shape he'd never seen before: two short, straight lines, one intersecting the other.

He switched his gaze to the circle of light cast on the ceiling. Circles...diameters...universal constants... questions...unbelief...cures...thoughts came and went, weaving their way through his tired mind like the warp and weft of a loom.

Finally, Raul's eyes closed. As he turned on his bed a lone floorboard creaked in protest. It was the last sound he heard before he slipped into a deep and exhausted sleep.

He was woken a couple of hours later by the tolling bell. Within the confines of the small room the peals sounded different, mellower. Alongside the tolling he began to hear the opening of doors along the corridor and the shuffling of feet outside. He glanced at the watch on his wrist. They must be heading for the *Gathering of Compline*, whatever that was. Raul slid off his bed, intending to open his door slightly and look out. He found it locked.

He went to the window but it was too dark outside to see anything. If Parens Island had any outdoor lights, they hadn't been turned on. All that punctured the darkness were pin-pricks of light from the distant mainland. The gatherings must take place inside the sanatorium rather than outside. Tomorrow he would find out for sure.

Raul settled back on his bed, wondering whether to undress or not. If Doron was going to return as promised then it was going to have to be soon. *9.00 pm Retire*, said the timetable.

As if on cue, a key scraped into the lock and the door swung open. Doron stood on the threshold, but only to announce, 'Raul, Doctor Tomas has come to talk you.' He stood back to allow a tall, slim woman to sweep into the room. Only then did Doron himself enter. He placed the package he was carrying at the end of Raul's bed, and squatted down beside it. He had the air of somebody not expecting to be called upon to speak.

Doctor Tomas had seated herself at the desk. She glanced quickly through the small sheaf of papers she'd brought with her, then laid them aside. Her clothes – a crisp tunic and matching trousers – were smart but plain. Her hair was short, an uncomplicated cut. The only sign of personal decoration was the pair of gemstone earrings reflecting the room light as she tilted her head forward. Everything about her spoke of directness and simplicity. Warmth didn't come in to the equation.

'You know why you're here?' she said abruptly.

Taken aback by the sharpness of her voice, Raul did no more than nod.

'Why?' said Doctor Tomas. 'Tell me. And look at me as you do so.'

Raul shifted uncomfortably. He could feel the woman's eyes on him, steady and unwavering, as if tunnelling deep into his mind. He forced himself to look at her, to avoid being cowed.

'I caused a disturbance in the Celebreon. I lost my temper.'

'Amongst other things,' said Doctor Tomas.

Her eyes were grey, Raul noticed, and showed the beginnings of crow's-feet. A trivial detail, but he'd found that absorbing such things made their owners seem less powerful. It was a technique he'd developed in the nurture-house, to help him stand up to the Guardian.

'I smashed a statuette,' he said calmly.

'Does that happen often? Losing your temper?'

'Now and again,' answered Raul. 'If I see something unfair happening, like somebody being cheated.'

'You believed somebody was being cheated in the Celebreon?'

'My sister, Arym. She was about to waste money on a statuette of the Blessed Dyna. And the trader was swindling her.'

'Waste?' responded Doctor Tomas. 'Why do you use that word?'

'Because…it was just plaster. Nothing more.'

Doctor Tomas lifted the top page of the sheaf of papers by her side. Long fingers, noticed Raul. Smooth fingers, pampered, like a musician's – the fingers of somebody whose hands matter to her.

'Is that why you decided to destroy it?'

'I didn't. It was an accident.'

'I think you *did* decide to destroy it,' said Doctor Tomas curtly. 'When you saw it in pieces, you shouted, 'as hollow as your precious Dyna!' Why would you say that if you hadn't intended to destroy it?'

Raul took refuge in a shrug. His mind was already beginning to swim with the effort of answering this woman.

'Let me suggest a reason. You are questioning the

Republic's doctrines concerning the recognition of individual human achievement. Yes?'

That much was true. But surely she wasn't suggesting he was ill simply because he asked questions?

'Maybe,' replied Raul uncertainly.

Another of the closely-printed pages was turned by those slender fingers. 'Did you or did you not say, in the hearing of others in your nurture-house, "I'm not interested in any pox-ridden Enshrinement!"?'

Raul did nothing other than nod, but now in his breast he could feel the spark of anger kindling.

'That sounds very much like questioning to me, Raul. Do you deny that?'

'No.'

'Good. So you no longer deny that you're ill?'

The spark became a flame. 'Yes, I do!'

'Then you are contradicting yourself, Raul. You've just admitted to questioning the Republic's doctrines.'

'Yes, I have. I'm no longer sure about what we've been taught.'

'Such as?'

'Loads of things. About how the world came to be. About how humans fit into it all. About how some humans are more special than others.' He swung round fiercely, deliberately forcing himself to look her in the eye. 'Having doubts doesn't mean I'm ill!'

Doctor Tomas's tone thickened, like ice forming on a pond. 'On the contrary, Raul, it means just that. The Republic demands that we believe in its doctrines with all our hearts and with all our minds. Those who cannot or will not do this are, by definition, unbelievers. And since unbelief is irrational they must also, by definition, be unwell.'

'But that's crazy. What's so wrong about being an unbeliever? What harm have they ever done?'

'Untold harm!' snapped Doctor Tomas. 'Have you been taught nothing? The history of our world is littered with the misery caused by violent unbelievers. Our own Wasteland is just one example from thousands. That is why the Republic, in its wisdom, has instituted policies to eradicate unbelief completely!' The passionate outburst had left Doctor Tomas flushed around the base of her slim neck. She seemed to sense it, adjusting the collar of her tunic as she stood up. She still had Raul locked in her penetrating gaze, though.

'That is why you are here, Raul, in this sanitarium.' Her voice was back to its former coolness. 'Do you know what the word "sanitarium" means?'

'Healing?' shrugged Raul.

'Close. It means "keep healthy". In other words, prevent the spread of disease. It's derived from the Latin word *sanus*, meaning "sane". Which makes it most appropriate, because unbelief is a disease of the mind.'

Raul was incredulous. 'You're saying I'm mad?'

Doctor Tomas's lips tightened in a show of distaste. 'This is not the nurture-house dormitory, Raul. We don't use that kind of language here. There is nothing shameful about your condition. The illness of unbelief is only shameful if it is concealed or denied, allowing it the opportunity to fester and spread. Our guests are here so that they can be cured, but it also prevents them having the opportunity of infecting others.'

'You make it sound like I'm carrying a plague!'

'Unbelief allied to violence is just as deadly.' Doctor Tomas plucked up the sheaf of papers detailing Raul's behaviour as if they too might have been contaminated. Before she had even got up, Doron hurriedly crossed to the door, opening it so that she could sweep out as briskly as she'd arrived. But Doctor Tomas paused on her way, the loose floorboard creaking beneath her heels. 'Raul, you should be thankful that you have been sent here. Would you have preferred the enclosure on Town Mount?'

'T-Town Mount?' stammered Raul, stunned. 'The ghetto?'

'The official term is "enclosure"; but, yes, that is the place I mean. So – would you prefer to be cured here, or confined there?'

'You mean they…those people everybody hates…'

'Unbelievers too old to be cured, Raul. You are being given a better way.' She addressed Doron for the first time since they'd arrived. 'Would you care to add anything, Healer Doron?'

Doron smiled and swept a curl of brown hair from his eyes. 'When we are children, we think as children. But when we are adult we put away childish things. That's what your doubts are, Raul – childish things. Those in the Enclosures were too set in their ways to be helped by us. You're not. You're young enough to be cured.'

It all sounded so reasonable, so convincing. The same hint of reassurance that Raul had felt earlier began to seep back, smothering his fears and anger in its warm embrace.

'You're sure?'

Doctor Tomas brushed the question aside as though it were a gnat. 'Raul, we are almost at the close of the

Third Century. Very few cases are incurable nowadays. It is the Republic's target that within two decades of the Fourth Century the illness of unbelief will have been totally eradicated.'

'You're one of the lucky ones, Raul,' added Doron.

'But you must play your part,' said Doctor Tomas.

She didn't elaborate. With a dismissive nod, she swept out and left him to it. Doron closed the door behind her, then handed Raul the package he'd brought in with him. Raul took it, knowing full well what it would contain – the kind of garments he'd already seen the other guests wearing.

'There are no distinctions between our guests,' said Doron. 'Each of you is in the same position. To emphasise this point, we find it helpful for you all to wear identical clothes.' Doron lifted out a long cream tunic like a buttonless coat. 'Remove your outer garments and put this on – it's called an alb,' he said, discreetly looking away.

Raul took off his shirt and trousers and slipped the tunic over his head. Made of smooth material and reaching down to his feet, it felt surprisingly comfortable. Doron now handed him a long strip of warm brown cloth with a hole in the centre. With Doron's help, Raul slipped his head through the hole so that the material hung down, front and back.

'It's called a scapula,' said Doron. He picked a belt out of the package. 'You keep it in place with this.'

Raul tied the belt round his middle. He felt odd, yet strangely free. It was as if the outfit had been designed with tranquillity in mind.

Now Doron lifted a heavy, full-length cloak with a wide

hood – and hung it on a strong wall hook. 'This is a cowl,' he said. 'What you have on now is for daily wear. The cowl is purely for the Gatherings. Put it on when you wake tomorrow morning.'

Raul's eye fell on the first line of the timetable, still on the desk where he'd left it. *Gathering of Lauds.* 'What does "Lauds" mean?'

'Praise,' said Doron. He smiled. 'Not easy at six o'clock in the morning, but you'll get used to it.' He swept Raul's discarded clothing up from the floor. 'Rest now,' he said. 'You've had a hard day.'

The healer left then, closing the door quietly behind him, Raul's grimy nurture-house clothing in his arms. He presumed the same thing had happened to Arym, and worried about just how much she would be hating him for it. As for himself, Raul felt that part of his life had just departed with his old clothes. He didn't know whether to cheer or cry.

The bell began to toll at 5.50 am precisely. Unbidden, the overhead light flickered, then came on. An indeterminate click accompanied it, coming from the direction of the door.

Raul eased himself out of bed. He looked out of the window. It was a typically dark December morning. In the distance, twinkling lights on the mainland divided the slate-grey waters of Craston Sound from the blackness of the sky.

The bell's ringing had quickened slightly. Subconsciously, Raul's own movements altered in time with it. He crossed to the sink and splashed a few handfuls of tepid water over his face. Then he lifted the heavy cowl from its hook and pulled it on. It was thick and warm, like being swathed from head to toe in a brown blanket. As he crossed the floor the loose floorboard creaked, but Raul hardly noticed it this time. He opened the door.

Along the dimly-lit corridor, others were doing the same. Cowled figures were emerging, turning silently towards the stone stairs leading down to the vestibule. Raul hesitated. Then the door of the neighbouring room opened. A black-haired, sallow-skinned boy of about Raul's age came out. But whereas other heads had been bowed, his was up. Their eyes met. The other boy gave a hint of a smile then, as he walked silently past Raul, inclined his head as if to say, 'this way.'

Raul slipped in behind him. In step with the Gathering bell's peals, they filed down the stairs. At the landing they were joined by others, the girls whose rooms were on the floor below theirs. One fell into step beside him. Raul glanced at her, hoping it might be Arym. It wasn't. Anxiously he scanned the now double file of shuffling youngsters. There she was – further ahead – leaving the bottom stair and stepping into the vestibule.

Had she been through a similar interview with Doctor Tomas, he wondered? Assuming so, what had she said? Would she be leaving on the next boat, declared by Doctor Tomas to be perfectly well, only here because of her wretched brother?

Raul reached the vestibule himself, there to file through the same door he'd watched the other guests pass through the previous day. Just as then, the two lines separated. Raul found himself turning to the right as the girl beside him followed her line to the left.

They had entered what Raul would later discover was called a cloister garth. For now, all he knew was that he was in what looked like a covered walkway. Above his head, lanterns hung from the beamed ceiling of an angled roof. Swinging gently in the chill morning breeze, the lanterns cast just enough light for Raul to see that the walkways formed an open quadrangle facing on to a central area of manicured grass. Plumb in the centre stood a statue. Raul recognised the figure even before his line had turned into the longer side of the garth, then stopped to face it. The statue was – could only be – that of the Saviour.

Next to Raul, the boy he'd followed down the stairs pulled up the hood of his cowl. As he did so he turned and whispered, 'My name's Micha. What's yours?'

'Raul.'

'Well don't let your brain freeze, Raul. Not in this place.'

Raul smiled, pulling up his own hood and feeling its warmth at once. He noticed that some of the others had their hands tucked into opposite sleeves of their cowl. Fleetingly he thought of how perfect the strange-looking garment would have been for Odam's food-stealing exploits in the nurture-house. Then he too slid both hands across. A comforting warmth began to suffuse his cold fingers, as if the cowl had been designed for times such as this.

'Here we go,' whispered Micha.

Healers had begun to file solemnly into the cloister to their right. Raul noticed Jenna and Doron stationed together at the far end. The moment they'd congregated, the statue of the Saviour had become bathed in a soft yellow light. It was, Raul saw, almost as tawdry as the one they had in the Celebreon. A bird rested on the Saviour's upturned palm. At his feet lay a turtle.

One of the healers stepped forward. In his hands he held a slim book, which he now opened.

'At this Gathering of Lauds,' read the healer, 'we celebrate the start of another working day. For, as we are assured in *The Writings*, Chapter Three, verse sixteen: "With labour and toil shalt thou work all the days of thy life."'

'We work in joy!'

The sudden shout from those around him caught Raul by surprise. Only when it happened for a second time did he realise that the guests were expected to play their part in the Gathering by making certain responses.

'"Thou shalt eat the herbs of the earth,"' read the healer.

'We eat in joy!'

'"In the sweat of thy face shalt thou eat bread till thou return to the earth out of which thou wast taken."'

'We will return in joy!'

'"For dust thou art and to dust thou shalt return."'

'Thus it is written!'

The responses may have been unfamiliar but the text was not. In the nurture-house the Guardian had used it frequently. Now, unbidden, the same questions as usual began to flood into Raul's mind. Had they been born for work alone? Had all life really begun the way *The Writings* said, from the very dust of the earth? Would it end the way they said?

Raul's thoughts were suddenly penetrated by the sound of a single note from a small reed pipe, blown by the

64

healer leading the Gathering. After the slightest of pauses, the combined voices of the assembly now began to recite the Lyrene Promise. Not in speech, though, but as plainsong. Taking up the healer's piped note, Raul could only listen as the familiar words rose and fell on the morning air like a bird in flight.

'We prom-ise *this* day
To be cheer-ful *and* kind
And cur-i-ous and brave *and pat-ient*
To study and think *and* work hard
All of us in our diff-*er-ent* ways.'

The song was hypnotic in its simplicity. Whenever they'd recited the Lyrene Promise in class it had been no more than a meaningless drone. What he'd just heard had been incomparable. The uncomplicated cadences had seemed to give the familiar words a power he'd never suspected. As the final note died, he realised that tears had formed in the corners of his eyes.

He brushed them away quickly, thankful that around him the lanterns in the cloister garth were being extinguished. Only the light focussed on the statue of the Saviour remained lit, bathing the benign figure in its glow. The healer who'd led the Gathering bowed low before it, then turned away to file out with the others. On both sides of the quadrangle a low murmuring confirmed to Raul that the service had ended.

Beside him, Micha turned and grinned. 'Breakfast time. I'm starving!'

Raul returned the grin, half-expecting the boy to spin on

his heel and race off in nurture-house style to wherever the promised food was being served. But no. Micha merely turned to his right and waited. Raul did the same – until, finally, their line moved slowly round to an open double-door in the centre of the west cloister.

Doron and Jenna were waiting for them, as were the other healers for their own charges.

'Table four, Raul,' said Doron. 'Show him the way, Micha.'

'Yes, Doron,' said Micha.

Raul followed the boy into a large room with four bare wooden tables, each widely separated from one another and laid with bowls and cutlery for eight. In the centre of each table a shallow wicker basket held a small collection of cereals and preserves. A pitcher of water sat encircled by eight upturned glasses.

'The refectory,' said Micha. 'My favourite place, already.'

Raul didn't need to be told why. Uninviting as the place looked, at that early hour even the plainest of meals was going to taste like a banquet.

Raul was led to one of the tables, opposite a triptych of high windows now letting in the half-light of a grey dawn. He sat down so that he was facing Micha. The boy threw back his hood.

'You said this is your favourite place, *already*,' murmured Raul at once. 'Haven't you been here long, then?'

Leaning forward, Micha held a finger to his lips. 'The Rule of Silence,' he whispered. 'We're not supposed to talk yet. But the answer's three days. Three days too many.' He glanced to one side. Others were approaching. He leaned back casually, so much so that Raul almost didn't catch his closing, softly-murmured promise. 'I'll talk to you later.'

66

The room was filling. Chairs scraped on the floor as the tables became occupied. The odd spoon clinked against a bowl. But nobody spoke.

Doron arrived at Raul's shoulder. Beside him stood a younger boy with a thin, pinched face. Raul smiled a welcome but the boy didn't respond. Doron directed him onto the chair beside Raul.

'This is Jack,' he said quietly. The Rule of Silence clearly didn't apply to the healers.

Then Jenna arrived with three girls, each of whom took a seat on the other side of the table. One, hesitant and timid, Jenna introduced as Sarih. She sat opposite Jack, her gaze remaining directed downwards while she silently twisted a small gold ring on the little finger of her left hand. The second girl sat heavily down beside her, opposite Raul. Introduced as Emily, she sat bolt upright on her chair as if she was ready to leave at any moment. With her full lips and wide mouth fixed in a glower, she at least gave Raul the impression of being frustrated at having to remain silent.

The third girl was Arym. She'd been given a cowl that was at least a size too big. She sat down opposite Micha, pulling up her sleeves so as to set free her hands. Raul mouthed, 'How are you?'

He received a half smile, half scowl – an Arym speciality – and the mouthed reply, 'Fine. There's nothing wrong with *me.*'

The way she accompanied *'me'* with a jabbed index finger against her chest suggested to Raul that Arym had had a successful interview with Doctor Tomas. It gave him some sort of relief from his feelings of guilt.

Doron and Jenna sat now, as did the other healers, at the head and foot of their table. It appeared to be the signal for the meal to begin – at least for Micha, who immediately reached forward to pluck a slice of toasted bread from the basket. In a movement that surprised Raul by its swiftness and strength, Doron stopped him by thrusting out his own hand to encircle Micha's wrist and hold it tight. The boy gasped in pain. Doron ignored him and nodded at Jenna.

'We give thanks for the food we eat and the cup we drink,' she murmured, head bowed, 'and remember those in the world who are hungry and thirsty.'

Only then did Doron release his grip on Micha and allow the breakfast to begin. It was conducted in silence, as if each of them were eating alone. Raul tried to make eye contact with the girls sitting opposite but even that failed. Sarih stared down at her plate, nibbling at her toasted bread with her front teeth like a rabbit. Arym looked into the middle distance, avoiding eye contact with anybody. Only Emily, still sitting bolt upright, fleetingly met Raul's gaze before turning her attention back to what was on her plate. On either side of him, Raul rubbed shoulders with extremes. Jack appeared to eat hardly anything, whereas Micha ate so hungrily he gave the impression that he'd chew on the table itself were it not for fear of Doron's reaction.

The meal lasted precisely thirty minutes, until an internal bell sounded, sharp and short. Under the direction of their healers, the six guests on an adjacent table left their seats and scattered mechanically across the refectory. A blank-faced girl solemnly swept Raul's plate and cutlery from under his nose and carried it away. Another added his empty glass to the top of a growing tower in her hand, smiling as if the simple task was giving her the greatest of pleasure.

Around them the other healers had begun to lead their groups from the refectory. Once their table had been completely cleared, Doron and Jenna stood to do the same.

'What now?' whispered Raul to the still-chewing Micha.

'Assessment,' came the soft reply. Micha held back Raul momentarily by the arm so he could get close enough to add, 'Don't tell them any more of the truth than you have to.'

They followed the others out of the refectory and into the flagstoned cloisters. Ahead, Doron turned towards the north cloister as if taking them back round to the staircase leading to the upper floors. But then, at a glass-panelled door, he stopped.

Ushered through, Raul found himself in what appeared to be a meeting room-cum-library. It was thinly carpeted, with plain chairs arranged in a horseshoe shape. The walls were lined with open shelving carrying ranks of dusty books. Raul spotted a few biographies of the greater Blesseds and, on a shelf of their own, a complete row of identical volumes detailing the life and teachings of the Saviour.

'Sit down, everybody,' said Doron, pulling a chair into the gap between the arms of the horseshoe. Jenna had taken her place directly opposite him, in the flattened centre of the curve of chairs. One by one they sat down. Doron smiled. *The Writings* sat in his lap. He appeared to be waiting for something. The door opened. Doctor Tomas entered. Without a word or a glance she settled herself on a lone chair beside the biographies of the Blesseds. Doron began.

'Let me begin by welcoming Raul and Arym to our little group.' He directed his attention their way, switching from one to another as he spoke. 'Sharing your troubles is an important part of your cure, Raul and Arym. In that way you all help to heal each other.'

'Everybody is at a similar stage,' added Jenna. 'Nobody in the group has been here for more than a few days.' She beamed at Jack. 'And some are already making wonderful progress!' Jack returned a wan smile at the compliment.

'Introductions, then!' said Doron. 'Jack, why don't we start with you today?'

'My name is Jack. I live on a farm in the north of the Region.'

'Tell us about it,' prompted Jenna.

Jack's dull eyes brightened slightly. 'On our farm we have sheep and goats. I help look after them. Sometimes I feed the baby ones with a small bottle of milk. That's my favourite time, when the babies are born.' His voice was becoming firmer, more alive. 'I've seen the babies being born. It's wonderful! The mothers cry out with pain but then their babies arrive, perfect in every way.'

'What word could you use to describe that, Jack?' asked Doron.

'Miracle?' replied Jack, frowning.

'Wrong, Jack,' said Jenna. 'Try again.'

The boy's head fell in thought. When it came up again the brief flicker of vivacity had gone. 'Natural.'

'Excellent, Jack!' said Doron. 'Birth is *natural*. Well done.'

'That's what it says in *The Writings* then, is it?' The speaker was Emily, the girl who'd briefly met Raul's gaze in the refectory. The impression he'd gained in that moment, that she at least had some fire burning within her, appeared to be accurate. Sitting on the edge of her seat, the girl jabbed a finger in the direction of the book nestling in Doron's lap like a contented cat. 'Is it?' she repeated.

'Of course,' said Doron mildly. '*The Writings* explain how all things came to be: us, the other animals, all living things – together with this world in which we live.'

'Well I don't agree,' snapped Emily.

From her corner seat, Raul heard Doctor Tomas give the slightest of coughs. He glanced round. The woman wasn't even looking their way and yet he was certain that that cough had been a signal.

'Are you saying *The Writings* are in error, Emily?' asked Jenna. 'That the genesis of our world and all we see can be explained in some other way?'

'No, what I'm saying is that it doesn't give the whole story. There are bits left out. *The Writings* don't tell me all I want to know.'

'And you said as much to others? Argued at school, and especially at home? Insisted you were right and everything you'd been taught was wrong?'

'You know I did! But was that reason to bring me here?' The girl was blinking back tears. 'The regulators came for me when my parents were out! I know I annoyed them, but I'm sure they'd have stopped it happening!'

'Emily!' It was Doctor Tomas, her voice as sharp as

71

the keenest blade. 'Who do you think asked for you to be brought here?'

A look of incomprehension crossed Emily's face. Then, as Doctor Tomas's words sank in and she realised how and why she'd been removed from her home, she crumpled like a dying leaf. Slumping back on her chair, Emily's shoulders began to shake in huge, gulping sobs. In the corner, Doctor Tomas calmly turned back to her notes.

As Jenna moved to Emily's side with whispered words of comfort, an unexpected voice sounded from beside Raul.

'My mother loves me.'

It was Sarih. Doron appeared delighted, as if a contribution from this quarter was either unexpected or overdue.

'Of course she does, Sarih. That's why you're here with us.'

Sarih gave no indication that she'd heard what Doron had said. Eyes seemingly fixed on the tips of her shoes peeping out from beneath the folds of her cowl, she droned on.

'My name is Sarih and I live with my mother. Our house is number 143. I am thirteen, which is one-eleventh of our house number. I love my mother. My mother is thirty, which is ten multiplied by three which also adds up to my age. My mother loves me. My mother thinks I am ill. And that is why she sent me here. I am here because my mother loves me and I am ill and she doesn't want me to be ill. She wants me to be better and here I will get better...' Her voice trailed away.

Doron smiled broadly. 'Excellent, Sarih! And you *are*

getting better, that much is obvious!' He leaned forward, trying to catch Sarih's eye. 'Is there anything else you want to say? About why your mother thought you were ill?'

No reply.

Doron answered his own question. 'She thought you were ill because you were questioning *The Writings*, Sarih. Do you question *The Writings* any longer?'

Sarih still didn't respond, didn't look up, as if the effort of delivering her short monologue had exhausted her. She simply shook her head.

It was enough to satisfy the healer. Raul found himself wondering how much of Sarih's little speech had been her own and how much had been planted by others – such as the satisfied-looking Doron himself. The healer was now scanning the little group again, deciding who to call on next.

'Shall we save our newcomers until last? Yes, I think so. Micha, then. Introduce yourself, Micha. How long have you been with us?'

'Two days,' came the reply, followed with the merest pause by, 'eleven hours and twenty minutes.'

Doron gave a thin-lipped smile. 'Admirably precise, Micha. Can you be equally precise about why you were admitted to our care?'

'Because I got caught.'

The healer sighed. 'Doing what?'

'Stealing from the collection boxes in the Celebreon.'

Raul was able to picture the scene without difficulty. It was impossible to take many steps in any direction in the Celebreon without meeting a donation box pleading for contributions towards the upkeep of the building. Most

73

had bulging padlocks on them. Stealing from one must have taken considerable ingenuity.

'That was sacrilegious,' said Doron curtly. He took *The Writings* from his lap and held it aloft. '"Thou shalt not steal".'

'Stealing shouldn't have been enough to get me sent here, though. Stealing doesn't make me an unbeliever, does it? It's not as if I said something bad about the Blesseds or the Saviour or anybody. All I did was try and take some money to buy food.'

'To steal from one is to steal from all. To steal from all is to steal from the Republic. An offence against the Republic is sacrilege – disrespect. Do you not understand that, Micha?'

The boy hung his head. When he spoke again it was in a voice that had been transformed from wilful to meek. 'I do now.'

'Are you sorry for your offence?'

'I was hungry,' he whimpered.

'Then you should have stayed at your nurture-house, not run away. In its goodness, the Republic provides food and shelter for those not fit to do so for themselves. Spurning her mercies is sacrilegious also. Do you understand that, Micha?'

'Yes, Doron.'

'It has been suggested that your attack on the Celebreon was a sign of unbelief. What do you say to that?'

'I was hungry, Doron. Hungry. Nothing more.' Micha hung his head lower, not daring to look up.

'Very well,' said Doron, glancing at Doctor Tomas and receiving a curt nod in response. 'We'll leave it there for today.'

74

Raul had watched this scene with a growing dismay. Of the other four, only Micha had seemed really different. Jack, Sarih – even the still-weeping Emily, in spite of her early fire – had all given the impression of lacking something that he hadn't been able to put his finger on until he compared them with Micha. Micha had an alertness about him that the other three hadn't. To see him suddenly crumple under Doron's probing had been horrible. Then he remembered the boy's whispered word of warning as they'd left the refectory: *don't tell them any more of the truth than you have to.* And in that moment he knew that he'd just seen Micha produce a remarkable piece of play-acting.

'Raul!'

Doron's smiling and unctuous calling of his name pulled Raul sharply back to the here and now.

'Do I have to say anything?'

'Of course not,' said Doron, spreading his hands in a gesture of understanding. 'Pouring out one's inner feelings is difficult. But – it cleanses. Why not try? Introduce yourself at least.'

No harm in that, thought Raul. 'My name is Raul. I'm fourteen. I live in Craston, in Nurture-House Eleven. I've been there since I was twelve.' At his side, Sarih gave tiny squeaks of pleasure on hearing each of the numbers. Raul turned back to Doron. 'Is that enough?'

Out of the corner of his eye Raul saw Doctor Tomas signal to Doron with the slightest shake of her head.

'Why were you sent to us?'

'Because I lost my temper and smashed a statuette of a Blessed.'

75

'Are you sorry?'

Don't tell them any more of the truth than you have to.

'Yes.'

'Good. What you did was sacrilegious, Raul. No less sacrilegious than Micha's theft. Worse, in fact, because it was accompanied by actual violence.'

'I realise that now.'

'That is a beginning. We must work to excise that violent streak, Raul. If it remains, it has only one end. You understand what I am saying?'

In spite of himself, Raul shook his head.

'Murder,' snapped Doctor Tomas. 'Make it clear, Doron.' She stood up, notes clutched in her slim fingers. 'That is where history has shown that unbelief and an inclination to violence will lead if it is allowed to develop.'

'The greatest of all the commandments, Raul,' said Doron solemnly. '"Thou shalt not kill."'

'Smashing the statuette of a Blessed doesn't mean I'm going to become a murderer!' Raul almost laughed at the absurdity of what they were saying.

Doctor Tomas had moved to the door. 'It is my responsibility to be sure of that, Raul. And until I *am* sure, you will not be leaving here.'

She paused to address the group at large. 'Doron and Jenna will be providing me with reports about each of you during the course of the next few days. It goes without saying, therefore, that you should co-operate with them fully. Only in that way will I be able to determine the programme of treatment best suited to your particular needs.'

'What about me?'

It was Arym. Silent and solitary until now, the impending departure of Doctor Tomas seemed to have triggered her tongue into action.

'What about you, Arym?'

'You haven't heard what I've got to say!'

'I don't need to. There's nothing at all wrong with you, Arym. That was quite apparent during our talk in your room yesterday evening.'

'You're one of the saved, Arym,' smiled Jenna warmly. 'One of us. A true believer.'

'Then – I can go home?' asked Arym. 'Back to the nurture-house?'

'No,' said Doctor Tomas at once. 'You leave when your brother leaves. Not before.'

Arym's glance at Raul was one of pure bitterness. 'But – why? Why!'

'Because your presence is part of his treatment,' said Doctor Tomas. She held up a hand as Arym began to argue. 'I don't expect you to understand, Arym. You will simply have to accept it. And trust me.'

She left then, closing the door softly behind her as if to avoid lessening the impact of her parting words. Doron allowed the silence to do its work, then took control again. He and Jenna alternated, as if they were playing some kind of game.

'Each of you has been given a timetable of the sanitarium day. It will not alter. Every day will follow that same timetable.'

Jenna took over. 'The four Gatherings, of Lauds, Sext, Vespers and Compline, are central to your day. You will not be late for them. At the sound of the bell you will leave whatever you are doing and proceed in silence into the cloister garth.'

'Participate with devotion,' said Doron solemnly. 'The liturgies of the Gatherings play a major part in attacking the dangerous thoughts to which you have fallen prey. They will help you to rediscover the true meaning of this earthly life.'

'The same goes for the Duties. These will begin tomorrow,' said Jenna. 'The Duties offer physical benefits, but they also serve the common good and remind us that we are only temporary custodians of this land.'

'Others will follow us and it is our duty to pass on to them a legacy which reflects our position as true followers of the Saviour,' said Doron. He held *The Writings* aloft yet again. '"The earth is the people's and its fullness thereof"!'

Doron sat back then, as if the trivial nature of what was to come next could only tarnish his triumphant quotation. Like half of a well-oiled double act, Jenna promptly leaned forward.

'You will now return to your rooms until the Gathering of Sext. Use the time for thought. Study *The Writings* or the other approved texts provided for you.' She smiled warmly at each of them in turn. Raul found himself smiling back. 'After lunch, and just for today, you will then be free to do whatever you wish until the Gathering of Vespers. Explore the island, walk along the beach – the choice is yours!'

'What if we don't come back?' asked Micha. He'd asked the question with a laugh, but somehow Raul suspected that he was deadly serious.

'You mean, what if you try to run away?' said Doron,

his absence from the discussion short-lived.

If he'd been stung at having the real meaning behind his question so quickly perceived, Micha didn't show it. 'If you like,' he grinned.

'The short answer is that you'd be wasting your time, Micha. And putting yourself in great danger. This is an island, remember. The cargo boat is the only feasible way off. And the boat master is on perpetual lookout for any guest trying to leave without – shall we say – permission. You would be detected and returned.'

Micha was keeping up the act. 'We could swim!'

'Three miles?' said Doron calmly. 'I wouldn't advise it. Not unless you want to suffer the same fate as poor Annie Dawkins…'

He paused, waiting for their faces to ask for the details as he knew they would. Raul had little doubt that what they were about to hear was a tale Doron had told many times before.

'It happened in 106 AD, long before this sanitarium was built, on a warm and sunny afternoon in the month of Tremon, when Annie walked out to the west of the island for a picnic. As you will see if you go that way, the location is delightful. From the small beach you have the most beautiful view across to Orb Island. A view, also, of the notorious reef which links that island to this…and which was to prove so deadly.'

Doron was telling the tale like a master. The group were listening intently. Even Sarih had lifted her eyes from the floor to look in the healer's direction.

'The tide was low and the waters tranquil. So poor Annie must have decided to cross the reef and picnic on

Orb Island. There, while she was eating and drinking, the tide must have turned. It is all too easy to imagine what happened next. A panic-stricken Annie setting out on the return journey; getting part way across the reef, only to find the way ahead transformed from a calm pool into a swift-flowing channel; discovering that it was too late to turn back; realising that she was doomed.'

Doron closed his story with slow emphasis. 'Annie Dawkins' bloated body was washed up on the beach next morning.'

True to form, Jenna stepped in to lighten the mood. 'Doron so loves to frighten our guests! But don't worry. The dangers are all outside. In here, there are none. Here you're safe.'

'Here we care,' said Doron.

'Here we cure,' said Jenna.

She turned on her smile for one, final time. And, once again, Raul found himself smiling back at her.

Raul and Micha set out just after two o'clock that afternoon.

They'd agreed to go together in the few moments they'd had to talk on the way back to their rooms. Or, rather, Raul hadn't argued when Micha had said bluntly: 'You and me. Looking around later. Right?'

'How about the others?'

'Forget the others.'

With Doron in close attendance, no more had been said until they'd parted at their room doors. Then, with Doron delayed by a dawdling Jack, Raul had just managed to whisper: 'You weren't joking, were you? About running away.'

Micha had shrugged. 'Depends.'

'On what?'

'On what we see when we look around.'

The Gathering of Sext had proved short and simple: not much more than an exhortation about not giving in to laziness during the second half of the working day, followed by the chanting of the Lyrene Promise.

Lunch proved to be likewise, simple and silent. Afterwards Sarih had retired immediately to her room. Arym had set off with Emily and Jack down the pathway leading to the jetty and beach.

Micha had watched them go then turned in the opposite direction. As Raul had noticed on the day they'd arrived, that same pathway continued on up past the western end of the sanitarium. That was the route they now took, climbing steeply uphill through an avenue of aged trees. Within no more than eighty paces they were clear of the others and at the brow of the incline. Within a further twenty the pathway, now descending sharply, had petered out into an unkempt patch of grass and scree. A primitive wooden railing barred the way.

'Don't worry about it,' said Micha. 'We're not going that way. Not unless you've got a pair of wings under that outfit!'

'There'd be enough room,' Raul laughed. Following the Gathering of Sext they'd changed from their cowls into the less cumbersome – but still bulky – albs and scapulas.

Beyond the railing was a sheer drop. Leaning forward slightly Raul could make out a clutch of black rocks far below, white-flecked waves circling them like ruffled collars. To his left, the cliff edge ran round and back until it almost seemed to merge with the eastern tip of the sanitarium building itself. It was clear that from that direction the place was as inaccessible as a fortress.

Micha had turned sharp right. He was now following no more than a track. Running parallel with the cliff edge – but, thankfully, a safe distance from it – it cut through banks of viciously-spiked gorse. More than once Raul had cause to thank the thickness of the clothes he was wearing.

Only half-a-mile wide, Jenna had said. It seemed like more until, suddenly, they broke free of the gorse and found themselves walking out onto what felt like a bulbous lump of crumbling cake. Small stones and fragments of rock littered the ground, which now fell away steeply on every side. This had to be the western tip of the island.

'Now what?' Raul asked.

Micha grinned. 'Now we go down!' He was already scurrying towards what looked like a wedge cut in the ground. Following him, Raul saw that it was a fissure in the rock that extended almost vertically to a patch of shingle beach. If Micha had managed it before – as it seemed he must – then the descent couldn't be as dangerous as it looked.

Part-sliding, part-squatting, part-slithering, Raul followed the other boy until finally the ground levelled beneath their feet and they burst out onto the beach like two corks from a bottle. But Micha didn't stop to enjoy the view. He kept on running, scattering pebbles and urging Raul to keep up as he scurried on round the tip of the island to the unseen far side.

And, suddenly, there it was: the reef. Black, slimy and covered with bladderwrack, it lay between them and the small island on the other side like a dozing crocodile. As dangerous as one too, judging by Doron's tale of the wretched Annie Dawkins. Looking at the reef now, though, that was hard to believe. Between the black rocks the water lay shallow and placid.

'Tide's out!' shouted Micha, still on the move. 'Perfect!'

He ran on, a further hundred paces or so, to where the shoreline curved again, to run parallel with the mainland. By the time Raul caught up, Micha had scrambled up onto a low rock stack. He pointed out across Craston Sound, like a mariner on watch.

'Doron was lying!' he cried. 'It's not three miles to the mainland. That's just the way the boat brought us from the harbour. Look, from here it's a lot less.'

He was pointing north-west. And it was true – from where they were the curve of the mainland seemed nearly close enough to touch.

'Can't be more than half a mile,' said Micha.

'So?' said Raul.

'So I couldn't swim three miles. But I could swim half a mile.'

Doctor Tomas had watched with a cool detachment as Doron and Jenna sent their charges off to explore their new surroundings. The faces were different but the problems were the same as ever. Her vocation was to cure them. More than that, to discover some method of preventing the illness from ever taking root in the first place.

She turned away from her curtained window and began to prepare for the meeting she had scheduled. There were conference rooms elsewhere in the building, of course, but she preferred to hold her reviews in a more congenial, relaxed atmosphere. It was so much easier to get agreement to her proposals that way, without being accused of imposing her will by diktat. She smiled thinly at the thought.

The room was tastefully furnished. A low circular table stood at the centre of a ring of plushly-cushioned chairs. The chair Doctor Tomas always occupied was subtly higher than the others. Her authority was thus emphasised before she'd uttered a word. And, often, she needed to say very few. Many a time an encouraging smile or a concerned frown had been sufficient to prompt the very proposal she'd wanted to make.

Doctor Tomas set the table with three glasses. She uncorked a small bottle of red wine – nothing special, rather rough in fact, more a sign of welcome than anything else. Finally she laid out a small selection of sweetmeats and savouries, little luxuries that were difficult to get hold of in these times, simultaneously showing her influence while making her junior staff feel a flattering degree of importance.

Her timing was immaculate. As she slid the last small plate into position there came a respectful knock on the door.

'Jenna, Doron. Come in. Take a seat, please. Wine?'

Anticipating their answer, Doctor Tomas poured and served. The two healers looked and sounded suitably grateful. She took her seat and began the meeting at once.

'Thank you for being so prompt. Time is always pressing but, as I'm sure you know by now, I do value these preliminary discussions whenever we have a new intake of guests. Your impressions are very important to me. So, Jenna, why don't you begin? Your views are usually so perceptive. What did you make of your group this morning? It seemed to me that Jack and Sarih were presenting similar types of doubt. Emily too, even though she was far more emotional. Would you agree with that assessment?'

'I think so,' nodded Jenna, as Doctor Tomas knew she would.

'The question is whether their doubts are due to poor education. If so, that is not our province. It can be corrected by remedial training elsewhere. Of far more concern is – well, what would *you* say?'

Jenna hesitated, clearly wanting to come up with a reply that would meet with approval. Doron confidently stepped in to answer on her behalf.

'Conscious rejection of truths they have been taught thoroughly and well?'

'Excellent, Doron. And it seems to me that Jack and Emily, certainly, have indeed been well taught. Sarih, too, in spite of her obvious preference for all things mathematical. Which makes their doubting a matter of concern.'

'But…' said Jenna, 'none of them seem the violent type.'

'Unlike Micha and Raul,' agreed Doron.

'Isn't *that* what we're most worried about, Doctor Tomas?' persisted Jenna.

Doctor Tomas paused. In their innocence the pair had

homed in on the crux of the meeting far more quickly than she had expected. But, she reflected, it had been they who'd raised it. Now to bend the discussion in the way she wanted.

'Of course you are quite correct, Jenna. Predicting those whose mental rejection will fester into a violent rejection is indeed our prime objective. But,' she added softly, 'not our only objective, surely?'

Jenna and Doron didn't answer. Doctor Tomas pressed on, filling the vacuum with her persuasion.

'Malevolence, the desire to inflict harm, is a living thing. It does not arrive fully formed. It grows. Do you think that those whose actions produced the Wastelands first revealed their true selves through violence? No. I would suggest that they did so initially through their rejection of the truths we hold dear. In other words, by revealing themselves as unbelievers.'

Doron was the first to concur. 'I'm sure you're right, Doctor Tomas.'

'So – what would you recommend?'

'I'm not sure,' said Doron slowly.

'You think it's better to wait, then? Until it's too late?'

'No, definitely not. I think – I think perhaps there should be medication for all.' suggested Doron.

'Pre-emptive treatment? Is that what you're suggesting? Integrating medication within the assessment programme rather than waiting until after it's finished?'

'I think so...' Doron then nodded firmly. 'Yes, I'm certain.' A most suitable phrase popped into his head. 'Prevention is better than cure!'

A shaft of pleasure pierced Doctor Tomas's breast. She

would have to nurture Doron. He was so pliable. Now to work on the other one. 'How about you, Jenna?'

'I – I don't know.'

'You disagree?' The calculated challenge was matched by an encouraging smile designed to give Jenna just enough confidence to continue.

'It's just that – well, the guests we're being sent seem to be getting younger. Once they were in their early twenties. Now they're barely into their teens. To administer medication before they've been assessed… ' At that point Jenna's courage failed her. She left the doubt hanging in the air. It was an easy target.

'Have you never heard of the Jesuits?' asked Doctor Tomas.

'I have,' said Doron, interrupting like a child in class. 'They were a sect of unbelievers.'

'They were indeed, Doron. A very effective sect, dedicated to propagating their superstitions. And their maxim was this: "Give me a child until he is seven and I will give you the man." Jenna, what do you think that meant?'

'Young minds are vulnerable,' acknowledged Jenna.

'Precisely. And so…'

'The younger they can be cured, the better?'

Doctor Tomas nodded thoughtfully. 'I'm sure you're right,' she purred, deftly turning Jenna's query into a proposal.

'Even if they've shown no hint of violence, like Sarih?' asked Jenna.

'Yes. The Republic's tolerance towards all unbelievers is wearing thin, Jenna. Valuable resources are being wasted in rooting them out and preventing their superstitions from spreading. Unbelief is like a virus, Jenna. It can infect anybody. Even you.'

Jenna shook her head firmly, almost violently, so anxious was she to regain the other woman's confidence 'No, Doctor. My belief is unshakeable.'

'And mine!' cried Doron. 'No unbeliever could ever make me part from the teaching of the first Commandment: "It is Science that hast brought thee out of the realms of superstition, out of the bondage of religion."'

His passion was taken up by Jenna, her voice joining with his to complete the quotation in unison. '"Thou shalt have no gods. Thou shalt not adore them, nor worship them, nor serve them."'

Doctor Tomas leaned forward to replenish their wine glasses, subtly rewarding their support.

'Your devotion does you both credit. You are right to refer to *The Writings*, of course. They lie at the heart of the matter. There must be, there can be, no deviation from their teachings. Unbelievers, those who persist in proclaiming the existence of a god or gods, are an evil which we ignore at our peril. Even before the Catastrophe occurred, history was littered with examples of how such people had employed violence in support of their superstitious creeds. That is why we are here. To save them – and to save us *from* them. To do whatever it takes to cure them.'

She smiled at the two healers, now visibly relaxing in the glow of her approval. '*Whatever* it takes,' she repeated, with the subtlest emphasis on the important first word. 'I'm sure you're both right.'

For the first time, Doctor Tomas took a sip from her own

glass of ruby-red wine. They would chat on for a few minutes but, for her, the meeting was over.

Raul and Micha hadn't been able to continue round the northern shoreline. From the point at which Micha had looked out across Craston Sound towards the mainland, they'd only walked on for a short distance before their way had been barred by a towering rocky outcrop stretching out into deep water.

'We could swim on round,' suggested Micha. 'It can't be that far from here to the jetty.'

Raul shook his head, then made the fateful admission: 'I can't swim.'

Micha stared at him for a few moments. 'No point asking if you want to escape with me then,' he said finally.

'No,' said Raul, though being able to swim had nothing to do with it. For him, escape wasn't an option. Where could he go? The nurture-house was the only home he had ever known. No, he'd have only considered escaping if that was what Arym had wanted – and, having been declared perfectly well, there was no earthly reason why she should.

In silence, the two boys retraced their steps back to the fissure in the rock wall. Levering themselves upwards by gripping both sides, they managed the climb without much difficulty. They were soon heaving themselves out onto the track they'd left earlier.

Micha stood for a moment gazing this way and that. 'I just hope I can find this place in the dark.'

'In the dark? You're not serious?'

'Of course I'm serious. They watch every move we

make, so when I go it'll be when I've got the best chance of not being spotted: at night.'

'But...' Raul's mind was swirling with conflicting thoughts. 'Don't you want to get better?'

'Better? I stole some money because I was hungry, and if I'm hungry again I'll do the same thing again. I'm not wrong in the head, Raul, I'm wrong in the stomach!'

'You don't...you don't believe in God, then?'

'God?' spat Micha. 'No, I don't. Nor do I believe in the Republic or Science. None of it. I just believe in *me*.' He looked at Raul. 'You mean you do?'

'I don't know. I just keep getting these thoughts. Wondering if there could be something more powerful than the Republic, or even Science. More powerful than anything.' He found tears pricking his eyes. 'And I just wish they'd go away. I want to be cured, Micha.'

'And you reckon they'll do it? You trust them? Even though they're liars?'

'Liars?' echoed Raul. 'How do you know that?'

Micha pointed. From where they were, the upper floors of the sanitarium were clearly in view. Bathed with dying sunlight, the weathered brickwork had taken on a pale glow.

'Does that place remind you of anywhere?'

It did. The rugged limestone blocks, the grey slate roof, the distinctive shape of the room windows, curving from straight sides to meet at a central point at the top – Raul had seen all these in only one other building.

'The Celebreon.' he said.

'Right. And how old is the Celebreon?'

Everybody knew the answer to that. The date was carved

in gold-leafed lettering above the great door: *346 BC*.

'Five hundred years, most of it,' said Raul.

'Chances are the sanitarium is about the same age then,' said Micha. 'Yet when Doron launched into his tale about Annie Dawkins this morning, he said it hadn't been built then.'

'It happened in 106 AD, long before this sanitarium was built, on a warm and sunny afternoon in the month of Tremon ...'

At that moment the bell for the Gathering of Vespers began to peal, its ordered chimes rolling out towards them like a mother calling her children home. Raul hesitated, thinking about what Micha had just said. The sanitarium *did* look remarkably similar to the Celebreon; similar in the way that he and Arym were similar, with many differences but with an indisputably common parentage. If that was the case, why had Doron made a point of saying that it hadn't been built that long ago? Had he been telling a lie, as Micha was suggesting? And if so, why?

A surprise awaited them as they hurried into the cloister garth. The Gathering of Vespers was not being held there, as those of Lauds and Sext had been earlier that day. Instead, the residents were silently filing towards the refectory. Raul and Micha joined them, their breathless panting soon slowing as if calmed by the measured pace at which they had to walk.

Emily and Arym gave Raul and Micha a look of recognition as they joined them at their table. Jack's eyes flickered their way, but no more. Sarih appeared to be checking the table settings for eight of everything. Jenna, too, was in her place. She motioned silently for them to sit down.

Doron was at the front of the room, looking down from a small dais. Raul assumed that it had to be the healer's turn to run the Gathering. The moment the door refectory door closed, Doron began.

'Sisters and brothers, the Gathering of Vespers is the hour when we celebrate our labours, the end of our working day. At this time we reflect on the joys of working for each other and for all humanity.'

The service proceeded just as the others had. They chanted the Lyrene Promise, its simple sing-song rhythms already insinuating themselves into Raul's memory. Doron summarised the work the different groups of residents had carried out during the day. But then the pattern changed.

'For the benefit of our newer residents, once a week we combine this meal with our Vespers celebration by listening to a passage from *The Writings* as we eat in silence. By tradition this passage is read not by a healer, but by a guest. The chosen guest therefore does not have time to eat. He or she willingly sacrifices their meal for the greater good of all.'

It seemed inevitable that Doron would select somebody from his own group. And as he looked their way, Raul somehow knew who it would be.

'Raul, please.'

Not knowing what was expected of him, Raul simply stood still until Jenna guided him away from the table and across to an elevated platform at the side of the refectory. She motioned him up the short flight of steps. There, Raul found the book already open, a tasselled ribbon marker stretched across the page.

'Until the end of the meal,' announced Doron, 'Raul will be reading from *The Writings*, commencing at Chapter 1, verse one.'

Raul looked down at the page laid out ornately before him. The large capital letter which opened the chapter was a blur of colour and curlicues but the words that followed it were no different to those in the mass-produced versions of *The Writings* they'd used every day in the nurture-house. Nervously, he started to read.

'*"In the beginning was the singularity..."*'

On he went then, as from the tables below began careful sounds of a meal being eaten with a minimum of noise. Above it all, like birdsong over a bubbling stream, he heard his own voice reading the words of life:

'*"...And, in the absence of time, the singularity blossomed giving forth quarks.*

'*"And the quarks begat protons and neutrons, which in their turn begat the nuclei of hydrogen and helium.*

'*"And thus it was for one million years..."*'

And yet, even as he read, Raul was unable to stop the thoughts from crowding in. He'd grown up with these familiar words, just as he had with those of the Lyrene Promise. They were revered. Scientists throughout the Republic had proclaimed them from their towers, in their papers and in their sermons. *The Writings* were the inspired work of such men and women, produced so that the humble and the lowly could understand the origins and meaning of their lives. Who was he to even begin to question them?

'"*Then to the nuclei were added electrons and so were formed atoms.*

'"*And the light of the photons was extinguished and darkness was all around for now the universe was opaque.*

'"*And thus it was for one billion years...*"'

Raul read on until the meal drew to a close. Beneath him tables were cleared. Guests and healers began to drift away. The refectory emptied, causing his voice to take on a light echo. Those on his own table were almost the last to leave. Doron and Jenna appeared to be insisting that they finished every final scrap of food and drop of drink. Then, one by one, they too drifted away with Jenna, until only he and Doron were left in the room.

'Thank you, Raul. You may stop reading now.' A smile. 'Well done.'

'Does anybody listen?' asked Raul, descending the steps.

'Of course. They all listen, even though they may not realise it. The power of the mind to absorb the spoken word is remarkable.'

Doron accompanied Raul along the silent cloister and up to his room. When Raul opened the door, it was to see a tray laid out waiting for him. Doron followed him in and pushed the door gently shut.

'It seemed rather harsh to make you forgo a meal so early in your stay,' he said. 'Eat and drink it now. Then I can remove the evidence before anybody is any the wiser.'

Exactly who 'anybody' might be, Raul didn't ask. But somebody *had* been into his room during the Gathering of Vespers. It had been tidied, his bed smoothed and his few possessions lined up in an orderly fashion.

And so, while Doron waited in silence, he ate the simple meal of bread and fruits, finally washing it down with the glass of sparkling water that accompanied it. The effervescence clutched at the back of his throat and made him splutter.

'What is it?' he coughed.

Doron didn't answer, for there was no need. Raul's eyes were already rolling in their sockets. Taking him by the elbow, Doron guided him across to the bed. Raul fell on to it.

He didn't see the healer gather up the tray, didn't hear the creak of the loose floorboard as he made for the door. He felt no more, knew no more, until he was woken much later by the bell for the next Gathering.

It was only when the healer leading the service intoned, 'At this Gathering of Lauds we celebrate the start of another working day,' that Raul realised that the darkness belonged to the morning and not to the night. A murmur from beside him told him that he hadn't been the only one.

'I missed Compline,' said Arym, who had reluctantly partnered him as they'd filed down the stairs.

'You mean you slept through as well?' whispered Raul.

Arym nodded, albeit uncertainly. 'I must have. I can't remember.'

They all had. Not only Raul and Arym, but Jack, Emily, Sarih and Micha as well. Their faces at the breakfast table showed a mixture of confusion and weariness. Doron dispelled it with an amused smile.

'I – we – ' he added, gesturing towards Jenna at the

other end of the table, 'have a confession to make. You were each given a sleeping draught yesterday evening. Either at table or—' he glanced at Raul, 'later.'

'Why?' asked Micha sharply. Of them all, he seemed the liveliest.

Doron smiled benignly. 'To ensure that you slept well. Today you will be undertaking Duties.'

'Why couldn't you have told us that straight out?' pressed Micha.

'In case you refused to take it.'

'You could have forced us.'

'We do not use force here, Micha,' said Doron. 'We care. We cure. The methods we use are all devoted to that end.'

Micha fell silent. Doron hadn't answered the question, Raul sensed that, but his mind was so foggy that he couldn't work out how. In fact, apart from a mild throbbing in the upper part of his left arm, his whole body felt as though it didn't quite belong to him. So he was quite pleased when, at a nod from Doron, Jenna brought the breakfast to a close with a reprieve.

'Residents often experience a slight reaction to the sleeping draught,' she said. 'Return to your rooms. We'll call you when it's time to begin Duties.'

The sun was up by the time the healers gathered the group together on the forecourt outside the vestibule. It was a pale and listless sun though, as if it too had overslept, and offered little warmth to counteract the effects of a biting wind. Raul, his hands tucked snugly inside the front of his scapula, reluctantly removed them to take one of the sacks Jenna was distributing.

They set off then, down past the grassy oval and along

96

the track which led towards the jetty. Before reaching it though, they were led off on to a sandy pathway running between an unkempt expanse of bracken and dunes. They were walking parallel to the shoreline, reasoned Raul – correctly. For, as they swung left and followed the pathway through a clutch of tall, knife-edged grasses which whipped at their robes, it was to find themselves emerging on to the flat, firm sand of the beach.

The tide was coming in. Away to their left, small in the distance, the jetty appeared and disappeared as the rolling waves threw themselves at it and shattered into clouds of spray. Closer, to their right, more waves were pounding against the huge rocks littering the base of the cliff face which marked the other tip of the crescent of sand.

'Nice pattern,' said Sarih.

They were the first words Raul had heard her utter that morning. Even Jenna hadn't been able to coax her into conversation as they'd walked along. She was pointing at the ranks of swiftly-running waves, their curving whitecaps identical to the contours of the beach itself.

'Science tells us all about them, Sarih,' said Jenna. 'Science explains how their motion is linked to the pull of the moon. Science gives us numbers to tell us when the tides are going to rise and fall.'

Micha was standing beside Raul. At this mention of tides he gave Raul a conspiratorial nudge – only to wince as he did so.

'What's the matter?'

'Nothing,' said Micha. 'Sore arm, that's all. Must have been lying on it all night.'

Doron strode close to the water's edge. He turned his

back to it, ignoring the fingers of water probing across the sand towards his feet.

'Look at this beach,' he cried above the roar of the waves. 'At the sea. At the natural beauty all around you. Science teaches us that it is all we have. It is our duty to preserve it.'

He gestured towards the sacks they'd each been given. 'That is your Duty task this morning. To give glory to Science and to honour the Saviour by collecting all that endangers life and disfigures beauty.'

'He means pick up any rubbish,' called out Micha.

Raul laughed. His head was beginning to clear and Micha's response to Doron's overblown speech had tickled him. He was the only one. None of the others so much as smiled. Meekly they separated, sacks in hands, to straggle up and down the beach.

For the next hour or so they collected whatever the waves tossed up on the glistening sand: fragments of splintered wood, knotted lengths of rope, containers of different shapes and materials. Soon Raul's sack was beginning to feel heavy in his hands. But at least his arm had stopped throbbing. He'd just laid his load down for a moment when an anguished cry came from further along the shore. It was Jack.

Thankful for the break, Raul hurried across. Jack's searches had taken him almost as far as the pockmarked cliff face at the opposite end of the beach to the jetty. By the time Raul reached him, the shuddering boy was backing away from a rock-strewn area at the water's edge, pointing. A bloated jellyfish was lying motionless on the soft sand, its tentacles waving randomly as the water ebbed and flowed around it.

'Nothing to worry about Jack,' said Raul. 'It's dead.'

'But that's the whole point!' cried Jack. 'Why is it dead? Why? Why do creatures have to die!'

He began weeping uncontrollably. Jenna arrived and put an arm round his shoulders. Jack buried his face in her tunic, only to pull away again as if the mental picture of what he'd seen was worse than looking at the real thing.

'It was the same on the farm at home,' he cried. 'I loved seeing the babies born. But I was always sad too, because I couldn't bear to think that one day they'd die.'

From behind them came Doron's voice, chill and hard. 'That is irrational, Jack. You must learn the lessons of Science. All living things must fade and die. Death is the absence of life, no more, no less.'

'But is it the end?' asked Emily.

Doron could barely disguise his contempt. 'You mean, is there some way, some incomprehensible and unprovable way, in which that jellyfish lives on? No, Emily. It will rot and decay; it will be eaten by carrion; it will be washed back into the sea from which it came. But it will not live on, any more than you or I will live on when the time comes.'

'So why was it born in the first place?' Jack retorted angrily. The sight of the dead jellyfish seemed to have snapped him out of his earlier torpor. He was more agitated than Raul had ever seen him before. If he could get into this sort of state about a floating blob, what might he have been like over a slaughtered lamb or a calf? Had that triggered Jack's parents into calling for help with him?

Gently Jenna led the shaking boy across to a low boulder and sat him down. 'It wasn't born for a reason, Jack,' she

99

said. 'Nothing is. That jellyfish, its ancestors, the fish that formed lungs and crawled on to land, those that grew legs and walked upright – none of us were born for a reason.'

'Science teaches that life has no purpose,' said Doron, following them. 'Only unbelievers deny this. Are you an unbeliever, Jack?'

Jack shook his head wildly. 'No! I just... I just...'

Looking satisfied, Doron softened his tone. 'You just want an explanation, is that what you're trying to say?' Jack nodded pitifully, wiping his eyes with the back of his hand.

The healer called the rest of the group close. They gathered round, laying down their sacks of detritus and spreading themselves on the age-old rocks like disciples congregating to hear the words of their master.

'No creature on earth, including we humans, evolved for a purpose – that's why questioning death is so foolish. On the contrary, creatures evolve for a different reason, one that's best illustrated by an example.

'There is an island far from here called Madagascar,' continued Doron. 'It's in the Indian Ocean. Most islands were once part of a bigger land mass, but Madagascar has been a separate island for so long that it's like a little world in its own right. Some of the creatures found there have been found nowhere else on our earth. I am thinking in particular of one called the aye-aye lemur.'

Jack was nodding and smiling now, noticed Raul, as if he was being told a well-loved bedtime story. It was a new one on him, though.

'The aye-aye lemur has a unique feature. It has an astonishingly thin middle finger that it uses to scratch for grubs beneath the bark of trees.' Doron smoothed back his hair as a gust of wind moved it marginally out of place. 'Now the other unique fact about Madagascar is that throughout the length and breadth of the island you will not find a single woodpecker. The bird is not known there.' He looked at them in turn, settling finally on Jack. 'Do you see the significance of that? What do woodpeckers eat?'

'Grubs,' smiled Jack. 'From under the bark of trees. They peck-peck-peck until they get them.'

'Exactly,' purred Doron. 'A source of food exists, and so a life-form develops to exploit it. In our country it is the woodpecker. On the island of Madagascar it is the aye-aye lemur. This is what happens. Life develops to fill gaps. Life is a consequence, not a beginning. It has no purpose.'

'So what gap did we fill then?' asked Micha. He'd clambered on to a higher rock than anybody else and was lounging on his side, head propped on one hand. His arm must have stopped hurting too, reasoned Raul.

'We humans filled no gap. Our distant ancestors did that, when they emerged from the sea to exploit newly-formed lands.'

'Did they grow legs before they came out, or after?' asked Emily tartly.

'Some did, some didn't,' answered Jenna at once. 'You are the product of two parents, Emily, but the human race itself has many parents.'

Doron had opened his ever-present copy of *The Writings*, leafing quickly through the wafer-thin pages to the verse he wanted.

'"And the earth produced by mutations every kind of living creature: cattle, reptiles and every kind of wild beast,"' he read solemnly, the words cast into the morning air as if they were precious seeds.

At the mention of one of those words, Sarih had begun to nod and smile. Now she repeated it. 'Mutations, mutations, mutations...' until Jenna stopped her.

'You like that word, Sarih?'

'Mutations is like per-mutations. I like permutations. Permutations tell you all the numbers you can get from other numbers.'

'That's right,' said Jenna. 'That's how life works. Humans are just one of the numbers from all the possible numbers.'

Sarih's face registered a frown. 'Are the possible numbers big?'

'Very big,' said Jenna.

'I do not like very big numbers. Very big numbers do not fit in my head. I have to write them down.'

'Don't worry about it, Sarih,' said Doron. 'The number we're talking about is so big you couldn't even begin to write it down.'

'How big? If it is too big then it becomes an impossible.' She fell silent, as if the thought had already begun to trouble her.

'Wrong, Sarih,' said Doron. He pointed away towards the glistening sand of the beach. 'Our world has millions of beaches like this one. Each has a huge number of grains of sand – so many, that you would have to say that the chances of my picking up any one of those grains on my finger was impossible. Yes?'

He didn't wait for an answer, but bent down to draw

102

his index finger across the narrow swathe of damp sand at his feet. He then held it up in the air, as if testing for the direction of the wind, and carefully brushed away the grains of sand until just one silvery speck remained on his finger tip.

'Impossible,' he smiled. 'But it *did* happen. In the same way, however impossible it may seem, life has developed mutation by mutation to produce us. That is what Science teaches us through *The Writings* and *The Writings* do not lie.'

Up on his standing stone, Micha scrambled to his feet and beat his chest proudly. 'Me the result of life! Me special!'

'No, Micha,' snapped Doron. 'We are not special. Humans are highly developed animals, that is all. We are not special in any way – not even in this puny world, let alone in the universe.'

'But how can you be so sure of that?' asked Jack. It sounded like a plea for help.

'Jack,' said Jenna soothingly, 'Tonight, during the Gathering of Compline, look up at the sky. Think about how enormous the universe is. Science tells us that there are a vast number of worlds similar to ours.'

'How many?' persisted Jack.

'As many as the grains of sand in all our planet's beaches?' suggested Raul.

'Thank you, Raul,' beamed Doron. 'That is an excellent comparison!' He turned back to Jack. 'There are as many worlds like ours as there are grains of sand in all our planet's beaches. And so the chances of this world being the only one supporting life are vanishingly small.'

Even as he said it, though, the healer found himself glancing down at the single grain of sand still glistening on the tip of his index finger.

And he heard Raul say, 'But it could have happened, couldn't it?'

The conversation seemed to jerk Sarih momentarily out of the trance she'd been in. 'That is called probabilities!' she cried. 'For a small probability you need lots of goes to make it happen once.'

'What are you saying, Sarih?' said Jenna.

'If there is a small probability of life...you need lots of worlds...to make it happen...once,' said Sarih, very slowly.

'Hey, that's a problem, ain't it?' chirped Micha from his perch on high, sounding pleased. 'I mean, if this world *is* the only one in the universe with creatures like us on it, then you have to wonder why? What do *The Writings* have to say about that, Doron?'

The healer looked up sharply, pointing *The Writings* at Micha as though it were a weapon. 'I can tell you what it says, Micha!' he spat. 'It says "you shall not take the name of Science in vain, for the people shall not hold him guiltless that takes the name of Science in vain"!'

He slid from his own perch then, gesturing angrily at their sacks. 'To work, please. Let us clean this beach of all offending material.'

Micha dropped down besides Raul with a soft thud. 'In other words,' he grinned, slinging his sack over his shoulder, 'he's talking rubbish!'

For the next couple of hours they roamed the length of the beach, filling their sacks. There seemed no limit to what people would dump into the sea, uncaring as to where or when it would be washed ashore. Even as they worked, they could see that more was being carried their way by the ever-strengthening wind whipping in from the sea.

'No swimming for it today,' muttered Micha.

They were beside some pitted, rusted-railed steps which led up to the jetty. The spot had proved to be a particularly fruitful source of flotsam, almost as if the jetty attracted it like a magnet. In reality, as Raul could see, the direction of the tide was responsible. The rolling waves looked like soldiers on the attack, relentlessly bearing down on the small landing stage before hurling themselves against it in a suicidal assault of spume and spray.

'Why are you even thinking about it?' asked Raul. 'You're crazy.'

'Why *aren't* you thinking about getting away?' asked Micha. 'That's even crazier.' He dropped his sack at Raul's feet. 'Do you feel all right?'

'How do you mean?'

'I mean, do you feel better than when you got up? I do.'

Raul nodded. The odd, detached feeling he'd had when he'd woken – as if a curtain had partly fallen across his mind – had definitely eased. It was still there, but now more like a curtain of gossamer than of thick velvet.

'Yes, that sleeping draught must have worn off. Same goes for them too, I reckon,' he said, nodding down the beach to where Jenna and Doron had allowed the others a short break. Sarih had drifted away to sit on the sand, head in hands, but Jack, Arym and Emily were at the water's edge. No longer the dull, listless youngsters of earlier, they were now waving and calling out to a solitary boat out in Craston Sound.

It was a sailboat of some kind, its brightly decorated sails full-bellied in the wind. Dipping and rising, the smallish boat looked no match for the heaving water. The lone sailor was clearly no fool, though. Expertly building up speed by guiding his craft into the white-capped waves he – or she, it was impossible to tell – would then swing it out again so as to make progress in the direction he wanted. This was clearly beyond the eastern tip of the island, well short of where they were. Perhaps that was why the sailor hadn't responded. As the boat finally disappeared from view behind the curve of the cliffs, Arym, Jack and Emily ceased their waving. Prompted by Doron and Jenna, they began to walk towards Raul and Micha.

Quickly, Micha returned to his question. 'You believe that sleeping draught was all they gave us, then?'

'Ye-es,' said Raul, but uncertainly. 'Don't you?'

'Feel your arm,' said Micha. 'Up at the top.'

Raul slid his right hand into the wide left sleeve, up his forearm, to the spot halfway between his elbow and shoulder that had been so sore before.

'It's fine,' he said.

'So's mine, now,' said Micha. 'So's Emily's, I bet you.' In the approaching group, Emily was swinging her bulging sack without any apparent unease.

'Three out of six,' murmured Raul.

'Could be more,' said Micha. 'I haven't asked the others. But I don't need Sarih to tell me that even half means it's probable that they did whatever they did to all of us.'

Raul fingered his upper arm. It felt perfectly normal now. No pain, no swelling, nothing. Was Micha right? Had something more been done to them while they were asleep, something Doron *hadn't* mentioned? If there had, it would mean they'd been put to sleep for that very purpose. But was that a reason for concern? Although he'd felt strangely detached that morning, at the same time he'd also felt very peaceful.

'Perhaps it's part of the cure,' he said.

On the pathway above the beach, a couple of older guests were trundling down a cart ready to receive the bulging sacks. Doron, Jenna and the rest of the group were close. Micha only had time for the shortest of responses.

'Well, whatever it is, I don't trust them, Raul. As soon as this wind drops, I'm going.'

The wind didn't drop, at least not for the next few days. If anything, it became stronger. As they worked on the beach, mornings and afternoons, the waves seemed to grow more powerful from one day to the next. Doron even declared the area beneath the cliff face out of bounds. They could only watch the waves pounding against the rocks from a safe distance.

'High tides as well,' observed Micha to Raul one morning. 'They're not helping.'

But Raul noticed that he'd said it with far less fire than he'd showed before. It was as though Micha's passion to escape was slowly shrivelling; as if he was starting to accept the position he was in; as if he was slowly allowing his heart and mind to be taken into care.

That was certainly how Raul himself had begun to feel. The days seemed to have a gentle, calming rhythm about them. The Gatherings of Lauds, Sext, Vespers and Compline were like anchors in the day, always bringing his mind back to the certainties of *The Writings*. The work sessions on the beach were also becoming strangely enjoyable. The physical, albeit mindless, activity left him glowing with a simple satisfaction. The group sessions were helping, too. Raul's memories of the nurture-house, the Guardian, the Celebreon – all the things associated with his growing unbelief – were starting to take on a new light under Doron and Jenna's guidance.

That morning, for example, Doron had greeted each of them with a smile and welcomingly gentle, 'pinch-punch, first day of the month!' The traditional cry, which in the nurture-house had always been accompanied by as vicious an assault as possible, had jerked Raul's mind out of the comfortably blank state it now seemed to be in whenever he awoke in the morning.

'December is over, everybody,' Jenna smiled. 'It's the first of Undec. Less than six weeks to go till the Festival of Darmas and the New Year!

They then led the group in reminiscences of the season, bathing the meeting in the warmth of happy times.

Arym was the first to contribute. 'I love the way the traders prepare for the Festival,' she said dreamily. 'All the lights and the decorations.'

'And the street players,' added Emily.

'We always put up decorations at home,' smiled Jack. 'I would even do the pig-pens and the chicken sheds.'

He looked to Doron. 'Well the Festival is as much for them as it is for us, isn't it?'

Doron nodded assent. 'Of course it is, Jack.'

'I like the way the Celebreon is all lit up,' said Emily. 'And the special services they have. Midnight on Darmas Eve is my favourite and walking home afterwards, all frosty and excited.'

Raul found himself caught up in the happy mood of recollection. 'Everything feels different on Darmas morning,' he said. 'Even the air. It's as if you can reach out and touch it.'

'Will we still be here at Darmas?' said Micha suddenly.

Doron and Jenna exchanged glances. 'Possibly,' said Doron finally. He didn't elaborate, but focussed instead on Sarih. 'Do you have any memories of Darmas to share with us, Sarih?'

The girl didn't respond, as Raul knew she wouldn't. Since that first work session on the beach, with its talk of permutations and probabilities, Sarih had hardly uttered a sound. Even the soothing Jenna hadn't been able to coax more than a few words out of her. The only time she'd said anything to Raul had been the previous afternoon, when they'd been working in the same dry and sandy area of the dunes. Raul had seen Sarih pick up a brittle piece of driftwood and, instead of adding it to her sack, she had slipped it inside her scapula instead.

'Why do you want that, Sarih?' he'd asked.

'Numbers,' was all she'd answered. 'Big, big numbers.'

Now, as the session ended and they were allowed some free time, Raul knew exactly what Sarih would do. She would return to her room, shutting herself in until it was time to come out. And whatever she was doing in there, it wasn't sleeping. Emily had complained quietly that she'd heard her through their shared wall, making squeaking and tapping noises whenever there was a free moment.

Sarih didn't appear at all for the Gathering of Compline.

As usual, they assembled in the cloister garth, facing in towards the candlelit statue of the Saviour. Above, dirty grey clouds were being propelled across the sky by the still-gusting winds. Raul pulled the comforting warmth of his cowl closer. A different healer, one working with an older set of residents, stepped forward to lead the service.

'Sisters and brothers, at the close of this day our community gathers together to celebrate the work we have done. We also examine our consciences. Have we helped each other? Have we made a fitting personal contribution to the good of all?'

The healer's voice was pleasantly melodic. She paused between each sentence, allowing her words to float away like a leaf in a rippling stream. Questions surfaced in Raul's mind. What was his conscience, exactly? Where did it come from? Was his conscience the same as Arym's or Jack's? Did animals have one? But whereas these questions would not so long ago have been tormenting him, now they were like will-o'-the-wisps: fleeting thoughts that failed to stay long enough for him to grasp them.

The healer-celebrant lifted a small pan-pipe to her lips and blew a single reedy note. From this simple lead, the community's plainsong chant took flight:
'Glory be to the Saviour,
And to his revelation

And to his guiding spirit…'

Starting gently, the voices quickly rose in intensity. Raul, his questions forgotten, joined with them. Swept up by some incomprehensible power, he sang as if the words and the music were food, passing their goodness to him, nourishing him.

'For as it was in the beginning,

So it is now,

And ever shall be…'

Raul suddenly felt free of doubts and uncertainties. His heart soared with his voice, seemingly reaching out beyond the sanitarium, the island, the Republic – beyond the very Earth itself – to probe for the stars.

'World till the end!'

Sarih's scream shattered the moment. It cut through the final notes of the plainsong like a knife.

'*The Writings* lie!'

Raul turned towards the sound. Sarih had run out from the vestibule entrance, but no further. Wild-eyed, she screamed her message again. Then the scream became a wailing, a keening, like an animal in distress. She fell to her knees, only to leap up again as Doron and Jenna moved quickly towards her. Then she turned and ran.

Raul wanted to stay, to soak up more of the power. But a more pressing desire was urging him to move, to find out more about what Sarih had screamed – and why. Pushing past the confused and murmuring guests, he followed the two healers along the cloister and up to the first floor.

Sarih had reached her room. She was squatting in one corner, rocking to and fro, her arms encircling her legs. Her wailing had become a low monotonic moaning.

Jenna knelt beside her. 'Sarih. What's wrong?'

'Science tells lies. *The Writings* tell Science. *The Writings* tell lies.'

Doron dragged Sarih roughly to her feet. 'Science does not lie! Science is truth! *The Writings* state this plainly. "Science is the Way, the Truth and the Life,"' he quoted, then bent low, forcing Sarih to look at him. 'Do you believe this, Sarih?'

Sarih struggled to break away, to get back to the sanctuary of her corner, but Doron's grip was firm. Cupping a strong hand beneath Sarih's chin he yanked her head up and back. 'Do you believe this!' the healer shouted into her face.

'No!'

With a manic effort Sarih twisted out of Doron's grip. The healer darted to one side, covering the door, but Sarih made no attempt to escape. Instead, backing into her corner, she pointed wildly around the room – at what Raul had already noticed.

The pale walls of Sarih's room were covered by a web of calculations. Figures had been piled upon figures. Some had been emboldened, some underlined. Massive numbers ran parallel then turned at strange angles, as if Sarih had discovered she'd needed more room than she'd expected.

It explained what Sarih had been doing at every available moment. It explained the taps and scrapes Emily had heard. They'd been the sound of crayon on plaster as Sarih had struggled with the problem that had consumed her, a problem that had brought her to the state she was now in.

'Science say humans come from apes,' she cried. 'Apes come from reptiles. Reptiles come from fish. So on and so on right back to when there was no life at all.'

'Billions of years ago, Sarih,' said Jenna. 'That's right.'

'And this all happened by mutations. A very big number of mutations, too big to fit in my head.'

'Deep time allows this to happen. Science has explained all this.'

'Then explain this!' screamed Sarih.

Tears streaming down her face, she scooped something from the small desk beneath the room's window and threw at it Doron's feet. It was a handmade dice. Crudely chipped from the sort of driftwood Raul had seen her slip into her scapula, the dots on each face were marked out with ink. It landed with a six uppermost.

Sarih pointed at it. 'Six chances of getting a six,' she shouted.

Again she lunged for the desk. It was, Raul now saw, littered with driftwood dice. A second one was hurled across the room, then a third and a fourth. They ended with a variety of numbers on show, none of them a six.

'Fail! Because odds of throwing two sixes is six times six equals thirty-six. Odds of three sixes is six times six times six equals 216. Odds of four sixes is…'

'I know how mathematics works, Sarih!' shouted Doron.

Sarih ignored him and began pointing at calculations on the wall.

'Keep going. Say you have forty dices. Say I throw them one time a second. How long would it take to get a throw of all sixes?' She leapt from her corner to slam a hand down on part of a huge number, littered with zeroes. 'Longer than what Science tells us is the age of the universe!'

'What are you saying, Sarih?' said Doron, hard-edged.

'What is easier?' shouted Sarih. 'To change a frog into a bird or to throw forty sixes? Sixes, of course. But if sixes can't be done in time how can mutations? Science lies! There must have been a Creator-God.'

Doron spoke slowly, moving nearer to the distraught girl with every word. 'You are wrong, Sarih. Nature throws its dice more than once a second. In that time millions of mutations might occur. To use your silly example, Nature could well be throwing all sixes once a day.'

The effort of arguing seemed to have left Sarih in tatters. She was holding her head, one hand on each temple, as if trying to stop it exploding. Jenna was at her side. With every step, Doron was getting closer.

'Do you believe me, Sarih?' he said fiercely.

'I don't know, I don't know...' wept Sarih, sinking to the floor.

Doron reached the desk. With a violent sweep of his arm he sent the remainder of the driftwood cubes hurtling at the crying girl. Some hit her and landed by her side. Others smacked against the calculation-strewn wall before clattering to the floor. Before they'd even come to rest, Doron was at Sarih's shoulder and pulling her head up by the scalp.

'There are your forty dice!' he shouted. 'Look at them. A random collection. And what are the chances of them turning up like that? I'll tell you. Exactly the same as for your precious sixes!'

They lifted her up then, Jenna on one arm and Doron on the other. Stepping to one side, Raul held the door open for them. Sarih appeared to be letting them guide her but, at the door, she began to struggle again.

'Take it easy, Sarih,' said Raul. 'It's for your own good. You're ill.'

'But the numbers…'

'Mean nothing, Sarih. Science says that everything happened on the first throw of the dice. Science can't be wrong.'

Hearing this, the girl seemed to lose the urge to fight. Her head fell to her chest, her arms went limp. Meekly she allowed Jenna and Doron to lead her out of the room and away.

After they'd gone, Raul returned to his own room. He crossed to the window and looked out. The grassy oval was bathed in a wan moonlight. Beyond it, the tree tops stood still and skeletal against the distant glow of light from the mainland. Still hearing the echo of the voice he'd heard advising Sarih, and still feeling surprise that it had been his own, Raul didn't even notice that the wind had dropped.

'Has anybody seen Micha this morning?'

The question was lightly posed but Doron, at the head of the breakfast table, looked at Raul with serious intent. When Raul shook his head – and Arym, Jack and Emily did likewise – the healer immediately got to his feet and hurried from the refectory. He returned a few minutes later to beckon Jenna outside. Raul knew then that Micha had swum for the mainland, just as he'd promised.

115

'He's gone,' he whispered to the others. 'Micha's gone.'

The response was muted. 'Gone? What do you mean?' frowned Emily.

'Back home,' said Raul.

'On the boat?' smiled Jack. 'I liked the boat.'

'By swimming,' said Raul. 'He said he was going to swim across to Craston.'

'He told you that?' hissed Arym fiercely. 'And you didn't try to stop him?'

Raul shrugged. He felt curiously uninterested, as if trying to decide whether Micha's escape was a good or bad thing was simply too much effort.

Jenna's return to her place at the table stopped any further discussion.

'Sarih is unwell,' she said to them. 'She will not be joining the group today. Neither will Micha. Foolishly, he appears to have absconded. Doron is going to look for him. Now eat. We've been given a new Duty this morning. It would have been hard enough with six but with only four…'

'Micha can do double the work when he's found then,' Arym interrupted sourly.

Jenna shook her head. 'When Micha is found,' she murmured, 'I doubt very much he will be fit for any work at all.'

The new Duty turned out to be far harder than scouring the beach for flotsam. After they had congretated in the vestibule, Jenna led them round the garth to a small, plain door set in the far corner of the south cloister. From this a short, dank-smelling corridor led to an outer door. Passing through this Raul saw that they'd been brought to an L-shaped area of walled garden. The longer part ran the whole width of the west end of the sanitarium building, parallel with the track that he and Micha had followed the afternoon they'd gone exploring.

Where is Micha now? wondered Raul.

Jenna, however, led them round to the shorter part of the L-shape. Facing south, this part of the garden had been tastefully cultivated. Tall shrubs of jasmine hung with yellow winter flowers. Drooping snowberries glistened in the pale sunlight. Spreading lilacs were already bulging with buds. Beneath them, spikes of daffodil and narcissus were showing green against the dark earth.

At the far end, perhaps sixty paces distant across the dank lawn, a low-railed fence marked the cusp of the land. Beyond it, as if cut by a razor, the ground gave way to the sky. A row of rustic benches faced out over the sheer drop of the cliff's edge. Raul could see calm water.

How calm was the water last night? he wondered, as Jenna led them on. Passing through a lichen-covered archway embedded in a towering cypress hedge they arrived at what Raul assumed was an extension of the garden area they'd just left. But where before there had been order, here there was only chaos. Trees, shrubs, vines, brambles, flowers, berries, shoots – all had merged into one tangled mess.

'This is your Duty,' said Jenna. 'To help make this area whole again.'

'How did it get like this?' asked Jack.

117

'Neglect,' answered Jenna. 'Just as an untended mind can become overgrown with errors and superstition, so it is with a garden. As you cut away what shouldn't be here, imagine that you're doing the same to those thoughts which trouble you.'

Jenna sent Jack and Emily down to a relatively clear area at the far end, close to where the railed fence continued on round to follow the contours of the cliff, telling them to start a bonfire there.

Before accompanying them, she said to Raul and Arym, 'You can begin work here.' Jenna indicated a vague way forward. 'It would seem logical that a pathway would have led on from here, don't you think?'

Left to themselves, Raul and Arym worked for a while in heavy silence. Arym finally broke it by asking, 'What happened with Sarih?'

Raul told her about the wall of calculations, and about what he'd said in support of Doron.

'Good,' said Arym. She hesitated. 'Are you starting to feel…better? Jack and Emily are, I can tell.'

Raul nodded. He *was* starting to feel better. Calmer, for certain. He'd felt none of the old surges of fire that used to flare within him, not since they'd been given the sleeping draught. Nor were the questions coming so often, as if the curtain across his mind was stopping them from getting through. He smiled. He felt good.

'Micha *wasn't* feeling better,' he said. 'He felt angry.'

'I wonder if they've found him yet?' said Arym. 'They're bound to have told the regulators to watch out for him on the mainland. Bet you they'll bring him back on the next cargo boat!'

118

But Micha's chair was still vacant at lunch. Doron was in his usual place, but offered no explanation. His only comment was that Sarih had been transferred to another part of the sanitarium for further treatment. Raul wondered where that was, but didn't say anything.

'Will she get better?' Emily had asked.

'Doctor Tomas is doing her best for her,' Doron had replied. 'When there is more news, I will tell you.'

He hadn't accompanied them when they returned to Duty, however. Jenna remained in charge, supervising the fire and helping Emily and Jack to carry the heavier loads to it. In their own area Raul and Arym worked on, making slow progress against the tangle of brambles and vines. They'd been given strong gloves to protect their hands from the savage thorns but, even so, one still managed to pierce the leather palm of Raul's glove and bite into his flesh. He then compounded the agony by snapping the thorn as he tried to pull it out. From then on, the black remnant beneath his throbbing skin was a constant reminder to take care.

But, by late afternoon, vague signs of a pattern were beginning to emerge. Jenna's intuition looked to have served her well. There did appear to have once been a winding path which threaded its way from the arch to some unseen destination deep in the jungle. More than once Raul's digging and raking had struck distinct pockets of stone chippings buried beneath the layers of leaf mould. By clearing the top layers aside, the first five or six paces of the pathway had been revealed.

On either side of it, though, the going had been much harder. Ferns and bracken grew to thigh level. Even after they'd been hacked away, it was only to find that the ground underneath was bulging with roots and vines. Much of the vine had insinuated itself into the trees as well, the green-laden tendrils winding around trunks and climbing high up into the branches. Raul yanked a pile down from a chestnut tree, prising the thick lower stems away from the trunk with the point of the sickle he'd been given to use.

'What do you think this place used to be?' he asked suddenly.

Arym looked at him, her arms laden with bracken. 'Same as it is now,' she said dismissively, 'a sanitarium. A place where they send weird kids who wonder if there's a God. And their poor half-sisters.'

'Micha didn't think that. He reckoned the building was as old as the Celebreon.'

'So?'

'The Celebreon was around before that girl Doron told us about, who drowned.'

'Annie Dawkins,' said Arym flatly.

'But Doron also said the sanitarium wasn't here then. Which means...' For a moment Raul struggled to remember exactly what it *did* mean, 'that if this place was around before then it must have been used for something else.'

Arym shrugged. 'The past doesn't matter. Today and tomorrow, they're all that counts. How we get this job done; how we get you out of this place.'

They'd built up a decent heap of dead wood and tangled vine. Laying it all on a wide strip of sacking, they took a leading corner each and dragged it through to where the bonfire was going well. Lobbing their load into the flames, they then retreated to watch it pop and crackle and send flakes of white ash floating into the air. Jenna had brought drinks flasks out with her, too. The others settled down with theirs, seated comfortably around the fire. Raul didn't stay. While Arym gratefully accepted Jenna's offer to remain and help prevent the bonfire getting out of control, Raul finished his drink quickly and went back to his work.

Different types of bushes and shrubs had begun to emerge in the part he and Arym had cleared. Raul began on an unkempt laurel bush, ruthlessly cutting back its wildest outgrowths and hacking out the dead wood. This done, he went round again, this time concentrating not on reducing length but on giving the laurel shape. Slowly it began to take on a tulip-like appearance.

It was as he cleared away the mass of clippings that Raul found the strange object. Digging down deep into the mound to gather up as large a pile as he could carry to the bonfire, Raul overestimated its depth. His gloved fingers plunged through the clippings and into the layer of leaf mould beneath. When he lifted his pile, the thing came up with it, to stick out of the ground like a sword.

Except that this wasn't a sword, only sword-shaped. Tossing the laurel clippings aside, Raul bent down and pulled the thing fully out of the ground. Humus and damp leaves came with it. Thin red worms clung to it, feasting on the wood. For that was clearly what it was made from – planed hardwood, badly rotted from however long it had spent in the sodden earth, but still with a sufficiently solid core to stop it falling apart in his hands.

Frowning, Raul held it upright. It comprised two pieces.

121

The longer of the pieces had a span of about a metre. It was badly charred at one end, the wood blackened and scaly rather than soft and pulpy with rot. The other piece was shorter, sixty centimetres in length at most. They were linked by a simple tenon joint, the shorter piece being attached crossways to the longer, about two-thirds of the way up. At this point, a diamond of four holes was just visible.

Raul was still studying the thing when Jenna came pushing through the cleared section to see how he was getting on. She stopped abruptly.

'Where did you get that?'

Raul pointed to the spot. 'There. It was buried under the leaves.'

'Let me have it,' said Jenna, stretching out a gloved hand. 'I'll put it on the fire.'

Something about the way she said it, the curtness of her tone, made Raul hesitate. 'Why, what is it?'

'Nothing. Rubbish.'

A flicker of the old Raul flared through the calm curtain across his mind. 'You know, don't you?'

Jenna hesitated. 'Yes,' she said finally.

'Why won't you tell me, then?'

'Because it won't help you to know.' Jenna moved to his side, taking his arm in the soothing way she had used with Sarih. 'Raul, you're getting on so well. Don't worry about what it is. You'll never see one again.'

'I've seen one already,' said Raul.

'Don't be silly.'

'I have, I tell you. In my room. There's a shadow on the wall the same shape, only smaller.'

Jenna looked shocked, but didn't back away. 'Let me have it then, and I'll tell you what it is.'

Slowly, Raul let her ease the thing from his fingers. Only then did she say, 'It's called a cross.'

'What's a cross?'

Jenna's eyes took on a haunted look, as if she were wishing that Doron was here to answer the question with his certainties and quotations. Raul posed it again. This time she responded.

'A superstitious relic. A memorial symbol used by a sect of unbelievers. One of many such sects. They all had their own special symbols. Crosses, stars, crescent moons...the list is endless.'

'Were they cured? Is that how that cross got here?'

Jenna didn't answer directly. 'They're extinct, Raul.'

She turned back, leading Raul towards the glow of the fire, the rotten cross held away from her body as if she was afraid that the corruption of the wood might spread to her. Raul followed, intrigued, his slumbering mind jolted awake by what he was hearing.

'Does Science have a symbol?' he asked.

'Science doesn't need a symbol, Raul. Science is all around us. We can see it, touch it, smell it. We don't need reminding that it's there for us. It makes itself known. It's visible, not invisible. We see its order everywhere.'

Raul was reminded of π, the universal constant. 'Symbols stand for things. What did the unbeliever's symbols stand for?'

'Their gods. All different, but they all came down to the same superstition in the end. That somewhere there was a god who loved them as individuals, one who would look after them because he could do anything.'

Raul felt another tiny surge of his old self. 'Like – create things?'

'Oh, yes!' Jenna's contempt was clear. 'That was the one thing they all had in common – each of them believed their particular version of god had created the whole universe. As far as they were concerned he'd done it all. God was all-powerful and all-loving.'

They'd reached the fire. Arym, Jack and Emily had just loaded on a fresh pile of bracken and the flames were spurting high into the air. Jenna lifted the cross above her head and cast it into the heart of the fire.

Raul watched as it sizzled, as the flames licked hungrily along both lengths of wood, as the despised symbol finally cracked and split and died in a shower of sparks.

By then, Jenna had called a halt to Duty for the day. They gathered together their tools and began to head back. The odour of wood-smoke clung to their scapulas and albs. There would just be time to change into their cowls for the Gathering of Vespers. Passing through the archway, Raul looked across with pride at the pathway he'd helped clear and the laurel bush he'd shaped.

And he wondered fleetingly why, if Science was solely responsible for the order in his world, the garden had looked more chaotic at the beginning of the day.

Doron still hadn't returned. Was he still tracking Micha? Had he taken the cargo boat to the mainland to look for him? Or was he still scouring the island, checking the caves and blow-holes in the belief that Micha wouldn't

124

have dared attempt the swim? Towards the end of the group meeting after supper, Raul asked Jenna for news. She was non-committal.

'Micha is in our thoughts. We want what is best for him. Doron has taken on that responsibility.'

Arym asked about Sarih.

'Sarih is in our thoughts. We want what is best for her. Doctor Tomas has taken on that responsibility.' The healer looked relieved when the Gathering bell began to toll for Compline.

Outside, as they grouped round the statue of the Saviour, Raul was again glad of the comforting warmth provided by his cowl. The wind was rising again, a chill wind this time, slicing down into the unprotected cloister garth in bitter gusts. Above, the half-moon was being quickly smothered by a vast black pillow of cloud.

The Gathering was conducted in some haste by a healer who obviously felt the cold. Within a few minutes, Raul was climbing the stone staircase to his room. He noticed the smell the moment he opened the door. It was a tangy smell, which invaded his nostrils and clutched at the back of his throat. It wasn't new to him, however. He'd known it before, at the nurture-house, on the infrequent occasions when the Guardian had decided their dormitory walls needed a cleaner look about them.

The shadow of the cross on the wall behind his bed was no longer there. It had been submerged under a still-damp splatter of whitewash.

Snow came that night. Raul was woken by the Gathering bell to discover that the clouds and chill wind of the previous evening had brought a whitewash of their own.

Outside, the grassy oval had become an oval of white, as pure as the body of a swan. The trees were cloaked, their branches dipping under the weight, only to spring up again as a fierce gust lifted the load and sent it cascading to the earth. For the wind had not dropped, nor the snow ended. It was still slanting down across his window, being driven into small drifts on one side of the frame. Down below, the same thing was happening, only on a far larger scale. The bases of every wall, fence and hedge were slowly vanishing as the snow piled high against them.

Raul's pang of excitement rapidly disappeared – the bell was calling. Washing quickly, he threw on his cowl, then stepped out into the corridor to file silently down to the cloister garth. Arym became the partner at his side. He returned her smile.

The Gathering of Lauds that morning made one concession to the weather. Instead of congregating around the Saviour's statue, the community lined the cloisters instead. The glistening quadrangle, white in the candlelight, seemed to add a quality of its own to the plainsong that morning. As the service ended, Raul had never felt more tranquil. Quietly, calmly, he walked to the refectory.

Doron was waiting at the door. He stretched out his arm, barring the way. 'Not yet,' he said sharply, and motioned Raul to one side, to where Jenna was already standing with a silent Emily.

In the same fashion Arym and Jack were both plucked

from the queue entering the refectory. It was Arym who asked the question.

'Have you found Micha?'

'Yes,' said Doron without emotion. He looked tired. He was unshaven and his eyes were dark-rimmed, as if he hadn't slept for some time.

Raul didn't know whether to be happy or sad. 'Is he all right?' he asked. 'Can we see him?'

Doron ignored the first question, responding only to the second. 'Of course you can see him. I'm sure he would like that. He's this way.'

At his nod, Jenna moved off – but not in the direction of the vestibule stairway leading up to Micha's room. Instead she led them along the south cloister, past the door in the corner which led out to the garden, and down to another door at the far end. There she halted, waiting for Doron to produce a key to unlock it. Once done, the healer stood back to allow them through. He then followed himself, but not before he'd locked the door behind him.

There were no rooms on the other side of this door, just a circular stairway. Raul tried to stir his lazy brain into fitting the whereabouts into his mental geography of the sanitarium. He was sure that this stairway couldn't be approached from any of the rooms along the south cloister, which meant that the door they'd just passed through had to be the only way of reaching it. That being so, the stairs they were now climbing had to be the only way of gaining access to the upper floors on the south side of the sanitarium.

Ahead, Jenna had reached one landing, then a second.

As they'd been climbing, a distinctive odour had been growing stronger: not the tangy odour of whitewash this time, but one of scrubbed cleanliness. It peaked as Jenna left the stairway and led them into a corridor totally unlike any other they'd seen.

Its walls were a brilliant white. Its floor was covered with a material so glossy and clean it reflected their images as they walked along it, their shoes squeaking. Above their heads lights glowed. Above doors, too. Sometimes red, sometimes green.

'In here.'

Doron had pushed past them to reach Jenna's side, just as she stopped at a door with an oblong glass panel at eye level. He swung the door open, then ushered them through. Jack went first, then Emily. Jenna followed them in, guiding them to the far side of the one item of furniture in the room: a bed. Doron then motioned Arym and Raul towards its near-side before closing the door. Doctor Tomas was there ahead of them.

'Everybody here, Doron?' she asked with more than a hint of sarcasm. She smiled bleakly, answering her own question. 'Yes, of course they are.'

She had been standing at the foot of the bed, waiting. Now she gestured towards the still figure lying there, as if she felt the need to draw their attention to it.

There was no need. Each of them had been staring at nothing else since they'd entered the room. Raul's eyes hadn't left the figure covered by the crisp white sheet: covered completely, in time-honoured fashion, from the tips of his toes to the top of his head.

'I have examined your friend's remains,' said Doctor

Tomas into the silence. 'He drowned. Sucked down by the fierce undertow in Craston Sound, without a doubt. Where did you find him, Doron?'

'On the rocks beyond the jetty. The tide had washed him into a crevice, otherwise I would have found him sooner.'

The healer looked at Doctor Tomas and received a nod of confirmation. 'Prepare yourselves,' he said. 'He's been dead for nearly two days.' Hesitating for no more than a moment, Doron slowly peeled back the sheet to reveal Micha's face and torso.

On the other side of the bed Jack stared, wide-eyed. Emily's hand flew briefly to her lips before she buried her face against Jenna, all the while casting horrified glances back at the corpse laid out before them.

But only Arym shed any tears. They rolled silently down her face until she was forced to brush them away with her sleeve.

Raul did not cry. At first he felt little emotion at all. The figure didn't look much like the Micha he remembered. This Micha's face was swollen and puffy. His eyes were closed. His lips were a deep, deep blue. His shock of black hair, still laced with strands of weed, was dry and matted. The rest of his body looked to have grown in size. His chest and stomach were bloated. His skin was blotched and discoloured. It was covered in lacerations – from being tossed back and forth against the needle-sharp rocks, Raul assumed.

He found his attention being drawn to surprising contrasts. To Micha's fingernails, white against the purple of fingers that looked as though they belonged on an old washerwoman rather than a fifteen-year-old boy; to the fine fair hairs along his misshapen forearms; to the small, raised circle of white, clearly outlined against the surrounding flesh of his upper arm...

'Take a good look, Raul,' said Doron, his voice hard-edged.

Raul didn't respond.

'Jenna told me you found an unbeliever's symbol in the walled garden yesterday.'

Raul nodded, but didn't look away from Micha's corpse.

'She says she explained one of their superstitions – their irrational belief in a god who loved them.'

Raul nodded again, only a portion of his struggling mind on what Doron was saying to him.

'Exactly how irrational, you can now see for yourself. Wouldn't an all-loving, all-powerful god have stopped a thing like this from happening?'

Only then did Raul react. 'I've seen enough!' he shouted. 'Let me go!'

'Of course,' said Doctor Tomas softly. She motioned to Doron, who drew the white sheet back over Micha's head. 'But do not forget what you have seen. Remember, here in the sanitarium you are safe.'

The refectory had almost emptied by the time they got there. Each sat in their usual places, knowing now that Micha would never join them again. As for the other empty seat – Raul suddenly wanted to know more.

'Where is Sarih?' he asked.

'Sarih is receiving special attention,' said Doron calmly.

'Is she up there? Where we've just been?'

'That is where Doctor Tomas provides for those with particular needs, yes.'

'So she *is* there? She's not dead as well?'

The suddenness of the question made the others start. Only Doron took it in his stride. 'Raul, please! Sarih is very ill. She is receiving the best treatment possible. Doctor Tomas feels that seclusion is part of that treatment. We must respect her judgement.'

'So Sarih's still alive?'

'Of course she is. She will be back with us just as soon as Doctor Tomas feels she is well enough.'

By the time they'd finished their meal they were alone in the refectory, those whose duty it was to clear the tables that day having been waved away by Doron. Raul volunteered for the task.

'Thank you, Raul,' said Jenna. She smiled sympathetically. 'I'm sorry if seeing your friend like that was a shock.'

Doron pushed back his chair and got to his feet. He motioned to the others to do the same. 'The weather is too bad for Duty today. And besides, Jenna and I have a meeting to attend. Return to your rooms, please. You can spend the remainder of the morning in quiet reflection, until the Gathering of Sext.' He produced his copy of *The Writings* and thumbed the pages. 'May I suggest the first commandment as a suitable text: "You must love the Republic with all your heart, with all your energy and with all your mind; and her teachings as your own."'

Raul watched them go, Doron with Jack and Emily, and Jenna saying something to Arym. Unhurriedly, he then cleared away the clutter from the food table, stacking the glasses and plates on a tray, gathering the soiled knives and forks together beside them, then placing the tray on a chair while he wiped the table top clean. Only once a deep silence had fallen over the sanitarium did he quickly carry the loaded tray out to the scullery.

There, he wasted no time. His mind still felt woolly, still felt as though it didn't completely belong to his body, but the shock of seeing Micha's corpse had had a douching effect. He knew what he had to do, and none of the knives he'd just cleared from the meal table would be sharp enough. Quickly he pulled open drawers and cupboards, scanning the contents before closing them again.

Finally, in the drawer beneath the large worktop used for food preparation, he found what he was looking for. Thin, almost stiletto-like, the black-handled knife had a point like a needle. He'd seen traders on the quayside using similar knives for gutting fish, so he knew it would do the job. Secreting it into the folds of his cowl as he left the scullery, Raul walked calmly towards the vestibule stairway.

Slipping out from her hiding place behind the refectory lectern, Arym followed her brother at a discreet distance. She watched him begin the climb up towards his room. Only then did she break into a frantic run…

Doctor Tomas stood at the window of her room, looking out onto a view that was growing more wintry by the minute. Swollen flakes of snow were tumbling from the leaden sky in thick bursts. Rarely had a blizzard like this struck the island. Not since the year 174 AD, according to the short island history she'd been specially authorised to read before taking up her post. That year the freezing conditions had lasted from early Undec into the first week of February, restricting movement to a minimum. The prospect of a similar period did not appeal.

A knock at the door brought an end to this reverie. 'Come in, sit down,' she said. Taking their customary places, both Doron and Jenna appeared relieved that her mood was not as icy as the conditions outside. But then, why should it have been? No harm had been done – yet.

'Arrangements have been made to dispose of Micha's remains?' said Doctor Tomas without preamble, taking her seat.

Doron nodded. 'The cargo boat will take his body to the mainland as soon weather conditions permit. And the cremation can be – er, unrecorded, if that is your wish.'

Doctor Tomas frowned. 'Certainly not. Micha died by his own hand. That can be recorded.'

'Won't questions be asked?'

'By whom? As a nurture-house child, Micha was owned by the Republic. Only the Republic could question the nature of his death. And as I represent the Republic and I do *not* question it, that is the end of the matter.'

'I can't help feeling sorry for him,' said Jenna quietly.

'Why?' snapped Doctor Tomas. 'He died doing what he wanted. Many in history would have been pleased to say the same.'

Jenna looked down at her lap. 'I suppose so. But when he jumped into the water he couldn't have *wanted* to die. Could he?'

'There is nothing in his file to suggest as much. But do not forget, Jenna, that ours is not yet a precise science.

133

There is a long way to go before we can say that we have solved the riddle of unbelief. Perhaps Micha's unbelief was so deeply entrenched that he was oblivious to personal danger; that he thought some higher power would guard him.'

Doron nodded firmly, as if he thought an insight of great wisdom had just been voiced. 'Is there another possibility?' he asked. 'That Micha was an adherent of the life-after-death superstition?'

'You mean he *wanted* to die?' gasped Jenna. 'He never once showed any sign of that.'

'No, I mean that death held little fear for him because he was under the illusion that there was an after-life.'

Jenna looked at Dr Tomas. 'Should we have assessed for that?'

Doctor Tomas shook her head. She didn't believe in criticising her healers if at all possible. Far better to have them on her side, supporting her at all times.

'That was not a priority, Jenna. After all, many of our own kind, firm believers in all that Science teaches, are nevertheless convinced that there must be something more than this one life. It is a very difficult notion to eradicate. What is of greater importance is *why* they think this. The superstition of heaven is what we need to unearth. Did Micha ever suggest this?'

Jenna and Doron exchanged glances. 'Quite the opposite, Doctor Tomas,' said Doron, 'Micha absconded from his nurture-house to live on the streets like an alley-cat. He lived for the day. We were virtually certain that he was not so much a non-believer as a non-thinker. He will not be missed.'

'Unlike…' Jenna hesitated.

'Sarih?' Doctor Tomas spoke the name for her. 'She is recovering. All the signs are good.'

Doron looked at her with undisguised admiration. 'You have cured her, Doctor Tomas?'

The woman raised a slender finger of caution. 'Time will tell, Doron. But – your recommendation to take all steps necessary was well-founded. I was able to locate the source of Sarih's obsessive behaviour without difficulty. This has now been neutralised.'

'Will there be any…' Jenna hesitated while she searched for the most suitable phrase, 'side-effects?'

'Inevitably, yes. But the priority was to break the link between her numerical processing capacity and the area of her mind in which that capacity became the tool of disbelief. That has been done.'

'And the side-effect?' persisted Jenna.

'Sarih will have less dexterity with numbers than before. But she will be much happier.'

'Happier? Are you sure, Doctor Tomas? Mathematics was the only topic that made her come alive.'

'Jenna!' said Doctor Tomas sharply. 'Scientific ability in whatever form is a great gift. Used wisely, it benefits us all. But when abused, when turned towards evil purposes, then it is right – it is our duty – to put a stop to it. You should be proud that, between us, we have ensured that Sarih will no longer abuse the gifts she was born with.'

'And that will make her happier?'

'It will make her fellow human beings happier,' said Doctor Tomas.

'Which will make *her* happier,' smiled Doron. 'For as it

is written, "Happy are you who respect Science, who walk in its ways! For you shall eat the fruit of your handiwork; happy shall you be!"'

Doctor Tomas uncrossed her legs. She leaned forward, as if taking the two healers into her confidence.

'Enough of Sarih. What are we to do about Raul? I expect you, like me, found his little outburst in the mortuary room – disturbing – shall we say?'

'He and Micha had become friends,' said Jenna.

'There was more to it than that. He felt compelled to leave.'

'You think that might have been a return of his aggressive side?' asked Doron.

'Possibly. The experience of a friend's death does affect the mind in ways we do not yet fully understand. It could promote mental activity capable even of neutralising his medication.'

'Allowing anger? He has been very calm since his medication began.'

'I am thinking at a deeper level, Doron. Anger has many sources. Is there any possibility that he will seek to blame us for Micha's death and avenge it in some way?'

'No. Not at all. He's more likely to feel guilty!'

The sharpness of Jenna's tone stunned Doron. It surprised Doctor Tomas also, but she was far too experienced at dealing with subordinates to let it show. 'You sound certain, Jenna. Why is that?'

Jenna bit her lip, as if wondering whether to explain fully. 'Arym,' she said finally, 'confided to me that Raul knew what Micha was planning.' She gave Doron a look of apology. 'I'm sorry, Doron, I should have told you.

136

But I didn't want to make Arym feel awkward.'

'Why not?' asked Doctor Tomas.

'Because she wants to become a healer!' cried Jenna, hardly able to contain her enthusiasm.

Doctor Tomas stood up and crossed to the window again. For once she was uncertain about what she wanted to do. Until a few moments ago, she had been in little doubt. But now...

'Advise me then, Jenna,' she said softly. 'How should Raul's treatment proceed?'

Her question wasn't answered. From outside came the sound of raised voices, as if somebody was arguing with the assistant responsible for vetting all who wanted a sliver of Doctor Tomas's time. There followed a shout, some scuffling noises. The next moment the door burst open.

'Jenna, it's Raul,' cried Arym. 'He's stolen a knife and taken it to his room!'

Raul turned on the tap. Hot water spurted from it, spluttering momentarily before settling to a firm flow. He watched it swirling into the white china sink.

He thought about what he intended to do, tried to keep it at the front of his mind, along with the memory of Micha lying cold and blue and rigid on the white sheets of his final bed. He tried not to think about whether it was going to hurt.

He glanced at the needle-pointed knife resting on his bed, then back to the sink. The knife would come later. First he had to prepare.

He lifted his brown scapula over his head and laid it on the bed beside the knife. He began to roll up the left sleeve of his white alb, then realised how awkward it would be to keep it in position for as long as he needed. He took it off instead.

Swathes of steam were rising from the sink. He assumed that hot water would work more quickly than cold. The floorboard creaked as he stepped across it. Raul took one look at himself, blurry in the mirror on the wall. Then he plunged his crooked arm under the water far as the shoulder.

That was how Doron and Jenna found him when they burst into his room just minutes later. While Jenna plucked the knife from the bed, Doron flew across to pull Raul roughly away from the sink. Then, as if relieved that they'd arrived in time, the healer led him much more gently across to the bed and sat him down.

'What were you going to do with the knife, Raul?' he asked.

Raul, his mind in a whirl, didn't know what to say. He was already starting to doubt his own thinking. So he said nothing, just watched the water trickling down his arm and dripping on to the mat at his feet.

'Did what happened to Micha upset you that much?' Jenna asked gently.

Doron was firmer, but even he had an unusual edge of sympathy. 'We have one life, Raul. To take it – to even consider taking it – is a crime.'

'Micha made his own decision,' said Jenna. 'Nobody else made it for him. Nobody else should feel responsible.'

'Did you think that by taking your own life you would be going to see him again, Raul?' asked Doron.

The words cut through the turmoil in Raul's head like

the knife he'd been planning to use. Was that what they believed he was going to do? Take his own life by slashing his wrists? He looked up. The concern – genuine or otherwise – on both healers' faces told him that that was precisely what they had believed.

'I was feeling confused,' said Raul. Another thought struck him. 'How did you know I'd taken the knife?'

Doron replied without hesitation. 'The healer designated to prepare today's lunch noticed that it was missing. As you had been the last person in the kitchen, the culprit had to be you.'

'I see.'

'Get dressed, Raul,' said Jenna.

Raul slipped his alb back on, followed by his scapula. 'Are you taking me for further treatment?' he asked quietly. 'Will I be with Sarih?'

The mention of that name appeared to trigger some doubt about what the healers had planned to do next. After an exchange of glances with Jenna, Doron laid a hand on Raul's shoulder and made him sit back on the bed.

'No. We are going to recommend to Doctor Tomas that you be confined to your room for a while.'

Jenna pointed out of the window at the still-falling snow. 'Not that there will be many Duty sessions for a few days anyway!'

'We will need to keep an eye on you, Raul, until we are sure that you are no longer a danger to yourself.'

'You mean I can't go out?'

'Only for meals and the Gatherings. Apart from that you will spend your time in here – with plenty of good reading matter, of course.'

139

'And I won't see anybody except you two?'

'No...' Doron gave Jenna another quick glance, then added, 'apart from Arym, that is. We will recommend to Doctor Tomas that Arym should be allowed to see you regularly.'

'She is your sister, after all,' smiled Jenna.

Arym stood leaning against his door, hands on hips. Since coming to his room, perhaps thirty minutes after Doron and Jenna had left, Raul's sister had appeared alternately upset, confused and angry. Upset, she'd said, that he'd even thought about killing himself, confused about the reasons why, and angry at the shock of hearing the news from Jenna. Now she was exhibiting all three emotions in parallel.

'I want to get out of this place, Raul! Can't you get that into your fat head? But they won't let me go if you're still here. And they won't let you go until you stop acting as if you *deserve* to be here!'

'I know,' said Raul.

'Do you? Do you really?' She came to sit beside him. 'Oh Raul, I thought you were getting better. Then you go and take a knife from a drawer and...' The words died on her lips. She sighed and shook her head.

'I *am* getting better, Arym,' said Raul. He turned to face her. 'Micha was wrong. He thought the people here couldn't be trusted. I don't believe that. I do trust them.'

Arym smiled. 'You do?' She ruffled his hair. 'Then maybe we do have some things in common,' she said, 'just like Science and *The Writings* say we should.'

'Science doesn't lie,' said Raul. '*The Writings* don't lie.'

Arym squeezed his hand affectionately, then stood up. The floorboard creaked. She pressed her foot down on it a couple of times. 'I don't know how you can put up with that, though!' she said.

She crossed to the door and knocked at it gently. A key turned in the lock. It swung open. Out in the corridor Jenna's shadow briefly darkened the wall. Arym waved a goodbye hand at Raul, comically waggling her fingers. Then the door closed behind her. The key grated again.

Raul lay back on his bed. It was strange how the sight of Micha had affected him. It was as if curtains across his mind had momentarily parted and what he'd seen through the gap had told him he had to find something sharp.

Another similar moment had come only a little while ago, when Arym had said, 'Then you go and take a knife from a drawer.' Had she been guessing? Or had she been watching? He didn't know, nor could he work out whether or not it was important.

What *was* important, what he knew he had to do before the curtains closed much further, was find the sharp thing he needed.

Raul shut his eyes and concentrated. Where else could he find such a thing? Not anywhere in the sanitarium building itself. They would be watching him now. Outside, then? Yes, the garden, the walled garden where he'd found the cross symbol. That had been rampant with just what he needed, from the short sharp thorns of brambles and wild roses to the vicious needles of berberis.

Yes, a thorn might do it. But how could he get to the garden unnoticed, even if was possible in this weather? He

141

looked down at the palm of his hand, still showing the tiny black remnant of the thorn that had made it throb so much – and a word burst through the cobwebs in his head.

Splinter!

Splinters were sharp, needle shaped. Splinters came from wood. Wood was used to make floorboards.

Quickly he levered himself off his bed, ripping aside the floor mat to reveal the bare boards beneath. He ran his hands over them, pressing down as he crawled along. A creak revealed the loose floorboard – which, Raul now saw, wasn't simply loose. Running the width of the room and beneath the bed, it was splintered and damaged, as if an incompetent workman had levered it up for some reason then hastily jammed it back into place again.

Easing his fingers beneath the unfastened end, Raul lifted and pulled. The board came away easily. It was better than he could have hoped. Sharp slivers of wood protruded from virtually its entire length. Pulling away the sharpest he could see, Raul pushed the board back into place. He stood up, crossed to the sink, and again turned on the hot tap. Then he began to roll up his sleeve.

It took him almost thirty-six hours.

His progress had been slowed by the need to ensure that everything was cleared away before either Doron or Jenna arrived to accompany him to the refectory for meals or to the cloister garth for the Gatherings. So, too, had he been held back by Arym's post-meal visits. But, far more than either of these, the biggest obstacle had been the pain.

Soaking his arm in hot water proved to be no use. He'd had to simulate the conditions in which Micha had met his end – and that meant cold water. Only after keeping his upper arm submerged until it was numb and blue with cold, did what he was looking for finally appear beneath his own skin: the round white pellet shape he'd seen on Micha's bloated arm.

Only then, taking up his splinter needle, had he been able to continue cutting it out.

Easing the splinter beneath his skin, he'd lever and twist. The numbness meant he felt little, the trickles of blood the only sign of the damage he was causing. But, all too soon, the effects of the cold water wore off. Then the pain began. Sometimes Raul was able to continue, at other times he found himself wondering why he was hurting himself so. Then he'd bathe the wound and wait for the pain to subside.

Finally, though, he'd managed to dig down and through to the object that could only have been inserted on the night they'd given himself, Micha – all of them? – the sleeping draught. The object that proved Micha had been right about not trusting them. How they'd managed to insert it beneath the skin of his upper arm without leaving a scar he didn't know. But there it was: a smooth, round, solid white pellet.

Pulling out the floorboard once more, Raul prised off a fresh, sharp-pointed splinter. He ran cold water over his upper arm until it felt as though the whole limb didn't belong to him. Then he returned to kneel by his bedside. Clamping his blanket between his teeth to stop himself from crying out, he gripped the splinter firmly. Then, before fear could stop him, he thrust it hard beneath the pellet and twisted it upwards.

He'd never felt pain like it before. He heard his own muffled scream, felt the bone-deep agony of his arm – but then, as he slumped away from the bed and on to the floor, he saw the pellet come away to fall beside him.

Raul lay still for some minutes, staunching the flow of blood with his handkerchief while he waited for the waves of pain to ease. Finally he got up and ran cold water over his arm until it was gloriously numb once more.

The pellet still lay on the carpet. What should he do with it? The Gathering of Vespers was not long off. They would be coming for him. Raul thought of washing it away down the sink, then changed his mind. He would hide it, to show Arym.

The gap left by the splintered floorboard showed him where. Under the floorboards the pellet would be well hidden, yet easily accessible. Hastily, Raul lay on the floor, holding the pellet between his forefinger and thumb. Thrusting his hand into the gap, he cocked his wrist and stretched until he felt the rough-sawn wood of a joist. There he allowed the pellet to slip from his fingers.

It was as he withdrew his hand that he found the book. It was the cheap spiral binding holding its pages together that Raul felt first, its end digging painfully into his palm. The rest of it he saw as he pulled it out into the light.

It was an exercise book, not unlike those they'd used

during their study sessions at the nurture-house – but clearly far older. Raul blew away the dust of time. The book's cover was plain and faded but the ink was still dark against it, the handwriting bold and clear. He could read the title without difficulty:

The Journal of Brother Mark

Book Two

Unknown reader – you have discovered my brief journal.

I don't know where you found it for the simple reason that, right now, I don't yet know where I'm going to hide it.

When is 'right now'?

It's officially Saturday 21st October in the year 225.

Today our community was condemned to death.

Sunday 22nd October

Who am I? Who are we? Why has the death sentence been passed on us, and on our way of life?

That's why I've decided to describe our final days: in the hope that, in the future, somebody will want to know the answers to questions like these. As I want you to make up your own mind about us, reader, I'm going to try to stick to the facts and not litter this journal with my own opinions. And believe me, that's not going to be easy!

So, who am I? My name's Mark Talbot. I'm twenty-six years old. I don't know how old you are, but here in the monastery I'm known as 'the young 'un'! Brother Conor – who must be sixty-five if he's a day – is as likely to call me 'baby brother' as he is to call me 'Brother Mark'!

We're a community of monks: people who've decided to

devote their lives to drawing closer to God. Simple as that. We're a family, of sorts – and, like any family, we have our rows and fights. Try borrowing one of Brother Henry's carpentry tools without his permission! But we live by what's called the Rules. That means accepting each other for what we are.

Our day revolves around worship and prayer. Take it from me, that's a lot harder than it sounds. We get up at three o'clock in the morning, for a start! Our first prayer service (called Vigils) starts at 3.30am and from then on we fit work and study around seven other services called Lauds, Prime, Terce, Sext, None, Vespers and Compline. Bedtime is eight o'clock – which might sound early till you remember we're up again at three to start the new day.

That's what we do in our monastery here on Parens Island: spend our lives giving thanks to God and praying for all the peoples of the world. *That* is what the Republic has decreed is so dangerous that it has to be put down like a mad dog.

We've known it was coming for some time, of course, but yesterday we found out exactly when. Abbot Romuald called us together to tell us that the Directive of Dissolution had been formally delivered. We've got to be out of here in ten days' time. We talked it all over yet again.

'Brothers, you must think of yourselves,' Abbot Romuald said. 'Do what you must to survive. Don't rule out the option of rescinding your vows if that's what it takes.'

He asked whether any of us would like to discuss that option with him. None of us did. Brother Conor, in his usual blunt way, spoke for us all.

'With respect, Abbot,' he growled, 'you can stuff your option where the sun don't shine!'

The laughter – Abbot Romuald's louder than any – cheered us up for a few moments. We briefly gave thanks for having survived so long. Every other religious community in the Republic was crushed and scattered long ago. If ours hadn't been so small – there's just twelve of us – and living on an island, they'd have come for us well before now.

The Brothers then took it in turn to outline their plans.

'When the dissolution squad turns up,' said Conor, 'I'm planning to offer peaceful resistance!'

The way he said 'peaceful' made everybody smile. Conor's built like a shed and was the landlord of a pub before he became a monk, so his idea of peace isn't always the same as everybody else's! But as Brothers Liam, Henry and Stefan went on to say they were going to do the same, I realised I was being unfair. I mean, Brother Stefan's eighty-three years old; he's hardly likely to be in there swinging punches!

No, as they explained, they intend to sit tight and force the squad to carry them to the jetty like so many sacks. They'll do the same when they reach the mainland, knowing the crowd's jeering will be ringing in their ears. Abbot Romuald looked worried and understanding at the same time.

'I am told that the new Enclosure should be ready on Town Mount,' he said. 'At least there you should be safe.'

'*They* should be safe, you mean,' scoffed Brother Liam. 'We're being treated like lepers.'

Brother Conor laughed one of his heartiest laughs. 'Look on the bright side, Liam. Our Lord was a good friend to lepers!'

Other brothers are going to leave over the coming days. Dominic and Pierre have safe houses to go to, they say. They're young, only in their thirties. They hope to find out more about the rumoured resistance movement, join it if they can, do their bit to keep the flame of faith burning. They'll need to be wary. Abbot Romuald said he expects the mood on the mainland to grow uglier by the hour. That's what's happened elsewhere. The Republic's dissolution squads always begin their task by whipping up hatred amongst the locals, often hiring them as helpers on the day itself.

Finally it was my turn. I told them my plan. I've been thinking about it for some time. There was nothing any of them could say that would change my mind – and they tried hard!

'Baby Brother,' said Conor bluntly, his pipe clamped between his teeth, 'You're mad.'

'You won't last five minutes,' said Dominic.

Brother Stefan was the most encouraging. 'Sweet ignorance of youth,' he smiled. At least I *thought* he smiled – behind Stefan's bushy grey beard it's not always easy to tell! He definitely chuckled, though, when he added, 'But if I was sixty years younger I'd be joining you!'

They may be right. Perhaps I am mad. Only time will tell. But living alone on Orb Island as a hermit is what I'm determined to try.

The death sentence on our community has come especially hard to Brother Stefan. He seems to have shrivelled overnight.

After Lauds I stayed behind to help him up the chapel stairs. Instead he patted the seat beside him, inviting me to sit down. For a while he said nothing, just gazed rheumy-eyed towards the glorious window at the end of the chapel.

'Did you know I made that window?' he said finally.

'Really?' I smiled. If I had a pound for every time he's asked me that same question, my vow of poverty would be much harder to keep!

'Oh, yes,' Stefan said quietly. 'Look at it.'

I couldn't help looking at it. Stefan's window is fantastic, a marvel of intricate design and painstaking craftsmanship.

'Every bit of glass,' he wheezed, 'and every scrap of metal, all found washed up on the beach. That was what made it so special, see? I was changing rubbish into something beautiful for God. Just like he changed me.'

I glanced at him. I hadn't heard this part before. I waited, hoping he would say more and was pleased when he did.

'You won't believe it to look at me now,' he chuckled, 'but as a teenager I was a bad 'un. Stealing, brawling, you name it. Till the day I nearly died in a knife fight.'

He rolled up the sleeve of his cowl to show me the scar running the length of his arm. Then he raised his chin, to show me the pale, thin line disfiguring his neck. I'd seen them both before of course, we all had, but this was the first time I'd heard him mention them. Nobody had ever asked him how he

151

got them. In our community we're not concerned with a person's past, only their future.

'I spent three months in hospital,' he went on, 'much of it thinking. Thinking that there had to be another side to life. That's when I started out on the journey which led me here.'

A journey which is going to end soon, I thought as I helped him up the stairs from the chapel and into the cloister garth. By the time we reached his cell he was badly short of breath. His face was pale and clammy. I don't know how Stefan's going to survive away from the monastery. Will the dissolution squad care about *that*?

Tuesday 24th October

We're trying to carry on our routine as normal. That's too much for Brother Stefan. For the first time any of us can remember, he's been taken ill. I carried some breakfast up to him. As I stood in his cell, I couldn't help thinking that the small room had been his home for the best part of sixty years.

It made me feel so young! I joined the community as a novice a mere seven years ago. I was nineteen then, having been born in what the law tells me was the year 199.

I wonder what your childhood was like, reader. Some good, some bad? Let me tell you a bit about mine.

Until I was twelve it was pretty normal. At school I was good at sport – and useless at geography and history! But the subjects which really fascinated me were science and, unlike most of my friends, religious studies. My teachers were always saying these two didn't go together, but I thought they did. To me they tackled the same questions but from different directions, like a town with two main roads leading to it. Some said that evolution had replaced creation. I thought it explained it.

Outside of school, I did the usual things: fooled around, partied, made lots of friends and not too many enemies. I was happy enough. Then, in one day, that all changed.

I lived with my parents on the outskirts of a city named Northam. Have you heard of this place? If you haven't, it won't be because it no longer exists – but because it's still contaminated and unfit for people to live in. Northam, you see, was the city at the very centre of what has since become known as the Wasteland.

If I close my eyes, I can still see and hear the newsflash being read out on television:

'There are reports coming in of a huge explosion in Northam Docks. Emergency services at the scene report that there have been many casualties. A religious extremist group have claimed responsibility. Their claim that the device was radioactive is yet to be confirmed.'

My parents died that day. Why they'd gone into the city I never knew, but I eventually came to realise that they'd been among the lucky ones. The unlucky ones weren't killed outright, only powerless to avoid the radioactive fallout. Over the following days, weeks, months and years, many thousands upon thousands succumbed to death from the cancers and other illnesses caused by that inhuman act. In all, the lethal dust contaminated an area of almost 200 square miles.

Maybe the Wasteland is now clean again and humming with life. Right now, that's not so. It's a foul place, years away from recovery.

I survived only because I had been holidaying with my cousin Glyn, here on Parens Island. In those days he lived here with his parents, my Aunt Ruth and Uncle Harry. They were employed by the monks to do all manner of odd jobs – from washing to farming! I'd been due to go back home to Northam the very night that bomb exploded. I never did. All I could do was watch the news bulletins on television. Eventually, the official letter arrived to say that I was an orphan. I didn't even get to see my parents buried. Mourners weren't allowed. All the victims were buried in sealed, lead-lined coffins like the nuclear waste they'd become.

Of course I wanted to know why God had let it happen. Who wouldn't? I cursed him and blamed him for it all. If he was supposed to be all-loving, then surely he couldn't have *wanted* it to happen? And if he was all-powerful, why didn't he *stop* it?

Perhaps I'll be able to give you some of the answers I finally came up with, but they're long and my time is short. For now all I can say is that I decided it wasn't sensible for me to blame God for the evil committed in his name – any more than it would make sense for anybody to blame my parents for something I'd done wrong.

Aunt Ruth and Uncle Harry took me in. I finished my education, with Glyn, in the small school the monks ran here on the island. In the evenings and at weekends I would help by doing odd jobs. One of these jobs, though he no longer remembers, was to collect glass for Brother Stefan! I saw the life the monks led. Its rhythm, its discipline began to draw me more and more. I asked the Abbot if I could join the community as a novice.

I made my final vows just over a year ago. As I write these words, I am a monk.

I will *always* be a monk. Doesn't the Republic understand? Only death will change that, not one of their warped Directives!

Wednesday 25th October

I've got to go to the mainland. It's going to be dangerous, but I've got to take the chance. The problem is that any boat leaving here will be met and searched.

It wasn't always this way. Holidaymakers used to come over to the island for a delightful day out. They'd buy some of Brother Liam's chocolate – guaranteed to put a smile on any visitor's face, and an inch on their waistline! Brothers Pierre and Dominic would sell their lovely perfumes, made from the flowers of the island's gorse. Most of all though, those visitors would return home with some peace in their hearts.

No more. Shortly after the Republic came into being, trips to Parens Island were banned. They thought they'd force us out by cutting off our meagre income. But the small band of islanders – which included Aunt Ruth, Uncle Harry and Glyn – who'd been forced to move to the mainland because the community could no longer afford to pay them, worked secretly alongside many others to help out. Donations of money and food began to arrive. The community grew more and farmed more. And so we survived. Our smallness and remote location put us way down the long list of churches, synagogues and mosques, religious houses and monasteries, being wiped out by the dissolution squads. They simply had too much work to do – until now. Now the Republic's will is to be done.

Will you know of the Republic, reader – and of the ruling Authority Party, who instituted it? Or will it and they have gone the way of many rulers by your time? My fear is that they will still be in power.

The Authority Party was elected in the wake of the Catastrophe. The fact that those responsible for the Northam bomb were members of a sect who'd ignored the clear teachings of their own holy books didn't matter. There were riots. Much more blood was shed. When, finally, order was restored it was to leave the way open to any party prepared to promise action and revenge. The Authority Party did just that.

'We will transform our country into an atheist, humanist Republic. Legislation will be introduced to make illegal the practice of any religion, or belief in any god.'

They were elected with an overwhelming majority.

Thursday 26th October

I am going to try and reach the mainland on Saturday. This morning I told Abbot Romuald what I'm hoping to do. A monk can't keep secrets from his Abbot: it says so in the Rules! He's promised to help.

A boat will be coming to remove the community's

possessions. They'll be examined, of course. Forbidden items such as holy pictures, prayer books and Bibles will be destroyed. Abbot Romuald is hoping that by voluntarily sacrificing much now, the Brothers will be treated leniently when they finally depart carrying the few things they own.

I'm going on this boat. Its master is an old friend of the Abbot's. He's agreed to travel back with one more in his crew than when he left. I'll help with the crew's duties, then merge into the bustle of life around the harbour. My return journey will be by a different route.

Today the monastery chapel was stripped bare. It was a heartbreaking task, but better done by us than by the dissolution squad. It didn't take long. Our chapel certainly wasn't dripping with gold, as the public have so often been told to justify the destruction and plunder by the infamous squads. But, to us, the little it contained had a value beyond words. We cried as we worked. The one good thing was that Brother Stefan was too ill to take part.

After we'd finished, I carried a bowl of hot soup and some freshly-baked bread up to his cell. He sipped the soup weakly, as if he was finding it hard to swallow. The bread seemed heavy in his hands.

As I went to leave he said, 'I think I may be staying with you after all, Baby Brother.'

Friday 27th October
Brother Stefan was right. He won't be leaving his beloved Parens Island. He died this morning.

157

When I looked in on him before Lauds he appeared to be sleeping peacefully, though his breathing was a bit laboured. But by the time I took his breakfast to him afterwards, his life on this earth was over. He was lying on his back, his hands folded, as if waiting peacefully to begin a journey.

I told Abbot Romuald at once. He informed the rest of the community. All thoughts of further packing and preparation vanished. Honouring our departed brother came first.

Stefan had no relatives. Most of us here have somebody, a family we leave behind as part of our sacrifice and theirs. According to Abbot Romuald, Stefan had nobody. We were his family. That being the case, there was no need to delay. Brother Conor and Abbot Romuald prepared Stefan's body. They dressed him in his worn, thin monk's cowl, then laid him in a simple pinewood coffin made in Brother Henry's fragrant workshop. Finally, Stefan's breviary was placed between his hands: in death as in life.

When all was ready, six of us carried our Brother down to the chapel. There our usual service of Sext became instead a Requiem. (This word, reader, means 'rest'). Abbot Romuald briefly recounted the details of Stefan's life that were common knowledge: of his childhood in a strife-torn country; of his family's journey to our country; of how he went off the rails as he'd told me himself; of his brush with death and his decision in hospital to seek the God he thought he'd lost; of how Stefan had been a monk for nearly sixty years.

No more was said then, for no more was needed. We simply sat in silence, looking up at 'Stefan's window', as we've always called it. The work of his hands, to the glory of God. I remembered him then, old but sprightly, beaming at a piece of glass or fragment of metal that I'd found for him on the beach. Remembered, also, my amazement as I watched this simple man realise his vision of transforming rubbish into a thing of beauty.

Nobody raised the question of how much longer Stefan's window would survive. We all know the answer: only until the dissolution squad see it. Then, just like so many others throughout the land, it will be smashed with whoops of laughter.

Do they think that will matter? If they do, they're fools! Smashing it apart won't lessen Stefan's work. We all know the image of Stefan's window will live on within us.

At the end of the Requiem we carried our Brother up from the chapel, through the cloisters where he'd walked, and out to the garden cemetery. There we laid him to rest along with those of our community who had gone before him. Stefan had apparently asked Abbot Romuald some time in the past if his grave could be close to a fine laurel which grows there. 'I never did have any laurels to rest on,' he'd joked, 'so it will be nice to rest *beside* some!'

The usual simple wooden cross now marks the spot, a diamond-shaped plate nailed to its centre. It says no more than is necessary:

Brother Stefan Kolbe

and the dates which marked his stay on this earth.

After some time praying beside Stefan's grave, I returned to my cell to prepare. Tomorrow I go to the mainland.

Saturday 28th October

The cargo boat reached the harbour just before noon. As expected, our packing cases were broken open and searched. Anything faintly religious was impounded, as was anything saleable. The boat master was quizzed, not only about his cargo but also about what he'd seen on Parens Island.

'Any sign of them hiding things? Planning to smuggle out any of their superstitious trash?'

Abbot Romuald had chosen well. The boat master shook his head at every question. After his interrogation was over though, I was made fully aware that the boat master considered his duty done.

'Go,' he growled at me. 'And don't come back again.'

I'd been hovering in the background. In place of my cowl I had on a thick turtle-neck jumper, corduroy trousers and a pair of Brother Liam's walking boots. A dark woollen hat was pulled down almost to my eyebrows.

On the boat master's order I started walking, mingling with other harbour users as they climbed the short distance up from the quayside to Trinity Square – or what used to be called Trinity Square. The 'Trinity' part had been blanked out. I was now in 'The Square.'

I passed a bar thumping out music. Like every other bar in the street it offered twenty-four hour drinking. A couple of men staggered out looking as if they had been doing just that. One almost collided with me.

'Watch where yer goin' for Christ's sake!' he slurred.

His friend was a bit less incapable. 'Shut up man,' he hissed at him. 'Don't you know there's a dissy squad on the way? Let 'em hear you say that and you'll wake up with a cracked head.'

I almost smiled. When the Republic's latest directive on anti-social behaviour had been issued, Conor had exploded in laughter as he'd read the small print about the penalties for using religious oaths.

'Don't you just love it!' he'd boomed. 'There was a time when Our Lord's name was used as swear word and nobody batted an eyelid. Now everybody's supposed to be an atheist and you get done for mentioning it!'

I headed on, away from the shopping area and into the housing quarter. Here, only ten years ago, the tall buildings had all been guest-houses. In summer they'd bulge with visitors, then hibernate all winter. No longer, by the sound of it. The garden of one large corner house was swarming with youngsters who only quietened and retreated indoors when a uniformed adult came out issuing orders.

Keeping my head down, I hurried along a narrow alley and into the adjacent street. The small house I wanted was here. I slipped in through a side gate leading off from the alley and tapped hesitantly on the glass pane of the kitchen window.

There was a long pause before the door inched open. Part of

a wary face peered out – enough for me to see how much she'd aged in the short time since I'd last seen her, on the day I'd made my final profession.

'Aunt Ruth...' I whispered.

The door opened fully and I was hustled inside. Only then did she feel free enough to squeal with joy.

'Mark! Mark, let me look at you!'

She hugged me and I hugged her. Beneath her cardigan she felt frailer than I remembered. In my mind's eye she'd always been so solid and doughty.

Uncle Harry appeared from the front room. We shook hands, grinning to see one another again. I looked an unfamiliar sight, I knew. He was the opposite, his trousers held up by a belt and probably the only working pair of braces in town. His weather-beaten, seafarer's face had gained a few extra lines.

They hustled me into the heavily-curtained front room. There, over tea and a plateful of Aunt Ruth's warm scones we exchanged news. I told them of what the Brothers were planning and of Stefan's death. They then told me their own joyous news – that my cousin Glyn and his wife had recently presented them with their first grandchild.

'Ruti,' said Aunt Ruth. 'After me,' she added with tear-filled eyes.

I knew why her joy was tinged with sadness. Her own name, like all names found in holy books such as the Bible, was no longer allowed for a new-born.

Selfishly I changed the subject. I asked whether my cousin

still had his own boatyard. Uncle Harry was about to answer when Glyn arrived. After greeting him and congratulating him on becoming a father, I asked my question again. To my delight he confirmed that his boatyard was flourishing.

'Moving out of fishing and into boat building was a good move,' said Glyn.

Uncle Harry nodded in agreement. 'I didn't like it at the time, but he was right. No future in fishing any more. The stocks'll all be gone soon.'

'Greed,' said Glyn. 'All down to greed.' He smiled. 'I shouldn't knock it, mind. It's greed that keeps us going.'

I must have looked confused because he explained without my asking. 'Everybody wants to spend what they've got on themselves, don't they? Giving to the poor ain't an option any more. The Republic takes care of all that. So what comes after a bigger house and a bigger car? A boat, that's what – even if most of 'em have never sailed before.'

Uncle Harry laughed. 'Out they go in the boat they've bought from him. But do they want lessons? Not on your life!'

'So the next time I see them is to earn more for repairing the damage they've done hitting the harbour walls!' said Glyn.

'Or when we hoist them out of the sea,' said Uncle Harry, far more seriously.

I remembered then that they were both members of the Craston lifeboat. Their bravery must have saved hundreds of lives over the years. Now I was going to ask them to take perhaps an even bigger risk and save mine.

I told them about the Directive of Dissolution – and about

my wanting to go to Orb Island to live as a hermit. They heard me out in a stunned silence. I'd drawn a small map showing the place I'd found and the way a small boat could thread its way in through the rocks to land supplies for me. I explained what I'd need delivered, and how often. What I didn't need to spell out was the need for secrecy or the possible danger to them.

Glyn shook his head. 'Mad,' he said. 'That's what you are.' I told him my Brothers felt much the same.

'Dunno about this God of yours,' said Uncle Harry. 'Hope he's worth it.'

'I think he is,' I said.

'Then we'll do all we can to help you,' said Aunt Ruth simply.

Over tankards of beer we went on to devise a simple system of signals and messages. Uncle Harry gave me a crash course in times and tides. Glyn spelled out the kind of weather conditions that would make sailing difficult or impossible.

'Winter will be the big test,' chipped in Uncle Harry. 'It may not be possible to get out to you for days on end.'

'I hope this place you've found is well sheltered,' said Aunt Ruth, in the same caring voice she'd used when telling me as a child to wrap up warm.

'I think it is,' I said.

I understand their concerns. I share them! But I've checked it out thoroughly. This is not just an exercise in blind faith. I wouldn't be asking them to take the risk of helping me if I didn't think I could survive.

Business complete, Aunt Ruth disappeared to the kitchen to return minutes later with a succession of steaming dishes.

Over a meal of home-made pies, succulent vegetables topped with melted butter and lashings of rich gravy we talked late into the night. We relived the better times, before my parents' death, before the Wasteland, before the Republic. Inevitably, though, we ended on the way things had turned out – and I learned what the noisy former guest-house I'd passed had become.

'They call it a "nurture-house", grunted Uncle Harry. 'Work-house more like.'

The nurture-house at the bottom of the street was the first of what Aunt Ruth and Uncle Harry feared would be many. It was rumoured that the Republic was buying property on a vast scale for the purpose of giving people the ultimate freedom: releasing their son or daughter to become a Child of the Republic.

What will the Republic do with the children it comes to own? I dread to think.

I retired to bed far later than usual. Back in the monastery my Brothers would have already completed the circle of the day in their service of Compline. Better late than never I joined with them in spirit, reciting the words under my breath:

'The Lord grant us a quiet night and a perfect end. Amen.'

Sunday 29th October
I left the house early – and alone. I said a sad farewell to Aunt Ruth. We both knew that we wouldn't meet again in this life. There were tears and heartfelt hugs.

I slid out through the alleyway in the half-light before dawn. For the next two hours I just wandered, trying to soak up some final memories. Turning through the Five Arches of the walled town I walked finally towards what was once St Mary's Church. I'd heard what they'd done to it but, painful as it would be, I had to see for myself.

The church is now called a Celebreon: 'The Celebreon of Our Saviour'. Like all Celebreons which have opened since the Republic came into being, it's a place where citizens can go to venerate the celebrities of the moment.

The great side door was open. Already a wave of talkative venerators were hurrying in. I followed them at a discreet distance. Just as well. If I'd been any nearer they couldn't have failed to hear me gasp or to see my tears. The place was unrecognisable from the church I'd once known.

The glorious windows had been ripped out and replaced by plain glass. Where once there had been side altars commemorating saints, there were now 'devotionals' celebrating the 'Blesseds' of the Republic. The figure of a sportsman stood proudly on a pedestal, surrounded by life-sized photographs showing scenes from his career. Pictures, books and statuettes were on sale.

On the other side of the Celebreon stood another pedestal. This one, though, was bare. The figure once mounted on it was now on its side, half-covered by a dusty tarpaulin. It had been broken as it had been removed and the female's head and shoulders – for it was the figure of a wild-haired pop-singer – had a large jagged crack running from top to bottom. As I watched, a Celebreon guard began to tear the devotional's tableau from its rail. I asked what was happening.

'You didn't see it?' The look I got was one of pure amazement. 'Voted out, weren't she?'

That is how 'Blesseds' are determined: through popular vote. Soon a new figure would be taking its place on the pedestal. Of the old, there would be no trace. That's how it works. Where once there were eternal saints, now there are Blesseds who remain only until the public tire of them.

There's one exception: the man whose figure looked down from where the main altar of the church once stood. Unlike most other Blesseds, he is long dead – but his influence lives on. His representation is compulsory in all Celebreons.

The figure I saw was dressed in a long frock-coat, his bald head in sharp contrast to the wild grizzled beard dominating his face. There were tacky extras: a pigeon resting on his outstretched palm, a turtle flopping at his feet. The statue was spotlit. High above it, suspended from the sanctuary arch by chains of gold, a huge electronic screen ran an endless loop of a programme. It began with the text of The Republic's Directive of Supreme Recognition:

CHARLES ROBERT DARWIN, by bringing to public notice the process of evolution through his inspired work On the Origin of Species, *thereby instigated the salvation of humanity by setting it free from the bonds of religion. It is directed that henceforth Charles Darwin will be known as THE SAVIOUR.*

There then followed sequences showing the passage of human evolution, mingled with horrific images of the Wasteland and its victims. The running commentary was pointed. Belief in Science means peace and prosperity. Belief in God leads only to war and catastrophe. There is no third way.

Did it mention that belief in God had also inspired countless works of mercy and charity? Of course not! Did it say that godless tyrants such as Hitler, Stalin, Mao-Tse Tung and Pol Pot had between them caused more butchery than all the religiously-motivated conflicts in history? Of course not!

I'd seen enough. Besides, Glyn and Uncle Harry would be waiting. They'd agreed to carry me back as a kind of dummy run for their future trips and the sooner they were free of me the better for them. I hurried out of the Celebreon and through the streets to their yard.

Their boat was launched and ready. It's a half-size fishing smack, designed so that it can be sailed single-handed. Neither of them looked up as I climbed quickly aboard and settled myself out of sight in the depths of the hull. I heard the roar of the small outboard motor, felt the craft chug out of the harbour and into the waters of Craston Sound. Once there the engine cut and Glyn hoisted the mainsail of tanned flax.

'You can come out now, Mark,' he said. 'But put that oilskin on first.'

Beside me was a bright yellow waterproof jacket, about six sizes too big. I slid into it then clambered up to join them. They'd raised the main jib sail too now, and the smack was picking up speed. I watched as the wind caught in the jib and made its large, colourful boatyard emblem – a barque on the open sea – look as if it was bursting with pride.

A sudden fear hit me. 'Won't somebody see that?' I said, pointing at the emblem. 'They'll know it's you going out.'

'Better that way,' said Glyn shortly. 'It's the boats they *don't* know that make them suspicious.'

The swell was making little impression on the smack. The boat was beautifully stable. Glyn, at the wheel, began to swing left, well short of Parens Island.

'Just in case we *are* being watched,' said Glyn, 'we'll go the long way round.'

We rode the tide well off Parens' eastern tip. Once beyond it, Glyn changed direction and began to steer a course parallel with the south shore. I gazed out and up towards our monastery; it looked as though it was ready to tumble down the south cliff, so close did it seem to the edge. The lowest level was partly shielded from view by rock plants and small shrubs that had seeded themselves in tiny cracks in the limestone. Even so, I could just make out the chapel window: Stefan's window. How dark and drab it looked from the outside!

Then it was gone and we were passing the western end of Parens Island. The sharp teeth of the reef were visible. Glyn lowered the sails and Uncle Harry fired the outboard motor. Still well off-shore, we eased past the reef to glide parallel with the shore of Orb Island. Now I took over as pilot. Following my instructions Glyn threaded the boat between submerged black rocks to where a group of standing stones in deep water formed a kind of natural jetty. Glyn jumped out and I threw him a rope. He looped it over an oddly-shaped rock, one that reminded me of a cockatoo's head. I heard the scrunch of the fenders as he pulled us close. Uncle Harry cut the engine.

'Welcome to my future home,' I smiled.

While Uncle Harry kept lookout, I showed Glyn the places I'd talked about: where he would leave things he brought, how I would signal if I needed him to come closer. Finally I showed where, with the help of God, I intended to live for the rest of my days.

To say he was taken aback is an understatement. 'There?' he gasped. 'You're going to live in *there*?'

I nodded. 'If Saint Simeon could live at the top of a pillar for thirty-seven years then I don't see why I can't cope in a cave – so long as you keep me fed and watered.' At that moment I wondered whether it was fair of me even to ask that of him.

I needn't have worried. 'I will,' said Glyn flatly.

We went back to the boat. Uncle Harry already had the motor fired up. Glyn and I shook hands knowing that, barring emergencies, it would be for the last time. He jumped aboard without looking back. They eased the smack expertly out through the shallows then raised their sails and turned for home. I sat and watched the billowing barque emblem until it disappeared from view.

I walked slowly to the reef. Kittiwakes and gulls were squabbling noisily over scraps being washed in on the foam. Low water had arrived and crossing the reef was as straightforward as walking the pathway beside Brother Stefan's laurel bush. Within half an hour I was back here in our monastery.

It really sank in, then. We've got very little time left.

Monday 30th October
Brothers Henry, Pierre and Dominic left this afternoon. Judging by the performance of the crude and foul-mouthed dissolution bailiff who came over on the cargo boat to supervise matters, tomorrow could be a brutal affair.

Abbot Romuald had to bribe the bailiff to turn a blind eye while we celebrated our final Mass together. It was heartbreaking. I don't mind admitting that I cried as we recited the Lord's Prayer:

'Our Father, who art in heaven. Hallowed be thy name...'
and tried to keep hate from my soul as we reached the words:

'Forgive us our trespasses, as we forgive those who trespass against us.'

Will you know this prayer, reader? Will you even know what prayer is? Not if the Republic complete its 'cleansing' you won't! It's said that even the destruction of every holy book isn't going to be enough. The torched mountains of Bibles, Scriptures and Qurans are to be replaced by its own book, *The Writings*.

But will people take *The Writings* to their hearts? Will they love the Word of the Republic as much as Brother Henry loves the Word of God? His breviary was found as the Brothers were searched before boarding the cargo boat. The dissolution

171

bailiff looked inside the cover, saw the inscription which revealed that it was over forty years old – given to him by his mother on the day of his final profession – and ripped it apart before his eyes.

'Good job I know it off by heart,' smiled Henry. It earned him a cut lip from the back of the bailiff's heavy hand.

At least during his short stay the bailiff didn't enter our home. He may be brutal, but it seems he's a stickler for the rules. He and his mob will turn us out of the monastery on the date directed and no sooner.

Abbot Romuald asked him what the Republic's plan is for the building. 'Will it become one of your Celebreons?' he said, unable to keep the contempt from his voice even at the risk of a punch. The bailiff was too full of his own importance to notice.

'Not decided yet,' he said. 'Me, I don't reckon so. Not unless they've got it down for somebody famous enough to warrant being buried on an island. Nah, they'll probably leave it to fall down. That way everybody'll forget you lot were ever here.'

'If you believe that, my friend,' Abbot Romuald replied with the quiet authority we know so well, 'then you do not understand the workings of God.'

That *did* earn him a blow. The bailiff lashed out, bloodying the Abbot's nose as he shouted, 'And you don't understand the workings of the Republic!'

Once the boat had left, taking our Brothers to their new lives, we came back to the monastery. The dissolution bailiff will return tomorrow. We spent the evening in the chapel, breaking our silent prayer only to say Vespers and Compline. At eight o'clock we retired to our cells.

Reader, this journal is almost complete. Tomorrow it ends. I'm going to hide it here in my cell. I've borrowed a hammer and chisel from Brother Henry's workshop and prised up a floorboard. I made a bit of a mess of it, but it's done.

Tuesday 31st October
4.20 am. I'm writing in haste. I must be on my way as soon as it's light. The dissolution squad will be arriving on the first tide and I'm certain they'll be ruthless in their work. I'm frightened they'll catch me. But I'm even more frightened about how they'll react when they discover what my Brothers have decided to do…

We rose and celebrated Lauds as usual. But, for the first and only time, we didn't walk up from the chapel together. As Abbot Romuald and I got up from our knees to leave, Brothers Conor and Liam just eased themselves back on to the stall seats behind them. There they sat, arms folded.

'We're staying put, Romuald,' said Brother Conor.

'We've decided to have a pray-in,' smiled Liam. 'A bit like a sit-in, but with Our Lord for company.'

'Oh, yes,' growled Conor, 'and with luck it's going to last a good while.' From beneath his cowl he produced the same hammer I'd borrowed from Brother Henry's workshop and dutifully returned. 'Basically, till they knock the door down and carry us out.'

Abbot Romuald closed his eyes, whether from fear or

despair I couldn't tell. 'Are you sure about this?' he said. 'You both saw how the bailiff behaved yesterday.'

Brother Liam nodded. 'We're sure.'

Beside him, Conor rolled up his sleeves, revealing his brawny ex-publican's forearms. 'Now if you and Baby Brother don't mind, Romuald,' he said as if he'd just called last orders, 'Liam and I have got a lot of work to do before our guests arrive.'

We said our farewells then. Not once did they suggest I stay with them. Nor did I try to talk them out of their plan. We all knew that their resistance would draw attention away from me, giving the dissolution squad more to think about than conducting searches. I told them I will pray for them.

'We'll pray for you, too,' grinned Conor. 'Now clear off and do your packing!'

'I'm frightened for them,' I said to Abbot Romuald as we left the chapel and walked along the east cloister. I've heard stories of the dissolution squads – of how they almost welcome resistance for the excuse it gives them to crush it with cold violence.

Abbot Romuald nodded thoughtfully, but said nothing as we continued on round to the vestibule. There, before I mounted the stairs, he stopped.

'Farewell, Mark,' he said then. 'God be with you.'

'And also with you,' I replied, almost automatically.

I turned away from him, my foot on the bottom step. Only then did it strike me that not once had I enquired about him. 'What are you going to do?'

He smiled. 'Old habits die hard,' he said. 'I was going to obey. I was going to travel obediently to the mainland and take my place obediently in the Enclosure.'

'*Was?*'

He nodded. 'I've changed my mind. I'm going to join Conor and Liam down in the chapel.' He laughed, and I saw a man at peace with himself. 'God gave them both stout hearts,' he said, 'but was perhaps a little sparing when it came to clarity of thought. They'll need some guidance in how to construct a decent barricade!'

6.50 am I'm writing this in my cell. Dawn is breaking. All too soon the boats carrying the dissolution squad will be leaving the mainland. Within an hour of their arrival our community will have taken its final breath. By then, God willing, I'll already be on Orb Island.

And so I end this journal. I'll be hiding it in the hope that one day my words will be read by somebody with an enquiring and open mind; somebody wanting to know who we were and how we lived. Even more, somebody wanting to know *why* we chose to devote our lives to growing closer to God and seeking his blessings on the world, believers and unbelievers alike.

Maybe my hope is in vain. By the time you see these words, reader, the Republic may well have destroyed all evidence that faith communities such as ours ever existed. Their directives are steadily moving in that direction. They're now proposing that even the names of some months should be altered.

'January', for example, is to become 'Undec' – purely on the grounds that Janus was a Greek god! And lunacies such as these will be accepted without dissent, just as the new calendar has been accepted.

By 'new', I mean the calendar based on the birth of Charles Darwin rather than that based on the birth of Jesus Christ. Under that calendar the date of Darwin's birth was 10th February 1809. But when the *Directive on the Darwinian Calendar* made it compulsory to date years from the new Saviour's birth, the year 1810 became Year 1 AD – AD for 'After Darwin'.

I expect there'll soon be an entry in the Republic's meticulous records to say that the Parens Island Monastery was dissolved on Tuesday 31st October in the year 225 AD.

But the date that will always be etched on my heart, the date I'll recall in my solitude for as long as I am able, is:

Tuesday 31st October 2034, Anno Domini – in the Year of Our Lord.

I could write much more but there's no time. My bag's packed with the few clothes I own. I've taken the crucifix from my wall. All that's left to do now is to hide this journal. I do it realising that my words may never again see the light of day, that age could wither this book or it could be destroyed along with our beloved building. I hope and pray that's not so and that you, reader, have learned something from what I've written.

If you do not – or cannot – pray for the souls of me and my

brothers, then please at least remember us. Remember that we lived and died in peace. Remember especially Abbot Romuald and Brothers Conor and Liam.

And, in your mercy, remember me.

Brother Mark

Book Three

Raul pulled the loose floorboard up. As he did so, the top of his arm caught on the bedclothes. He hardly noticed, so well had the wound healed. He put Brother Mark's journal back into its hiding place. Since finding it he'd read the monk's words so often that he felt a bit like Brother Henry had with his breviary: that he now knew them by heart. Replacing the floorboard, Raul gazed briefly around the small room – the small *cell*; Brother Mark's cell. Then he stood up to look out of the window that the young monk must have stood beside so often.

At last, a slow thaw had begun. The freezing conditions had lasted for over three weeks. Undec – January, as Brother Mark would have known it – had ended. They were now into February. Throughout that period, a series of blizzards by day, followed by bone-hard frosts at night, had made much of the island impossible to reach on foot. The various Duties had been for the most part replaced by just one: a daily scraping away of the fresh snow and ice which covered the pathway down to the jetty. Except during the worst of the weather the cargo boat had been able to make regular deliveries. Doron had said that, if necessary, supplies would be air-dropped to them by helitransport, but it hadn't come to that. Jenna had observed tartly how, even as the final quarter of the third century beckoned, a fall of snow was still able to bring the whole Republic to a standstill.

The thought turned Raul's eye down to the desk, and the scrap of paper he'd used to convert the dates in Brother Mark's journal.

If their Year 1810 had become Year 1 in the Republic's new calendar, then in the old system today's date would be 6th February 2084, not 275 AD as Raul knew it.

Other dates littered the page:

Brother Mark must have been born in 2008.

The 211 Catastrophe (as his nurture-house history lessons had always called it) would have happened in 2020 by Brother Mark's calendar.

Brother Mark had entered the monastery in 218AD/ 2027, made his final profession in 224AD/2033 – and then had his community destroyed by the dissolution squad in 225 AD/2034: fifty years ago. At the sound of footsteps, Raul snatched up the paper and screwed it into a ball. By the time Arym had knocked on his door and simultaneously thrown it open, the dates were buried in the pocket of his tunic.

Arym. Along with Doron and Jenna, she had been a regular visitor to his room over the past weeks. She'd escorted him to group sessions and to the refectory. On the way they'd talk about nothing much. She'd ask how he was feeling. He'd be non-committal, trying to suggest that he was recovering from the shock of Micha's death.

He'd also – and this had been much harder – tried to give the impression that the pellet of medication they'd implanted beneath the skin of his upper arm was still working on him just as it clearly was on Emily and Jack. Their sparks of individuality were almost dead. He could see it in their eyes across the meal table, hear it in the calm acceptance of their voices. Acting as they acted hadn't been easy, for with every passing day he'd felt his own mind growing sharper.

'Ready?' said Arym.

'What is it this time?' he said, trying to appear slightly forgetful.

'Group meeting,' said Arym. She sounded quite keen.

That was another thing he'd noticed. Arym had changed. Her anger at being there had dissipated. But not through medication, he was sure of that. Not once had she shown the same signs of detachment as Jack and Emily – nor of himself, he now realised, before he'd gouged the pellet from his arm. It was as if she was becoming interested in what Doron and Jenna had to say.

That was borne out when the meeting began. Doron was in the chair, Jenna immediately opposite him. Jack and Emily were together on one side of the circle. Arym picked the empty seat closest to Doron. It seemed natural, therefore, that when the healer said, 'We are going to talk about *The Writings*,' he should hand his black book to her.

The words of Brother Mark's journal flicked unbidden across Raul's mind: *The torched mountains of Bibles, Scriptures and Qurans are to be replaced by their own book,* The Writings.

'Listen,' said Doron, 'to the story of Adam and Eve. Thank you, Arym.'

Arym had taken Doron's book gingerly, as if handling something precious and fragile. But as she began to read, it was in a voice that surprised Raul: soft and lilting but at the same time infused with conviction.

'Adam lived in a garden of pleasure wherein was brought forth from the ground all manner of trees, fair to behold and pleasant to eat therefrom. In the midst of them grew the Tree of Knowledge. But Adam was afraid of this tree, for the owner of the garden had said to him, "In the day thou eat of it thou shalt surely die the death." Adam believed this.

'Now the serpent was wiser than any of the beasts in the garden. And he said to Eve, the partner of Adam: "Why dost neither you nor your man eat of the fruit of the Tree of knowledge?" Eve replied, "Because the owner of the garden hast commanded that we should not eat its fruit, lest we die the death."

'And the serpent said to the woman, "No, you shall not die the death! The owner knows that in the day you eat thereof, that day shall you possess the knowledge he wishes to gather unto himself alone."

'Then Eve saw that the fruit was good to eat and fair to the eyes and delightful to behold; and she took of the fruit thereof and did eat; and gave to her partner Adam, who did eat also.

'Thus were their eyes opened by knowledge. They saw that the owner had left them naked. So they sewed together fig-leaves and made themselves aprons. Then they found the owner, hiding in the garden. He straightway cursed them, saying: "Who told thee that I left thee naked? Hast thou eaten of the tree from which I forbade thee to eat?"

182

'And Adam said, "Yes. My woman gave me, and I did eat."

'Then the owner said to the woman, "Why hast thou done this?"

'She answered, "The wise serpent told me the truth. And I did eat."

Then the owner cursed them, telling Eve that henceforth all women would suffer the pains of childbirth, and that the stain of Adam's sin would be punished by a life of toil. But they cared not. They straightway sewed themselves clothes and went forth from the garden in the joy of knowledge, leaving the owner in sorrow and loneliness.'

Arym silently handed the book back. Doron cradled it in his lap, stroking its gold-tooled cover.

Will the people take The Writings *to their hearts? Will they love the Word of The Republic as much as Brother Henry loves the Word of God?*

In that moment Brother Mark's question was answered for Raul. Yes, some people at least would take them to their hearts – just, it seemed, as different books had been revered for different reasons throughout time.

Doron looked up. 'How many of you think that story is literally true?' he said. 'That it really happened?'

It was Jenna who broke the brief silence that followed. Like the other half of a well-rehearsed double act she said brightly, 'Well I certainly don't! I don't believe that two people named Adam and Eve ever existed!'

Arym looked genuinely shocked. 'You're saying the story isn't true? It's a lie? *The Writings* contain a lie?'

Jenna laughed. 'No, of course not! *The Writings* do not lie, Arym, never doubt that. But some of its truths are symbolic, not factual. That's what we've got in this story. The Tree of Knowledge, for example, isn't a real tree. It's a symbol. It represents the glories of Science.'

'More than that, Jenna,' added Doron. 'The Tree of Knowledge also represents the mental ability we humans have developed so that we can understand Science. Consciousness, of course, but also things like awareness and reasoning, feelings and emotions...all the different abilities we use to make sense of the world around us.'

'The abilities that have made the human species supreme!' laughed Jenna.

Doron again corrected her, like a teacher dealing with a pupil whose understanding of a subject contained gaps. 'We only dominate on land, Jenna. I doubt very much that we'd survive for long on the ocean bed. Our greater intelligence would count for little there.'

'So...you're saying that's how we came to be in control on land?' asked Arym. 'Because we've evolved greater intelligence?' Singers and film stars aside, Raul had never heard her sound as interested in any subject.

Doron smiled encouragingly, 'You remember my story about the lemurs of Madagascar, Arym? How, because a food supply existed, the power of evolution gave those creatures the physical attributes to fill a gap in nature and use that food. The same principle applies everywhere. Fire, fossil fuels, raw materials – these are what we consume. By slowly developing the abilities we needed to master them, evolution has used us to fill a gap.'

Throughout all this, Emily and Jack had sat silently.

Now they each made simple, giggly contributions.

'Who's the garden owner, that's what I'd like to know?' said Emily. 'He sounds a right misery!'

'And mean,' added Jack. 'Wanting to keep it all to himself like that.'

'The owner of the garden isn't a real person either, Emily,' said Jenna in a tone more suited to an infant nurture-house. 'None of the characters in the story are. They're all symbols.'

She switched her attention to Arym now, talking directly to her as if Raul's sister was her own personal pupil. 'Adam and Eve represent humanity – you and me, all of us. The serpent, of course, represents Science in its never-ending pursuit of truth and knowledge.'

'As for the owner of the garden,' interrupted Doron, 'can you be in any doubt that there you have the god of superstitions throughout history; the so-called 'creator' that time and again unbelievers have accorded the honour that belongs to Science alone!'

A fleck of spittle dropped on *The Writings* nestling in his lap. The healer took a handkerchief from his pocket and wiped it away from the black cover.

'But...' said Arym, with the look of one who wanted a small dark stain of her own wiped clean, '...if our minds evolved to help us survive, how is it that superstitious unbelievers are still around? I mean, if somebody thought their god would save them if they walked into a lion's den, they wouldn't last long, would they?'

'I'm not sure I understand what you're asking, Arym,' said Doron.

'I'm asking why, if superstitions don't help us

survive, they haven't died out.'

'That is an excellent question,' said the cool voice of Doctor Tomas. Unnoticed, she had eased open the door and was standing half in and half out of the room. 'Superstition appears to affect only humans. There is no evidence that apes, for instance, offer petitions to invisible gods.'

'Why do unbelievers still do it then?' persisted Arym. 'Why are *The Writings* still being doubted?'

Doctor Tomas now stepped fully into the room, even as she continued talking. 'I don't have all the answers, Arym. There is still much work to be done in discovering which parts of the mind generate such thoughts. But we're making progress – as you're about to see.'

Turning to look back out into the corridor, the doctor said. 'Come in, Sarih. Don't be shy.'

Slowly, head downcast, Sarih did as she was told. Once inside she kept her head down, just as she always had. For a moment Raul thought that nothing had altered about her in the weeks she'd been hidden away. Until, that is, Doctor Tomas spoke again:

'How are you feeling, Sarih?'

Immediately Sarih lifted her head. Gone was the permanently quizzical look on her face. In its place was a smile. A simple, contented smile.

'I am happy,' said Sarih.

Doctor Tomas addressed the group. 'You will remember that Sarih was anything *but* happy. Her mind was obsessed with mathematics. This obsession was leading her towards questions that she could not answer.' The doctor turned back to Sarih. 'Sarih, what is ten times five?'

Sarih looked at her. The girl's smile faded. She began to

bite her lip as she tried to focus on the question she'd been asked.

Doctor Tomas placed a hand on her arm. 'You don't know, do you?'

Sarih shook her head. Her eyes welled with tears.

'Good, Sarih!' Doctor Tomas's tone was as soothing as honey. 'It's good that you don't know! It makes me happy! How does it make *you* feel?'

The smile of contentment flowed back into Sarih's face. 'I am happy,' she said.

Doctor Tomas led Sarih across the room to the seat she'd always taken. She sat her down and made sure she was comfortable, then she turned to Arym.

'Superstitious thoughts will soon yield in the same way,' she said. 'That is what we are here for, Arym. To root them out. To make people happy.'

Beside her, Sarih smiled on.

When they were dismissed a few minutes later, Raul left the room so quickly that Arym had to hurry to catch him up.

'You're supposed to go straight back to your room,' she hissed.

'So, I'm going the long way round,' snapped Raul.

He stalked on, past the deserted refectory to turn into the north cloister. Only as they reached the far end, to swing left into the shorter east cloister, did Raul slow.

Arym drew him close. 'Calm down!'

Raul took audible deep breaths. Slowly he relaxed his arms and unclenched his fists. He looked around, as if he was absorbing the peace and silence of the cloister to compose himself. Arym was fooled.

'That's better,' she urged. 'Now, let's get back to your room and talk about it.'

Raul waited for a short while longer, his body still but his eyes darting everywhere. Then he turned and headed for the vestibule stairs and his room.

Once there, Arym's own composure evaporated. 'What was the matter with you?'

'Sarih, of course! They've turned her into an idiot!'

'Don't be so stupid, Raul. You heard her. She's happy.'

'She can't multiply ten by five!'

Arym shoved him then, hard, causing him to totter back and land heavily on his bed. The shriek of the floorboard acted to damp down Raul's temper slightly. The last thing he wanted right now was to have that investigated. He fell silent, allowing Arym to say her piece.

'Doctor Tomas is a pioneer, Raul! Doron and Jenna have told me all about her. She's leading the way in solving the problem of unbelief once and for all! Just think about it: no more arguments, no more wars! Everybody believing the same truth! The truth of Science!'

Raul reacted then. 'What's got into *you*? Before we came here you didn't care about any of that stuff.'

'Well I do now. I've seen how important it is.'

'So important you see nothing wrong in turning people like Sarih into idiots!'

'*Happy* idiots, Raul.'

'Better happy than unhappy, is that what you're saying? Whatever the price?'

'Yes, because it's not just Sarih's happiness that matters. It's everybody else's. And besides, it won't always be like that. Doron says Doctor Tomas is perfecting her techniques. One day the side-effects won't be so bad.'

'And that makes everything all right, does it?'

'It's how progress works, Raul. Success is built on failure. Surgeons like Doctor Tomas don't let failures put them off. They learn from them. That's what makes them special. Doctor Tomas will be a Blessed one day, you'll see.'

'Surgeon?' Raul repeated the one word that had stung him like no other. 'She's a *surgeon*?'

'So Jenna says. Patients who don't respond to therapy are taken on by her. The hopeless cases. She operates on them. She cures them, Raul.'

'She hasn't cured Sarih, Arym! Sarih's as dead as Micha, can't you see that?'

In spite of himself, Raul's fury had bubbled to the surface. Arym's sheer unquestioning acceptance of what had happened had rankled him, tearing through his resolve to stay calm and not reveal that, along with clarity of mind, his short-fused temper had also returned.

Arym stepped back, alarm written across her face. For a moment he thought she might have guessed what he'd done. If Jenna and Doron were being as open with her as it seemed, she must surely have been told about the medication implants. If she suspected him of tampering with his...

'I'm sorry, Arym,' he said quickly. 'I...I'm just frightened they'll do the same to me.'

The trick appeared to work. His sister's look of alarm was replaced by one of compassion – the sort that Jenna manufactured so well. She sat beside him. He felt her slide an arm round his shoulders and lightly press her fingers into the spot where the medication pellet had been. When he didn't flinch, she gave him a hug.

'Don't worry, Raul. Just stay calm and you'll be all right. Jenna's told me they're pleased with you. If you get through the Rite of Scrutiny you'll be going home.'

'The Rite of Scrutiny?'

'Doron will explain more about it. It's a kind of test and a ceremony all in one. Nothing to worry about.' She turned him towards her. She seemed to have outgrown him while he wasn't looking. 'Now is there anything else you want to tell me?' she said.

What did she know? Did she suspect anything? There was nothing Raul would have liked more at that moment than to share Brother Mark's journal with someone. To talk it over with Arym, ask her what she thought about everything the Republic stood for, had done and were doing. Only one thing stopped him: he simply wasn't sure whether the journal's claims were true.

His earlier performance, of leaving the meeting abruptly and making her hurry after him had been just that – a performance. He'd wanted to study the east cloister and the act he'd put on had simply been to disguise the fact. While he'd been pretending to calm down, he had actually been studying the cloister for signs that it had once contained an entrance to Brother Mark's chapel. For as the 'monk' had written in his 'journal':

'I'm frightened for them,' I said to Abbot Romuald as we left the chapel and walked along the east cloister...

But there had been no evidence at all. The building appeared to end at that wall. It held no entrances at all, only a row of clerestory windows high up beneath the beams of the sloping cloister roof. What was more, Raul had seen nothing to suggest that it ever had held an entrance: no outline of a doorway in the rough plastered texture, no subtle change in the colour-washed plasterwork: nothing.

And yet...there was no doubting that the building had once been the home of a sect such as the journal described. Now that he was looking for them, Raul had begun to see the palest shadows of crosses everywhere. There'd been one in the meeting room they'd recently left, above the doorway, visible when the light caught it at a particular angle. The reading pulpit in the refectory had once held one too, he was certain of it. The damage to the ornate carvings at the pulpit's front, as if a section had been hacked out, was of the same rough outline.

Beside him, Arym was repeating her question. 'Is there, Raul? Is there anything else you want to tell me?'

Raul almost did. He almost slid from the bed to pull Brother Mark's journal from its hiding place. Almost. He desperately wanted to show Arym the journal, to talk about it and the questions it raised. But he couldn't. Not until he had some hard evidence to convince her that it was genuine.

He shook his head. 'No. I'm fine. Just confused, Arym. I don't want Doctor Tomas to do to me what she's done to Sarih.'

Arym's tone was like a balm. 'They won't Raul. I'll work with you on the Rite of Scrutiny and then, as soon as Darmas is over, you'll be out of here.'

She left then, leaving Raul to wonder exactly what the

mysterious Rite of Scrutiny involved. And then, as his mind returned to Brother Mark's journal, to wonder what kind of evidence might be able to support it.

He looked out of the window. The thaw was accelerating. Blotches of green were spreading across the oval. The trees had lost their white coating and had returned to winter brown.

And Raul suddenly knew that what he was looking for might be in the overgrown garden.

Arym was descending the stairs after leaving Raul's room when she met Jenna coming up. The healer smiled warmly, but briefly. Then, quickly checking that they were alone, she drew Arym into an alcove.

'Raul hurried away from the group meeting this morning,' she said. 'Doron and I both noticed.' She added one more name, making Arym shiver involuntarily. 'And so did Doctor Tomas.'

'Yes,' answered Arym quickly. 'He – he wasn't feeling well.'

'He looked angry. Was he?'

Arym shook her head. 'Not – angry,' she hedged. 'More disturbed. He was shocked to see Sarih like she was.'

'Sarih was happy, Arym. She will always be happy.'

'Yes, I know. But…'

'Raul doesn't want the same treatment? Or is it that you don't want him to have it?'

Arym paused. 'Both, I suppose,' she said finally.

Jenna lowered her voice to a whisper. 'Both may not be possible, Arym. You may have to choose. Help your brother through the Rite of Scrutiny and all will be well. But if he fails it...'

'What?'

'If he fails it, Doctor Tomas will have Raul on the operating table within twenty-four hours.' Jenna tilted Arym's face up towards her own then, as if wanting to send her closing message straight into her mind. 'And if you want to become a healer, you will have to support that decision.'

Raul's chance came two days later, on Darmas Eve. As a sign of the increasing faith that Doron and Jenna had in Arym, she had been detailed to lead the group down to the beach for Duties. After handing out the sacks, Raul's sister had led the way.

She'd enthused about the difference of this Duty compared to the usual. 'We're looking for suitable things to turn into Darmas decorations! Jenna says it's a tradition to make new ones every year.'

Jack and Emily had squealed delightedly. Sarih's smile had widened. 'Happy!' she'd slurred.

Raul had waited until they'd almost reached the end of the sand dunes before calling out to Arym. 'I've left my sack behind. I'll go back and get it!'

Without waiting for a reply he'd returned quickly to the sanitarium building and retrieved the sack he'd deliberately dropped behind a potted plant in the vestibule. Then he quickly slipped out through the silent cloister garth and into the garden. Within a few seconds he hurried along beside the sanitarium wall and then through the towering hedge to the jungle they'd begun to clear.

Only as he passed through the gap did it occur to Raul that there might be other residents working here. He stopped suddenly, ready to dart back should he be seen, only to discover that there was, in fact, no danger. The garden was exactly as they'd left it. No further clearance work had been done. *Since the day I found the cross*, realised Raul. Why not? Had Jenna and Doron been ordered to stop Duty work here for fear of more being found? Because somebody knew what they perhaps hadn't known – that this place used to be the monastery's graveyard?

Raul hurriedly retraced his steps to where he thought he'd found the cross. The snow had mostly melted now. The earth felt soft and spongy. Occasional drips landed on him from overhanging branches. He stood, searching for a clue. There! A small volcano of leaf mould showed him where he'd pulled the cross from the ground like a rotten tooth from its socket. Rotten – and *charred*.

Dropping to his knees, Raul scraped at the ground with his bare fingers. Out came more layers of mould, accumulated over fifty autumns. And then...ash. Black-grey ash, still dusty where the solidified leaf-mould had kept the moisture at bay. The remains of a bonfire.

The torched mountains of Bibles, Scriptures and Qurans...

The words of Brother Mark's journal sent an imagined scene tumbling vividly into his mind's eye: of the dissolution squad, running amok and destroying every despised sign of the monks' faith – even the simple wooden crosses which marked their graves. Ripping them from the earth and tossing them, laughing, onto

194

a crackling fire. But what if, before doing that, they had shown an ingrained respect for the dead by prising the nameplates from the crosses and leaving them to identify the graves?

The usual, simple wooden cross now marks the spot, a diamond-shaped plate nailed to its centre.

Raul now turned back they way he'd come, back to the laurel bush he'd shaped. If that nameplate was anywhere to be found it would be there.

Stefan had apparently asked Abbot Romuald some time in the past if his grave could be close to a fine laurel...

But the base of the laurel looked too close to the path to allow sufficient room for a grave. Surely Brother Stefan's last resting place would have been on the far side of the laurel, facing the walls of the monastery where he'd spent the majority of his life. He checked his watch. If he was gone much longer, Arym was going to start wondering where he'd got to.

Think! he told himself. Would there be anything else that might show where a grave would have been? Anxiously he scanned the ground around the laurel for some clue. And then he saw. The merest indentation. A short stretch of cleared ground which seemed to dip and rise again as if something beneath it had rotted and collapsed under the weight of the soil – like a simple coffin...

Raul dived across to where the indentation began. The thaw had left the whole patch soft and boggy. He clawed at the ground, digging down through the leaves and thin roots to where the earth felt solid. As he dug, and found nothing, Raul inched his way along the length of the

195

indentation. Suddenly his fingers struck something hard. It could be a stone, a gnarled root, anything. He'd pulled out plenty of both. But this time it wasn't.

Embedded in a clod of earth, as if it had been pressed down by a heel, the diamond-shaped piece of metal was tarnished and greened with age. Raul rubbed it with the hem of his scapula. The words appeared:

Brother Stefan Kolbe
22nd February 1951–27th October 2034
Requiescat In Pace

Tucking it into his pocket, Raul hurried from the garden cemetery. He had his evidence, the answer to one question. Brother Mark's journal *could* be believed. But so many questions remained.

What had happened when the dissolution squad stormed the chapel? How were Romuald, Conor and Liam treated? Were they carried out, to spend the rest of their days in the ghetto?

As he ran towards the beach, though, one question gnawed at Raul more deeply than any other. Had Brother Mark realised his dream?

Raul hadn't been missed. When he hurried through the gap in the sand dunes it was to find the beach more crowded than he'd ever seen it before. Almost everybody – residents and healers – seemed to be there. There were groups searching the dunes, others the shoreline, yet more on and around the limestone rocks at the foot of the cliff. Quickly he found a rock pool to wash the mud from his hands before anyone noticed him.

It was near here that he spotted Arym. She was leading Jack, Emily and Sarih along a protected spit of sand. Every now and then a large wave would crash on to the rocks between them and the sea, sending them scurrying back with squeals of delight. Arym's charges reminded Raul of the one time he could ever remember being taken to the beach. That day he'd run squealing from the waves himself. He'd been seven years old – and, apart from Arym, that was how the others struck him: as though they'd become young children again. Pausing only to load a few shells and a frond of dried bladderwrack into his sack, Raul hurried across to join them.

Arym greeted him with a hoot of derision. 'Is that all you've found?' She pointed at his meagre collection. 'That lot wouldn't decorate a bonsai tree, let alone one for Darmas!'

Jack was grinning childishly at him. He rattled his sack to prove how well his shell-collecting had gone. Emily and Sarih waved the seaweed they'd accumulated before collapsing into fits of giggles as they began slapping it at each other.

'I wasn't sure what to look for,' shrugged Raul, hoping that would be enough to explain his extended absence.

Arym made a face for the benefit of the others. She was already in a festive mood. 'Anything!' she cried, 'so long as it's natural, not human-made. You heard what Jenna said after Vespers last night.'

Raul remembered. 'The Festival of Darmas is the highlight of the year,' the healer had enthused.

Doron had added his usual touch of austerity. 'Too many

197

people have forgotten what the day is all about. They've turned it into an excuse for one big party. Here we do things properly. On Darmas Day we celebrate the Saviour's birth, we recall his teachings – and we rejoice in the freedom those teachings brought us.'

'So we don't decorate the sanitarium with any of that cheap glittery stuff they sell on the mainland,' Jenna had said.

'Plastic shells,' scoffed Doron. 'Rubber seaweed. Artificial grasses that glow in the dark...'

'We decorate with natural things,' said Jenna automatically, 'the fruits of the earth – evolved, not created.'

Yes, Raul remembered. And he wondered again: created or evolved, God or no God – did it really matter? He found himself imagining the dissolution squad landing on this very beach, fuelled with hatred for humble monks who'd done nothing but live quietly and pray for others.

Now another boat was coming in to berth – a cargo boat. Amidst great excitement it was slowly drawing closer. In his wheelhouse the boat master looked anxious, as well he might. The waves were white-capped. What had begun as a gentle breeze when he'd left the mainland had become a strong wind. Waves were surging against the jetty. Slowly, and with much shouting, the cargo boat berthed safely. It was immediately surrounded. Hands reached out to help unload, for this was the eagerly-awaited Darmas delivery – the festival gifts given by the Republic to those in need. Back on the shore, Raul knew, similar deliveries would be taking place at every nurture-house.

Sarih brushed past him, trying to get nearer. Emily and Jack, sticking close to Arym, had already reached the jetty steps. Raul didn't move.

Out in the swirling waters of Craston Sound, another boat had attracted his attention. It was well to the east of them, its course set due south. Soon it would disappear from view behind the cliffs at the end of the beach. From there, who knew where it was headed? Raul sensed that the sailor knew the way well, though. In spite of the difficult conditions the craft was making good progress, tacking into the adverse gusts then running with the wind when it became favourable.

That was when he saw it. As the boat was hit by a crosswind the sailor expertly swung it round to reap the benefit. The jib ballooned – and the brightly coloured emblem of a sailing ship on the open sea stood out against the sail as clearly as black ink on white paper.

I watched as the wind caught in the jib, and made its large, colourful boatyard emblem – a barque on the open sea – look as if it was bursting with pride.

The craft was carrying the very emblem that Brother Mark had mentioned in his journal! And it was going 'the long way round', exactly as he described it.

Raul's fingers felt inside his scapula, touching the nameplate he'd found less than an hour ago in the garden. *Two* pieces of evidence. Arym would have to take him seriously now.

From the sanitarium, the bell began to toll, calling them to the Gathering of Sext. Raul joined the excited throng as they began to hurry away from the beach. Like theirs, his own mind was in a whirl – but for a different reason. Behind him, he had no doubt, the boat he'd seen was continuing on its journey to Orb Island.

For not until that moment had it occurred to him that Brother Mark might still be alive.

Raul had little chance to speak to Arym in the hours that followed. The afternoon was spent in the same way, scouring the beach and other areas for Darmas decorations. Then, after the Gathering of Vespers, they were all detailed to festoon different quarters of the sanitarium. This took them until the bell tolled for the Gathering of Compline. In a change to routine they congregated not in the cloister garth but in the refectory.

One group had spent the afternoon decorating the traditional Darmas tree – the Tree of Life. Freshly cut, it had been adorned in the fashion that Raul had known since his very first Darmas in the nurture-house. The lower branches carried many of the items they'd collected from the beach – fronds of seaweed and shells hanging on twine – all representing the teeming life in the waters of the world. On the branches above them the central part of the tree was layered with feathers and fur, representing the bird and lower animal kingdoms. The upper reaches were draped with relics – bones, claws, teeth – of humans and other mammals.

They gathered round the Tree of Life. By the glow of candlelight they read the well-known lessons from *The Writings*. Then refreshments were served, scalding hot sweetmeat pies and glasses of ruby-red mulled wine to wash them down. Finally the Gathering ended with an announcement that the following morning would be free time. They could do whatever they wanted until the special Darmas lunch with its traditional opening of the Republic's gracious gifts.

Raul used the delighted applause as cover to take Arym's arm and draw her near.

'Come to my room,' he whispered. 'I've got something to show you.'

Arym sat on the chair by the window as Raul pulled out the floorboard and recovered Brother Mark's journal. He'd spent the past few minutes explaining what he'd found and what he'd learned from it: about the monastery, about who Brother Mark was, about the life he'd led. Now Raul handed the yellowed book to her.

'Read it, Arym and you'll see. All the things we do here – these cowls, the silences, the Gatherings – they had it all and more.'

Arym slapped the book aside. 'That can't be so. You said they were God-followers. That means they were unbelievers.'

'No, they weren't!' said Raul. 'Read it and you'll see. They accepted Charles Darwin's teachings just as much as anybody else. But they argued that evolution didn't do away with God, it explained more about how he worked.'

'So did the maniacs who caused the Wasteland!'

'But not everybody who believed in God was a fighter. That's what we've always been taught, isn't it? But it's not true. Brother Mark and the rest of them were peaceful. They didn't start wars or anything.' He picked the journal up from the floor and put it back in Arym's hands. 'Read it.

Please. That's all I'm asking. Just *read* it!'

Arym paused, then slowly opened the faded cover. For the next hour she read. For the most part, Raul sat silently beside her, interrupting only to point out things he thought she might not have noticed, or to give his interpretation of words she couldn't read. When she reached the part which mentioned Brother Stefan's burial he produced the nameplate he'd found in the garden. Exactly how he expected Arym to react, Raul didn't know, but it wasn't in the way she did when she finished reading.

Handing the journal back to him, she simply said, 'So?'

'What do you mean, 'So?' Don't you understand what they did to this place?'

'Of course I understand. It – those monks – got what they deserved.' Raul was shocked into silence. Arym seemed amused. 'Raul,' she smiled, 'I knew most of that stuff already.'

'What? How?'

'Jenna told me. You're wrong about her and Doron, you know. They're not trying to hide things. They don't hide anything from me.'

'And you don't hide anything from them, do you?' snapped Raul. 'Will you be telling them about this like you told them about the knife?'

It was Arym's turn to look shocked. 'I – I was scared, Raul. I didn't know what you were going to do.' She'd already recovered her composure and her tone was altering. 'I thought you were going to hurt yourself. I was worried about you, little brother.'

It was like being back in their early days in the nurture-house when all had been new and frightening.

Then he'd only had to run to her and she'd soothe him with honeyed words. But that was then. Now he was able to fight his own battles.

'You haven't answered me,' hissed Raul. 'Will you be telling them about Brother Mark's journal?'

'Why? I've told you, they know it all already!'

'So where's the chapel, then? Have they mentioned that?'

'No, of course not.'

'Why not? I thought they told you everything.'

Arym's look of amusement had gone, to be replaced by one of scorn. 'Maybe they've said nothing because there's nothing to say. Use your head Raul, please. When that dissolution squad finally broke in, do you think they'd have left their precious chapel in one piece? Of course they wouldn't. Once they'd got those unbelievers out—'

'They had names,' interrupted Raul angrily. 'Abbot Romuald. Brother Conor. Brother Liam.'

Arym didn't back down. 'Once they'd got them out,' she repeated, 'that chapel wouldn't have lasted five minutes. They'd have gutted it. That window would have lasted just as long as it took a sledgehammer to go through it.' She stood up, adding one final thrust. 'And it wouldn't surprise me if, when they'd finished there, they hadn't gone out and found your Brother Mark.'

'They didn't. I know they didn't.'

'So he ended up as a pile of bones in some cave, then. Good for him.'

'Wrong again, Arym. I think Brother Mark's still alive.'

Raul's sister snorted. 'After fifty years? Not a chance, brother. They'd have tracked him down. Packed him off to the ghetto with the others.'

Her derision rankled. He felt his old temper flaring, a sure sign that the effects of the medication pellet he'd prised from his arm had truly worn off. 'Wrong for a third time, *sister*!' he shouted. 'Because I've seen that boat!'

Before he knew it, Raul had told her about the smack he'd seen with the boatyard's emblem on its sail, taking the same route described in the journal.

'And that's it?' scoffed Arym. 'That's your evidence for thinking he's survived for fifty years in a cave?'

'That's it for now,' snapped Raul, 'But I'm going looking for more – tomorrow morning.'

'Oh, yes? Where?'

'Orb Island. I'm going to see if I can find him, Arym.'

'And you offered to go with him, Arym?' said Jenna.

'There's no danger. He's checked the tides. It will be low most of the morning. We'll have over three hours.'

'I don't think Jenna was referring to the physical danger,' said Doron.

Arym felt uncomfortable. Hurrying straight from Raul's room to Jenna's, she'd expected to find the healer alone. Instead Arym had found her discussing the details of the forthcoming Rite of Scrutiny with Doron.

Arym had hoped that Doron might leave, but was hardly surprised when he'd stayed firmly put. Clearly she was going to have to persuade both of them.

'I am in no danger,' she said firmly. 'My faith is strong.'

'And Raul?'

'When he told me what he wanted to do, my first

thought was to try and talk him out of it,' said Arym.

'Then why didn't you?' asked Jenna.

'Because I'm hoping that if we find this man – or his remains – it will help him.'

'Explain,' said Doron. 'But be warned, Arym, the Rite of Scrutiny will determine his state of mind. If you are trying to help him because of your blood ties then you are misguided. Remember what *The Writings* say in prophesy: "The truths of Science will set people against their own kin; and their enemies will be those of their own household".'

'Doron,' said Arym, 'if this man is dead then he can't influence Raul for the worse. But surely finding his dried bones in a squalid cave can only be an influence for the better.'

Jenna nodded approvingly. 'By showing Raul the end of a wasted life? A fool abandoned by the God he followed? I think you're right, Arym.'

'And if by some chance this monk *is* still alive?' asked Doron thinly. 'If he speaks? If he seeks to persuade Raul? What then?'

'Then Raul will have to decide for himself,' said Arym. 'I can't help him. He will have to face the Rite of Scrutiny on his own.'

Now Doron smiled his approval. 'Excellent, Arym.' He leaned forward to rest his soft, white hand on her arm. 'Spoken like a true healer.'

Arym smiled in return. They were persuaded. What's more, they didn't appear to have seen the obvious.

'Of course it would be good in another way to find this Brother Mark alive,' she said quietly.

Jenna and Doron exchanged glances. 'Why?'

'Because he's a criminal, isn't he? Old as he is, he could be arrested and tried. And we would get the credit, wouldn't we?'

They left an hour after dawn, while the rest of the sanitarium slumbered. The air was crisp and clean. There had been a hard frost and the skeletal trees were rimmed with silver. The track which ran parallel with the cliff edge was hard underfoot. The sky was a pale, morning blue, but with a hem of grey from the layers of cloud already gathering on the horizon.

Beneath it all there was something else. It was Darmas Day, a day so special it felt like you could reach right out and touch it.

Raul pushed along the track as quickly as the banks of encroaching gorse would allow. Behind him, Arym was already struggling to keep up. More than once he stopped to wait for her, checking his watch as he did so.

They had three hours at the outside. The tide should by now be approaching its lowest point, the reef sufficiently exposed for an easy crossing. They needed to be back to it well before the probing fingers of water made their own return. The moment Arym caught up with him Raul turned to hurry on towards the western tip of Parens Island.

When they reached the fissure in the rock it seemed as if Arym was regretting her decision to come with him. She shrank back, alarm on her face as she saw the steepness of the descent to the beach.

'You want to hold hands?' offered Raul.

'No.'

In that one word, Raul realised how much Arym had changed in the short time they'd been in the sanitarium. It wasn't that she'd grown up – more that she'd grown away, as if the months which separated their ages had been transformed into something hard and unyielding.

He didn't look back to see how she was coping. When he scrambled out from the fissure and onto the beach he kept on going until he reached the shoreline. The waters were still, barely rippling up towards his feet. It couldn't be a better morning for a crossing to Orb Island.

Timing was Raul's only worry. They were already running late and Arym's painfully slow descent to the beach wasn't going to help matters. The moment she struggled out on to the shingle Raul turned and hurried on. Within a hundred metres the shoreline had curved enough for him to see the bird-carpeted rocks marking the south of Orb Island. Another hundred and the far end of the reef was in sight. A hundred more, and he was at the point where it began. Any further, Raul knew, and he would be close to where Micha must have dived into the chill waters that drowned him. Suppressing the thought, and without waiting for Arym to catch him up, he stepped out from the spongy sand and on to the black-stoned reef.

The crossing was far easier than Raul had expected. Many of the rocks were flat and wide. He could jump across the shallow pools between them. Others, though, were jagged, peaking a good half metre above the water level. But even these weren't difficult to move over if he first made sure he'd got a good foothold on the slippery surface. Around and between them all, the water gently eddied and swirled. A soft zephyr of breeze riffled Raul's hair. He was well over halfway across. The gobbling of the gulls on the opposite shore was growing louder. Some appeared to stop their foraging to watch him. Others waddled away across the sand. Only when Raul jumped from the shallow rocks of the reef's tail and on to the shingle beach, did they all rise into the air and wheel away.

'Where now?' asked Arym not long after. Crossing the reef had been so straightforward she'd managed to make up some of the distance she'd lost.

'That way. The journal said they came in on the south side.' Raul did his best to sound confident. Now that they'd arrived he wasn't sure about anything. If Brother Mark's hideout had kept him hidden for all these years, how was he going to find it in a couple of hours?

They followed the shoreline around to their left. Gulls and kittiwakes rose, squawking into the air, as they passed through, only to regroup behind them like foam in the wake of a ship. Arym was looking up towards the body of the island. Sloping sharply from the beach, it passed through a belt of thin firs to a flat, bare plateau.

'His cave must be in the side of the cliff,' she said. 'Or on top, even. Anywhere but down here where it'll fill with water twice a day.'

She was right, knew Raul. The caves at the base of the rock face were shallow and sodden, little piles of soaking driftwood washed to their tapering ends. But he had a reason for not climbing at once.

'I want to find where they landed first,' said Raul. 'Then we'll know we're close.'

...a group of standing stones in deep water formed

a kind of natural jetty, that's what the journal had said. But there were so many. The whole of the off-shore area was littered with peaks and slabs of black stone. The group that Brother Mark was referring to could be any one of them. Then, as they reached a spit of sand at the foot of a steep incline, he saw it.

The spit itself ran sharply downwards before disappearing into water that quickly changed from light to dark – a clear sign of how quickly it deepened. Bisecting the water, like a natural pontoon, ran a huge finger of fissured rocks. Some were flat, some were angled – and one that *reminded him of a cockatoo's head...*

'Here!' shouted Raul. 'They landed him here!'

Arym hurried to his side. 'You're sure?'

Raul pointed. 'It's deep enough there for a boat to come right in. That's where they tied up. So...' he hurried across to where the rock pontoon angled down to the beach, '...this is the way Brother Mark must have brought Glyn.' The passage from the journal sang in Raul's head as if it were being spoken aloud:

While Uncle Harry kept lookout, I showed Glyn the places I'd talked about: where he would leave things he brought, how I would signal if I needed him to come closer. Finally I showed where, with the help of God, I intended to live for the rest of my days.

Were the places near or far away, though? It didn't say. But surely one had to be near by: the place where Glyn would leave the things he'd brought. The agreement hadn't been for him to go as far as the cave Brother Mark had settled in. The monk hadn't expected to see him again.

209

Glyn and I shook hands knowing that, barring emergencies, it would be for the last time.

That's what being a hermit must have meant: living completely alone. So the arrangement had to be that things – food, toiletries, letters and newspapers, maybe – would be left somewhere for Brother Mark to come out to collect later. At night, probably, when there was no danger of him being seen.

Arym had seated herself on the base of the rock pontoon. She was facing the sloping beach, the curtain of cliff face rising behind it.

'Up or nothing,' she sighed. 'Or, more likely, up and find nothing.' Arym rose reluctantly to her feet, dusting the damp sand from the back of her scapula. 'How about that way?' she said, pointing without enthusiasm.

Straight ahead, an alley of firm damp sand rose up towards a shelf littered with small rocks and scree. Raul remembered again the boat he'd seen heading this way the day before. If anybody had landed here, their footprints would have already been washed away by the night tide. The high-water mark was clearly visible, a ragged line of dampness and stranded weed like the ring of grime on a nurture-house bath, just below the level of the shelf ahead.

...I showed Glyn the places I'd talked about: where he would leave things he brought...

There'd be no point leaving anything here on the foreshore, where it could get soaked or washed away. Arym was right, it had to be up.

'Come on, then,' said Raul, urgently.

They plunged forward, toes digging deep into the wet

sand as they climbed towards the high-water mark. After ten metres or so the sand began to give way to wet scree and smooth, slimy rock. Then, suddenly, there was no more dampness underfoot. Sand, scree and base rock were all bone dry. Still following the alley, Raul and Arym swung round behind a clutch of large boulders. And there, wedged firmly beneath a formation offering shelter against unexpected rain, they found a sealed cardboard box and a canister of oil.

Words were unnecessary. From the stunned look on Arym's face Raul saw that she'd come to the same conclusion as him. They weren't looking for a resting place marked with the cross symbol; they were looking for a cave, home to a monk for the past fifty years. Both the box and the oil canister were clean. Whoever had delivered them had known what they now knew for sure: that Brother Mark was indeed still alive.

'That way?' asked Arym quietly.

Raul nodded. Ahead of them the narrow alley threaded its way round to the left and out of sight. Bounded by what had now become a dizzying drop down to the beach on one side and the sheer rock face on the other, there was no other way. Leaving the box and the oil untouched, Raul led Arym onwards, the path not wide enough to allow progress in anything other than single file.

Within thirty metres it didn't even allow that. After cutting its way through a natural crevice between two steepling walls of rock the alley narrowed into non-existence. They'd reached a dead end.

'We must have missed something,' murmured Raul.

'Like what?' Arym had already turned, ready to head back the way they'd come. 'Can you see the way in to a cave anywhere?'

Raul couldn't. At the far end, the sea and the glowering sky were visible between the two sides of the crevice the path had led them into. But that was all. There was no sign of an opening, large or small. With Arym ahead now, Raul began to retrace his steps.

It was the cough that stopped him.

Hard and racking, though faint, it seemed to come from within the very rocks themselves. Raul stopped abruptly. He gestured to Arym with a finger across his lips. She came back slowly, frowning. Then she heard it too. This time the cough went on for longer, as if it was seizing hold of its owner's chest and wouldn't let go.

Raul studied the wall of rock. It appeared to be indented, with one length ending and another beginning a very short distance behind it. On first passing Raul had dismissed the gap between the two sections as nothing more than a fracture in the rocks. He'd been so focussed on looking for a recognisable entrance that he hadn't realised the fracture was more like the gap between a pair of overlapping curtains.

Turning sideways he eased his way in. The gap was narrow. Within a couple of metres the walls became enjoined like a pair of Siamese twins. For a moment, Raul thought he could go no further. But, after ducking beneath the join, he found himself able to inch further and further...until slowly he realised that the gap was widening, as if it was an isthmus linking the outside world to another, inner world.

212

Then, suddenly, Raul had reached it. He saw an opening, head-high; a chamber, cool and dry. Beams of natural light filtered in from somewhere above. Deep inside he could see the warm glow of a lamp, standing on a shelf rough-cut into the limestone wall. And beneath it, on a simple pallet made from driftwood and dried grasses, an old man, his white hair illuminated.

'Brother Mark?' murmured Raul. His voice sounded loud, but couldn't have carried clearly.

'Glyn? Is that you, my friend? Is Ruti with you?'

The three questions were accompanied by thin, laboured breathing, as if the speaker was finding it almost too much effort to draw air into his lungs. In spite of this, his voice sounded mellow and calm.

Raul drew closer. As he did so, Brother Mark reached out to turn the lamp up brighter before falling back onto his pillow with a sigh. Raul saw then that his white hair was matched by a beard of the same colour. Neither was wild and unkempt, though. They'd been trimmed regularly. In the glow of the lamp it was easy to see – and smell – that the old monk hadn't allowed himself to sink into filthiness and squalor.

Brother Mark hadn't repeated his question. Even with his eyes closed, it seemed that he knew the answer. Now he simply said, 'Peace be with you, whoever you are.'

Hesitantly, Raul moved into the circle of light thrown out by the lamp. 'My name is Raul. I'm with my sister, Arym. We've come from the monastery. I found your journal, Brother Mark.'

For a moment Raul wasn't sure if he'd been heard – or, if he had, whether the old monk remembered even having written the journal. His face remained impassive, its strong outline deathly pale in the lamplight. Raul knew in that moment that Brother Mark was dying. Then the monk's eyes opened, flicking Raul's way. A smile briefly played across his lips.

'Welcome to my home, Paul,' he said.

Raul knelt, assuming that Brother Mark hadn't heard his name properly. 'Raul, Brother Mark. My name's Raul.'

On its pillow the white-haired head gave the slightest of shakes. 'That is the name given to you by the Republic. A single change of letter to conceal a name once carried by a great man of God. Before they banned it, your name would have been Paul. And your sister is Arym, you say?'

Far from not hearing, Raul realised, the monk had absorbed his every word with a mind that was still active.

'That's right.' It was Arym, now stepping into the pool of light herself.

'Welcome, Mary,' smiled the old monk. 'Your name took them rather more effort to alter. Only fair, really. Your name has been glorified by so many wonderful women…'

'Well I'm not one of them,' said Arym sharply, as Brother Mark's voice was engulfed by a racking cough.

By the time the monk had recovered, Arym's barbed reply appeared to have been forgotten. With a grunt of effort he turned on to his side to face them. The worn brown covering that Raul assumed was a blanket moved with him: Brother Mark was wearing his monk's cowl. This symbol of his life seemed to add extra weight to what he said next.

'My journal. Did it make any sense, Paul?'

214

Raul nodded. 'Yes. Lots.'

Brother Mark leaned forward, a note of urgency in his voice. 'Has it helped you?'

'How do you mean?'

'Paul, I may live in isolation but my heart and mind are still in this world of ours. My friends provide me with letters and newspapers. I know what goes on. How else would I know what to pray for?'

Another bout of coughing racked him to a halt for a few seconds. 'So,' he went on when it was over, 'I know what our monastery home is used for now. I know why you are there. You have been blessed with the spark of faith, Paul. They want to extinguish it. They can't control it and that frightens them, just as it always has.'

Brother Mark looked at them keenly, his eyes still young and alive. 'But the future lies with you, Paul. And with you, Mary. Remember that.'

'Not with me it doesn't,' said Arym curtly. 'Not your kind of future.' Beside the kneeling Raul, Arym stood stiff and unbending. 'Your journal changed nothing in me. Your God is an invention. My brother is flirting with belief in him. I'm not.'

Brother Mark nodded slowly. 'Honesty is a great virtue, Mary. But remember that being honest with others is often easier than being honest with yourself.'

'I am being honest with myself. I don't believe in a God. Nothing will ever make me believe in your stupid God.'

The old monk didn't react to the insult – but neither did he back down. 'You may be right,' he said softly. 'But then again one day you might see something, hear something...experience something: something that tells

215

you you're wrong. It might be a breath of wind, a snatch of music, the love of another person, a cry of fear – anything. That's when you'll have to be honest with yourself. That's when you'll have to follow, like I did.'

'You? said Raul. 'You're saying there was a time when you didn't believe in God?'

Brother Mark tried to laugh. It made him wince. 'One time? *Many* times! Do you think when a man becomes a monk his doubts vanish? That he just goes blindly on?'

'But you still believe?'

'Yes, I still believe. Faith has to be renewed or it's worthless.'

'I don't understand,' said Raul.

'A refusal to face facts isn't faith, it's stupidity,' said Brother Mark. 'And atheists are just as guilty of that as anybody. We all believe in something beyond our imagining.'

'All right then,' snapped Arym. 'What made you believe?'

The answer came back without hesitation. 'Stefan's window.'

'The window you help collect glass for,' said Raul. 'The window in the chapel.'

...I would help by doing odd jobs. One of these jobs, though he no longer remembers, was to collect glass for Brother Stefan!

Brother Mark seemed to be struggling for breath. His chest heaved briefly. 'It helped me every time I saw it.' He looked up at Arym. 'It might do the same for you, if you can get into the chapel. If you *wanted* to get in.'

Raul didn't know what to say. How could he tell the

monk that there was no longer any sign of the place he'd held so dear? Arym had no such qualms.

'There's no chapel to get in to,' she said abruptly. 'It's long gone.'

'Not so!' responded Brother Mark at once. 'Glyn and Ruti would not lie to me.'

'They – they've been there?' said Raul. 'Since you left?'

'Not been there. But their notes mention it often. Whenever they see Stefan's window from the boat they offer a prayer for the souls of all who lived in our community.'

From the boat? They could still see it from the boat? A passage from Brother Mark's account of his journey to Orb Island with Glyn sprang to Raul's mind:

I could just make out the chapel window: Stefan's window. How dark and drab it looked from the outside!

And yet when he'd searched the cloisters...

'Brother Mark. Where was the chapel?'

The monk seemed to have anticipated the question. With difficulty he'd levered himself on to his side and was reaching out towards the same rough-hewn shelf the oil lamp was standing on. Beside it, their old worn covers barely reflecting the light, stood a row of books. Thin fingers trembling with the effort, Brother Mark pulled one down. It looked for all the world like Doron's copy of *The Writings*, its gilt-edged wafer-thin pages bound in a cover of black – except that the legend on the front of the monk's book read *Holy Bible*. He removed a folded sheet of paper from inside. It was a diagram, its lines blurred through overdrawing each time they'd faded too much to be read.

'This is a plan of the monastery as I left it,' he said. 'I've looked at it often. To remind me of them...' He seemed to have slipped back in time. 'So that I can pray for them...'

Raul took the sheet from the monk's fingers. He saw at once that Brother Mark was no draughtsman. He'd tried to show all the floors on one diagram. The result was something of a jumble. Even so, and despite the names against various areas being different too, he could see that the sanitarium was unmistakably the same building. The outlines of the cloister garth, the refectory, the vestibule, the stairways – Raul was able to identify them all. Only one eluded him: the one that Brother Mark's finger was now resting on, marked 'chapel'.

It was shown as a large room with its entrance in the centre of the east cloister. But it stood precisely where Raul had looked, in vain, for signs of just such an entrance. Arym had to be right.

'Arym's right, Brother Mark. Your chapel's gone, It's not there any more.'

'If the window is still there,' said the monk firmly, 'then the chapel is still there.'

'But I've looked,' said Raul. 'The entrance was in the east cloister, wasn't it?'

'Yes. Down a flight of steps.'

'Down—?'

Raul choked off his intended echo. How could he have been so stupid? How often had Brother Mark's journal given him the clue? And he'd missed it every time.

After Lauds I stayed behind to help him up *the chapel stairs...*

When all was ready, six of us carried our Brother down *to the chapel...*

We rose and celebrated Lauds as usual. But, for the first and only time, we didn't walk up *from the chapel together...*

'The chapel is underground,' breathed Raul. It was a statement rather than a question, and more for Arym's benefit than anything else.

'Beyond the east cloister,' said Brother Mark weakly. 'The monks who built it were workers of genius. It's made from a natural cavern that reached almost to the cliff face. They opened it at both ends. At the cliff end they put in a blown-glass window to give light; that was the window Stefan replaced. At the monastery end they built a flight of stairs up to the cloister garth.'

The old monk sank, coughing, back into his pillow, as if the speech had been too much for him.

How to tell him? wondered Raul. Honestly, he decided, before Arym did the job for him.

'Then the entrance has been blocked up, Brother Mark. There's no way in from that cloister any more.'

For a moment the monk didn't react. Then, slowly, tears squeezed out from behind his eyelids. A wrinkled hand wiped the first few away, but ceased to bother when they kept on coming.

'So it is true, then,' he said, his thin voice cracking with emotion.

It was Arym who asked, 'What's true?'

Brother Mark opened his eyes. When he spoke it was directly to Raul's sister. 'It was some time before Glyn could bring himself to write down what was

219

rumoured: that after the dissolution squad repeatedly failed to break down my Brothers' barricade the bailiff ordered his men to seal the entrance.'

'Seal it?' Arym couldn't keep the horror out of her voice. 'You mean he left them to starve to death?'

The old man nodded, the tears flowing freely now. He seemed to be wrestling with his memories, struggling to force words out. Finally they came, half-cried, half-shouted. 'It was my fault they died!'

'No, Brother Mark,' said Raul at once. 'It was their decision. You wrote down what they said to you in your journal. Abbot Romuald and Brother Conor and Brother Liam made their own decision to stay. It couldn't possibly have been your fault.'

The monk clutched fiercely at Raul's hand. 'But you don't understand! There was another way out of that chapel. And I didn't tell them!'

Neither Raul nor Arym had to ask for the details. They tumbled from Brother Mark's lips as if their weight had been crushing him for years and this was his last opportunity to be free of them.

'I'd discovered it years before, when Glyn and I were teenagers. We were larking about in the monastery's cemetery.' He smiled briefly. 'Strictly forbidden. We saw Abbot Romuald coming through the garden. Glyn raced off but I tripped. By the time I'd picked myself up it was too late to follow. Then I saw a circular metal plate close to the monastery wall. I assumed it was a drain. At that age I thought a smelly soaking was preferable to being reprimanded by the Abbot!'

'That was it?' asked Raul as Brother Mark had to

pause for breath. 'The way out?'

The old monk nodded. 'Under the plate was what looked like a drain shaft. You know, for inspecting the things. There were rungs embedded in the side. I scampered down them to find that the hole was as dry as a bone. And there was an opening. It led into a low passageway which passed right through the foundations and came out into the chapel.'

'Just like that?' said Arym. 'So why didn't anybody else know about it?'

'Because it was well hidden, of course. I didn't find it that day. I came back another time, on my own, with a torch.' Again his smile flickered, giving Raul a brief glimpse of the boy Brother Mark had once been. 'There was a small lever on the tunnel side. When you pulled that lever, a false part of the chapel's wood panelling sprung loose. Five minutes earlier and I'd have interrupted Vespers! Thankfully the chapel was empty. But I was so terrified I'd damaged something I pulled the panel back into position and ran for it. I never went down there again.'

'And you're saying you didn't tell any of the brothers about it?' said Arym coldly. 'Not even when you became one of them yourself?'

Brother Mark answered her directly. 'It didn't even cross my mind that they would need to know. This is not the first age to have practised persecution, Mary, but in my innocence I never imagined that such times would ever return.'

He broke down again then, his racking cough echoing round the walls of the cave. Finally he was able to bring his confession – for that's what it sounded like to Raul – to a close. 'The one regret I've had for all these years is that if they'd known about that passage they could have escaped.'

'They could have, Brother Mark,' said Raul. 'But they wouldn't have.'

'Of course they would,' snapped Arym.

Raul ignored her. His whole attention was focussed on Brother Mark. The old monk's last bout of coughing seemed to have left him spent. His breathing seemed shallower and more laboured than at any time since they'd arrived.

'They wouldn't have left that chapel even if you *had* told them,' said Raul again. 'Brother Conor said as much. You wrote it in your journal. He said that he and Brother Liam were going to stay in the chapel "till they knock the door down and carry us out". Remember?'

Brother Mark's eyes remained closed, but his eyelids were flickering as if he was reliving the scene. Slowly his laboured breathing became calmer, almost peaceful. He gave the faintest of smiles. 'I remember,' he said. 'Thank you for reminding me.'

'Raul!' Arym was tugging at his arm even as she was checking the luminous face of her watch. 'Look at the time. We've got to move!'

Raul knew she was right. Stay any longer and the tide would be swirling round the reef. He leaned closer to the old monk. 'I'll come again.'

The old monk's head gave the slightest of shakes. 'No, Paul. My time is near.'

'We could fetch a doctor!'

'Or somebody to arrest me,' smiled Brother Mark at Arym. She spun sharply away towards where they'd come in. The monk laid his pale hands on Raul's. 'Glyn and Ruti know what to do. It won't take much to bring down enough rock to seal this place. It's been my home. Soon it will be my tomb.'

'No!'

The soft hands were placing something in Raul's. He glanced down at what it was. 'Bellows for the spark,' smiled the dying monk. 'My need for it is over.'

'I can't just leave you...' said Raul, thickly. It was as if he was being told to abandon an old friend, when all he wanted was to talk to him for hours.

'You must. My bags are packed. I'm ready for my journey. Please God, yours is just beginning. Now go.'

Arym was already on her way. Reluctantly, Raul got to his feet. Pausing only to slide what Brother Mark had given him safely inside his scapula, he stumbled out of the cave. The moment he got outside he could tell the weather had changed for the worse. The grey clouds that had been lazing on the horizon when they set out were now scudding ominously above their heads. As he hurried down the scree-strewn slope, past the box and oil canister he knew Brother Mark would not live long enough to collect, a raw wind bit at his tunic.

The foreshore had narrowed alarmingly. The rock Arym had sat on earlier was already under water. Fingers of foam were probing their way up the beach. The tide had turned.

Raul's sister hadn't waited for him. She was running, stumbling round the shoreline to where the reef joined it.

Raul chased after her, urgency in every step. They could wait until the tide turned again, of course, but that would mean missing the Darmas Day celebrations. Questions would be asked – questions he'd prefer not to face until he'd thought more about what Brother Mark had told him.

As he caught sight of the reef, Raul breathed a sigh of relief. The rising tide hadn't made much of an impression on it yet. Some sections looked a little less prominent than before, but there still seemed enough to get them safely across. Arym clearly thought as much. She was already out on the rocks, pausing and jumping, pausing and jumping. Raul followed quickly, leaping lightly from rock to rock.

But all too soon his feet were kicking up water where earlier there had been none. It was becoming harder to keep up the pace. The black stones of the reef were now slick with spray. The more he tried to hurry, the more his feet slipped and landed in the lapping waves. Ahead, Arym had stopped. Raul edged his way to her side – to find that the next section was now submerged beneath thick, dark water, like a gap in a row of teeth.

'I can't jump that far!' cried Arym.

'We'll have to step into the water! Feel our way! The rocks can't be far below the surface!'

Hands linked, Raul and Arym waded forward together. Water coursed around their ankles and into their boots. Only when they felt sure of their foothold did they step forward again. But their progress was slower now, much slower. The gaps in the reef were widening. Whereas water had been pressing at their ankles before, now it was pounding at their calves. Raul was finding it ever harder to remain upright, let alone feel for the rapidly vanishing rocks that were their path to safety.

And then, as they got to a point some forty metres from the safety of the beach, they found that the low-lying rocks had vanished completely. The tide was now surging through the gap between them and the beach. Occasionally the tip of a rock might appear, like the hand of a drowning man, only to disappear immediately beneath the swiftly-flowing waters.

'Get down on your hands and knees, Arym!' shouted Raul.

They'd reached the easy section, the part with the large, flat boulders they'd leapt across so nimbly earlier that morning. Perhaps they could crawl the rest of the way?

Still clinging to his sister, Raul dropped to his knees. He gasped as the cold waters penetrated his alb up to the elbows. The waves were pounding at his thighs and sucking at his legs, trying to pull him off balance, as if they were engaged in a wrestling match. He and Arym began inching forward, crab-like.

'It's too deep!' screamed Arym, almost at once.

She'd plunged her free arm in as far as her shoulder and touched nothing. Panic-stricken, she let go of Raul's hand and tried instead to drag him to his feet with her. Feeling firm rock beneath him, Raul made it into a crouch but no further. As a sudden swirling surge of water hit them both, he felt Arym let go of his hand. He just caught a glimpse of her toppling into the foam before he too lost his balance. Then the taste of salt was in his throat and the waters closed over his head in a roar. A single thought flicked through his mind. This was how it had been for Micha.

Then Raul was kicking and fighting, thrusting for air even as the thick material of his saturated clothing tried to drag him down. Breaking the surface, he filled his lungs. Where was Arym? A scream from nearby gave him the answer. He saw his sister clinging desperately to the one visible high point of the reef. Raul thrashed hard in her direction, desperately trying to reach her outstretched hand.

But before he got there, Arym was hit by another wave. Raul saw her wrenched from her life-line, heard her terrified scream. For a moment he thought he'd lost her completely, until her bobbing head broke the surface close by. Lunging forward, Raul grasped the sleeve of her alb.

In that way he was able to cling to her, but Raul knew from his aching limbs that he could do so no longer. The fight was over. The sea had won. All they could do now was try and keep their heads above water for as long as possible, then hope that the end came peacefully. He heard Arym scream something, but the roar of the water drowned it out. The current was taking them now, dragging them to wherever it wanted, like the rubbish they'd collected so often…like the glass bottles Brother Mark had collected for Brother Stefan's window…all tossed ashore by the tide…

In a last, desperate act, Raul swung his floating legs downwards – and felt the swirl of sand.

'I can feel the bottom!' he screamed.

Whatever Arym herself had been screaming, it hadn't been that. Raul's shout provoked action in her too. The effect was that of an anchor being plunged into the sea bed. Buffeted, thrown from side to side, Raul and Arym used each other to stay upright and allow the waves to steer them closer to the shore.

Slowly their shoulders emerged from the foam. Then their chests, their stomachs...until finally they were wading, thrusting with every muscle in their legs against the shingle sucking at their feet, staggering forwards and backwards like a pair of drunkards, again and again, until with heaving lungs they'd climbed away from the water's clutches and were struggling up to the safety of Parens Island.

They reached the sanitarium to find the cloisters silent, the residents having just filed excitedly into the refectory for the special Darmas lunch. Hurriedly, both went to their rooms and changed into their warm, dry cowls. They met again on the stairs.

'How are you feeling?' asked Raul for the umpteenth time since they'd dragged themselves ashore.

And, for the umpteenth time, Arym simply snapped, 'I'm fine, Raul!' This time she added vehemently, 'Forget it, eh?'

Raul decided not to push it, much as he wanted to relive their meeting with Brother Mark and, yes, even their terrifying struggle in the water. But experience told him that if Arym didn't want to talk about something, there was no point in trying to force her. Perhaps the Darmas celebrations would help.

Doron and Jenna smiled warmly as they hurried into the refectory and sat down.

'Happy Darmas!' they trilled.

Arym responded with a subdued 'Happy Darmas!' of her own.

Raul too said, 'Happy Darmas!' but found it hard to enjoy the meal, special as it was. He was anxious to return to his room, to recover the book he'd hastily stowed beneath his mattress: the book Brother Mark had pressed into his hand before he'd left him.

Miraculously, from the brief inspection he'd been able to give it while getting changed, it had come through the ordeal on the reef remarkably well. The gold foil edges of its pages were soaking wet, of course, but their closeness must have formed a bond which had stopped the water seeping any further in. The text was still perfectly readable. The cover too, had survived intact. The simple gold lettering on the front had still been clearly visible:

Holy Bible

The plan, too, had survived. Raul had left it tucked inside the Bible's cover. He didn't need it. He now knew where the chapel had been – still was, if Brother Mark was right. As soon as he was able, he planned to look again in the east cloister. And then he was going to search for the way in.

The opportunity to check out the first part arrived much sooner than he'd expected. At the conclusion of the Darmas lunch they were allowed free time for an hour.

'Then return to the meeting room,' Doron had told the group, the solemnity of his face made to look faintly ridiculous by the paper hat perched on his head.

Raul returned to his room. After putting the Bible under the floorboard alongside Brother Mark's journal, he slipped quietly back out into the corridor. Passing loud sounds of giggling from the girls' floor, he hurried through the vestibule and into the east cloister. Once there, his eager eyes were searching, searching.

Not at the wall, this time – but down at his feet. Down at the solid flagstones of the cloister walk, each a metre square, laid in stretcher bond rows with each flagstone's edge extending to the middle of its neighbour's. Except for where he was now standing, halfway along the cloister.

Here a two-metre square of flagstones had been butt laid, with no overlap. Reaching no more than a third of the way out into the cloister, at first glance they looked hardly any different to the others. But now that he examined them more closely, Raul could see that they were. They were newer. The flagstones around them were more worn, faintly hollowed by the countless feet of monks shuffling silently down to their beloved chapel. Raul's eye ran across the floor to the cloister wall. Now he saw that there was some evidence of this too having been altered. Not at head height as he'd assumed before, but at ground level. There, the faintest of lines of newer plaster ran horizontally beneath the plasterwork.

It all became clear, then. He saw what Brother Mark must have seen so often in his solitude. The sadistic dissolution bailiff giving his order. The stairway down to the barricaded chapel door being filled in up to the level of the lintel. The heavy flagstones laid on top. The lintel being roughly concealed beneath a layer of plaster. And three men being left to choose whether to live or die.

Yes, *choose*.

For Raul had also since realised what Brother Mark hadn't. That it hadn't mattered that Abbot Romuald, Brother Conor and Brother Liam didn't know of the secret exit from the chapel. For, after being sealed in and left alone, as hunger gnawed at them and they grew gradually weaker, they must have realised that they did have a way out, a possible escape route.

All they had to do was smash Brother Stefan's window.

'What happened, Arym?' asked Jenna.

Arym had gone to the healer's room immediately they'd been dismissed after the Darmas lunch. It had come as no surprise to her to find Doron already seated there, *The Writings* cradled in his lap.

'We nearly drowned,' shuddered Arym. 'The tide had turned and—'

'Save the story for another time,' interrupted Doron sharply. 'You are here now. So, did you find this man, this unbeliever? Was his journal accurate or a pack of lies like the rest of their writings?'

Arym didn't answer directly, but with a question of her own. 'You said you knew all about what happened here, Doron. Was that true?'

'Of course.'

'How?'

The healer didn't attempt to hide his conceit. 'Before my transfer here I was allowed access to the dissolution archives.'

'Were some of the monks killed?' asked Arym.

'Many unbelievers died in the dissolutions, Arym,' said Jenna. 'Some gave up easily – the Christian superstition was no more than a veneer for many of its supposed followers – but others offered fierce resistance. Deaths were inevitable if the struggle was to be won.'

'That's exactly what the Wasteland bombers said in the suicide notes they left behind!'

'Their cause was deluded, Arym,' snapped Doron. 'The Republic's cause was – and still is – right.'

'Did people die here – in this place?'

Doron answered with hesitation. 'Yes.'

'In cold blood?' asked Arym, her voice trembling. 'Walled up in their chapel?'

This time Doron did pause. 'Is that what this monk's journal says?'

Again Arym deflected the question. 'Is it true?'

'No. It's not true.'

'But there was a place here called a chapel?'

Jenna gave the softly-quiet answer. 'Yes. It was where the unbelievers congregated to enact their superstitions, Arym.'

'And it's been sealed?'

'Long ago. The dissolution squad would have had orders to do that. The intention would have been to ensure that the place could never be used again.'

Doron made to rise. 'I think this journal needs to be in our hands. Now.'

'No!'

The intensity of Arym's cry stopped the healer's movement. 'Why not?' he asked coldly.

'If you take it from Raul now, he'll know I've told you everything about it. I – I don't want him to know. He trusts me. Leave it there – please.'

Jenna leaned across to place a hand on Doron's arm.

'Another twenty-four hours won't make any difference, will it?'

Doron gave every impression of weighing the argument in the scales of his mind. If so, it came down in Jenna's favour. 'Very well.' He turned to Arym. 'In case you've forgotten, your brother undergoes the Rite of Scrutiny tomorrow. If he passes then he will be leaving here anyway. If he fails...' The healer left the remainder of his sentence hanging in the air as if expecting Arym to say something.

When she didn't, Doron smiled bleakly. 'So, to return to my original question, Arym. Did you find this man, this unbeliever?'

For the first time since the meeting had begun Arym looked him directly in the eye. 'We looked everywhere, that's why we took so long. But the unbeliever's journal didn't have enough detail. We didn't find the place it said he was going to live in.'

'You didn't find this Brother Mark, then?'

'No, Doron. We didn't.'

'In the name of the Saviour and of his Revelation and of his Guiding Spirit.'

'So be it.'

'Welcome to the Rite of Scrutiny.' Doctor Tomas looked down at them from the lectern. 'To those who are to be examined, I say only one thing. Have no fear. This is merely one further step – hopefully the final step – on your road to recovery.'

She turned then, and calmly made her way down from the lectern to the body of the refectory floor. There she ushered Jenna forward to assist her with the flickering equipment laid out on one of the refectory tables. Beside it, a high-backed chair stood ready for its first occupant.

Raul adjusted his cowl. He felt – what? Nervous – certainly. But more than that – bitter. Bitter about what he'd learned from Brother Mark, about what had happened in the past and was still happening. He wasn't ill. He never had been ill, no more than those who'd decried the monks' way of life had been ill. The sickness had been in their prejudice against it.

'Emily!'

Doron's solemn call provoked the first stirrings of anticipation. Every resident was watching, all more recent arrivals than Raul's group. The Scrutiny was theirs and theirs alone.

Emily edged forward, moving slowly, so altered from the bright-eyed girl Raul had first seen sitting opposite him at the meal table. Jenna sat her in the chair, but didn't move away. Doctor Tomas then stepped forward. In her slim fingers she held a crown-shaped device, trailing wires. With Jenna's help this was placed on the frightened Emily's head. Doctor Tomas moved back to her table. Jenna made some adjustments, then nodded. Raul heard the click of a switch. Behind Emily's head, across the top of the chair's high back, a display pulsed wildly green, amber and red, before settling on green.

'I will now ask the Questions of Scrutiny,' said Doron. 'Emily. Did a supernatural being make you?'

The girl in the chair answered slowly, mechanically reading from the sheet they'd all been given.

'No supernatural being made me. My biological

ancestors made me, countless numbers of them dating back to the dawn of time.'

Above her head the display grew sideways, as if measuring the volume of her reply – except that it wasn't. That had all been made quite clear. The display was a measure of the sincerity of their responses, gleaned by sampling impulses from the brain.

'Emily. Were you made for any purpose?'

'I was not made for any purpose. I am the product of blind chance.'

Again the display grew, long and green. The congregation murmured in approval.

'Emily. Do you have an immortal soul?'

'I do not have an immortal soul. I am flesh and blood, no more.'

'Emily. Is there a life after death?'

'There is…there is…'

A hush fell over the congregation, turning to a low moan as Emily hesitated and above her head the display flickered and the green became heavily tinged with amber. But Emily's stumble was short-lived.

'There is no life after death!' she affirmed suddenly and loudly. 'There is no world to come. This life is all we possess.'

The display returned to a glowing green. The congregation hummed its pleasure.

'Emily. Do you have faith?'

'I do not have faith. Faith means believing in something that cannot be proved. Faith is irrational and forbidden.' The display still shone green.

Doron allowed himself a smile, for this girl's triumph

was his triumph also. 'Excellent, Emily. And, finally, say The Anathemas.'

Emily's face was a mask as she recited the ritual condemnations decreed by the Republic. 'Anathema be on any god, any almighty, any supposed maker of what is seen or unseen. I am a human being, set free from superstition by Our Saviour, Charles Darwin.'

Above her head the display bar went suddenly blank. The room fell silent – then broke into whoops of delight and applause as it lit up again in a panel of solid green.

Jenna hurried forward to help remove the headset from Emily and reward her with a tender hug. Doctor Tomas made a note in her file while, in the background, Doron recited the formula by which a successful Scrutiny was declared over:

'Rejoice and be glad Emily, for you were dead and now you live again. You were lost and now you are found. You were stricken and now you are cured!'

Jack was called. Again the pattern was repeated. The same droned responses generated the same green approval from the equipment measuring their sincerity. Jack returned to his place with a simple smile on his face.

'Sarih,' called Doron.

The smiling girl looked up at the sound of her name. Jenna stepped forward to take her by the hand and led her to the chair. But she helped attach no headset to her. No wires trailed from Sarih's skull to the equipment on Doctor Tomas's table. It was the doctor who spoke next.

'By the authority of the Republic vested in me, Sarih has been declared eligible for the Alternative Rite of Scrutiny.'

Doron's script had changed. 'Sarih,' he began, 'if I ask

a question you can't answer then just say you don't know. Do you understand?'

Sarih nodded. Her smile didn't wane.

'Sarih. Did a supernatural being make you?'

A pause, then, 'I don't know.'

'Were you made for any purpose? Do you have an immortal soul? Is there a life after death? Do you have faith?'

After each question, Sarih echoed her smiling answer, 'I don't know.'

'One last question then, Sarih. Are you happy?'

Now Sarih did react, like a dog who'd just heard a word she recognised. She nodded. 'I am happy!' she said, repeating the words like a mantra as Doron declared formally, 'Rejoice and be glad, Sarih, for you are cured!'

The excited buzzing from the assembly slowly died down. Raul felt eyes turn his way.

'Raul!'

Raul rose from his place and crossed the refectory floor towards the high-backed chair. Doctor Tomas and Jenna were ready for him.

Without a word the healer guided him into the chair. Standing before him, she began to attach the headset. Raul felt it pressing down on the top of his skull. Jenna made various adjustments, tightening the headset's rim until it felt to Raul as though a thick rubber band was squeezing his head. He looked up and saw Jenna nod. At the table, Doctor Tomas pressed a button on the control panel before her.

Raul didn't find the sensation unpleasant – no darting pin-pricks or dull throbbing as he'd anticipated. Just a steadily growing warmth and, from above his head, residual beams of flickering green light shining out from the display panel. Beyond the light he could make out the others – Jack and Emily, contented, Sarih smiling her simple smile. And Arym; Arym with her eyes downcast, as if she was afraid to watch.

'Raul—' Doron's voice seemed to carry through the headset and burrow into the centre of his skull. 'Did a supernatural being make you?'

'I don't understand the question.'

A loud murmur arose from the seats around him. Raul saw Doron exchange glances with Doctor Tomas. And above his head the rays of colour flickered amber.

'The question refers to origins, Raul. All you have to do is read the answer from the sheet you were given.'

Raul threaded a hand into the folds of his cowl. He didn't remove it. 'My biological ancestors made me, countless numbers of them dating back to the dawn of time.'

The display above his head was flickering between amber and green, as if uncertain where to settle.

'That is an incomplete answer, Raul.' Doron's voice was like iron. 'You must give the complete answer. Read from the sheet you were given.'

Now Raul's hand did emerge from his cowl. But instead of a sheet of paper it held a book, the edges of its pages feathered and curled from the effect of sea water. 'I'll read from this instead,' he said calmly.

And in the hush he heard his own unwavering voice, rising up to the vaulted roof of the refectory just as he imagined Brother Mark's voice would have echoed around the walls of his lonely cave whenever the gentle monk had read the same passage aloud.

'"In the beginning God created the heavens and the earth. Now the earth was a formless void, there was darkness over the deep, and God's spirit hovered over the water…"'

It took the listeners a few moments to realise what they were hearing. Even then the initial reaction was one of stunned amazement. Nobody moved. Raul read on, aware only of the power of the words on his lips.

'"God said, 'Let there be light', and there was light. God saw that light was good, and God divided light from the darkness…"'

Now things began to happen. From the body of the room a low moan began to rise, as from mourners at a funeral. Arym looked up, her head shaking from side to side and her mouth open in a silent scream. Doron too, Raul realised, had come out of shock. He'd abandoned his lectern and was moving swiftly across the refectory floor towards him. He had little time left. With a steady finger he turned to the next page of Brother Mark's Bible. The verses he wanted almost leapt out at him.

'"God created man in the image of himself, in the image of God he created him, male and female he created them. God blessed them… "'

Then Doron was on him. The wrinkled Bible was wrenched from his hands and hurled to the side before the healer, eyes blazing, began lashing at Raul's face with the flats of his hands. The assault was short-lived – moments later Doctor Tomas was at Raul's side, some instrument in her hand. He felt a sharp jab in his upper arm, the briefest pain, then lost consciousness.

His fading memory was not of a voice or a face or

a sensation. It was of a colour. Above his head, the display was glowing a fierce and accusing red.

'Everybody is disappointed in you, Raul. Doron and Jenna hoped it wouldn't come to this, I'm sure. Arym too. They all tried their hardest with you.' A thin smile formed on Doctor Tomas's lips. 'I must be honest, however. I am *not* so disappointed.'

She looked down on the unblinking Raul. How young and vulnerable they always looked on her operating table. How dependent on her skills to cure them.

'I am going to cure you, Raul,' she murmured. 'Your illness is severe. Far more deep-seated than I imagined.' She ran a finger lightly over the round, pink scar on Raul's upper arm. 'Never before has a resident rejected our help in so extreme a manner.' The finger continued journeying upwards, tracing a gentle path along Raul's neck, over his jawbone, up the side of his motionless face, to come to rest on the side of his now shaven head. 'But my instruments can cut through to the very source of your illness.' She bent low to whisper in Raul's ear. 'I can destroy it once and for all.'

Humming lightly to herself, Doctor Tomas pulled a small trolley closer to the operating table. It carried an instrument not unlike the one they had used at the Rite of Scrutiny. Coils of differently-coloured wires sat beside it, all terminated with electrodes. Doctor Tomas began squeezing small blobs of a clear gel across the surface of Raul's shaven skull. Into each blob she carefully pressed an electrode.

'Soon, Raul,' she said gently, 'all will be well. Your life

will be one of peace.' Smiling, she touched Raul's forehead with the tips of her gloved fingers. 'A peace only I can give to you. A peace the world cannot give.'

Doctor Tomas straightened up. She was almost ready. As ever, she gave silent thanks that she was living in the age she was. Less than a century before she would have been preparing for a major task. A team of assistants would have been at her beck and call, an armoury of scalpels, drills and other chilling instruments sterilised and ready to hand. Now, she could work alone. With laser-guidance and ultrasound scalpels, operations could be performed without blood or scars. Afterwards there would be no physical signs that Raul had ever undergone psycho-surgery.

She checked the anaesthesia control unit opposite. A thin tube ran from it to a point behind Raul's left ear. A small pulsing display showed that all was well. 'You're doing fine, Raul,' she murmured.

Now she reached across to the instrument beside her. She dabbed at a heat-sensitive pad. Immediately opposite, on an arm projecting up from the side of the operating table, another display burst into life. Doctor Tomas studied it carefully. The sight of the irregular oval shape thrilled her as much as ever. The ultimate triumph of evolution: the human brain. The brain of the boy on the table before her.

Doctor Tomas pressed a button controlling the tiny recording unit attached to the lapel of her tunic. When she spoke this time it was in clipped, formal tones. Preserving her work for posterity was vital. As she was following in the footsteps of pioneers, so others would follow in hers.

240

'Research on unbelievers has shown conclusively that their supposedly 'religious' experiences involve two areas of the brain in particular. Firstly, the parietal lobes. These provide a human's sense of time and place. Unbelievers, absorbed in what they called 'meditation', will contrive to shut down the activity of their parietal lobes. This results in a trance-like state, accompanied by feelings of insignificance and a consequent 'oneness' with some perceived "other" – their so-called God.'

The surgeon slipped her tone down a notch. Adding little digressions, she'd found, both lightened the academic detail and demonstrated the depth of her learning.

'In this regard, the arch-unbeliever Jesus of Nazareth was a classic example. Students of superstition history will find that he regularly claimed, "My Father and I are one."' Now she injected a little warmth. 'Sadly our present-day techniques of analysis were not available to the physicians of his day! If they had, a self-stimulating parietal implant would almost certainly have been the recommendation. Such implants promote the feeling of self-worth. Had Jesus of Nazareth come to realise that selfishness is a virtue, much of human history could have been altered.'

Doctor Tomas reached across and picked up a lightweight, pen-shaped object. She was almost ready to begin.

'However the second area of brain activity offers, in my view, a far more fruitful line of attack. I refer, of course, to that of the temporal lobes.'

She lightly, almost idly, ran the pen around and over

Raul's temple as she spoke on. The next part would be common knowledge to her audience, but was necessary for the sake of completeness.

'The temporal lobes are situated in the temporal cavity, behind the eye sockets and underneath the temples. They operate as seats of memory and experience. When these lobes malfunction, many problems can occur. Of most interest to the diagnosis of unbelief is that the afflicted can suffer from abnormal sensory perceptions and religious or moral preoccupation. If we are to cure the scourge of unbelief it is my contention that modifications in the temporal lobes are necessary. That is what I propose to do with the subject of this report: Raul of Nurture-House Eleven.'

That was sufficient description. The mere mention of a nurture-house would be understood as consent for her to operate on Raul in the name of scientific progress. Raul was owned by the Republic, had been brought up by the Republic. It would be assumed that he would want to show his gratitude in this way.

Neither was it strictly necessary to spell out the dangers faced by the patient. But Doctor Tomas did so. After all, highlighting the difficulties would only serve to maximise the appreciation of her talents.

'Locating the precise regions to be modified is crucial, of course. My analyses of the tempora are all carefully collated and will be available when the work is complete. At this stage let me say that I can locate the dysfunctional area within the bounds of reasonable certainty. The danger of collateral damage has been reduced as far as possible. Haemorrhage remains the highest risk.

242

I believe the benefits to the Republic outweigh the risk to the patient.'

This formula of words, accepted – indeed, insisted upon – by the Republic, would normally be the final pre-operative sentence. Doctor Tomas would now have been expected to commence surgery. She had one further statement to make, however. Dated this day, it would be the first evidence of her declaration of intent: evidence that would in future years place her amongst the Blesseds of the Republic.

'My work is designed to eradicate more than a belief in an unseen God. Its eventual aim is to remove belief in *any* form. Is there that much difference between declaring, "In the beginning God made..." and "In the beginning was the Singularity"? I suggest not. Both involve a declaration in support of the unimaginable. And why is that possible? Because we allow free will. And yet what good does free will serve? Free will leads to disobedience – and disobedience leads to misery. *That* is the dysfunction I seek to root out: the potential to disobey. The result will be the ultimate in human happiness: joy through obedience!'

Her heart singing, Doctor Tomas brought the Gamma Knife across to Raul's temple. The name was a misnomer. With this knife there would be no blood. All she had do was depress a button with her forefinger to deliver a finely-targeted dose of radiation to where she wanted. On the display before her, a cross-hair tracer moved slowly across the image of Raul's brain.

'Don't worry, Raul,' she murmured, 'you won't feel a thing.'

243

On the operating table, Raul heard her clearly. The anaesthetic had left him exactly as it was designed to. It had immobilised his muscles while leaving his brain activity unimpaired. He couldn't move his arms or his legs, but he'd heard everything Doctor Tomas had said. He couldn't move his head, blink his eyelids even, but he'd seen her every move in the muted light. He couldn't speak, but he could think – for that was essential, of course. How else could the activity of his brain be monitored if not by leaving it capable of responding to stimulus during the operation?

So now Raul fought in the only way he could fight: with his mind. He tried to flood it with memories and thoughts: of the distant stars, of the shells on the beach, of universal constants, of Brother Mark's journal, of the image in his mind's eye of Brother Stefan's window. Whatever part of his being this woman was going to remove, he didn't want it to go without a fight.

He was doing this as, beside him, Doctor Tomas applied the necessary pressure to the control button of the Gamma Knife.

Raul heard not a sound. He felt not a thing. And, mercifully, he didn't see what Doctor Tomas saw as, on the screen in front of her, a small section of tissue shrivelled and died.

Raul looked normal.

Arym hadn't known what to expect. A boy with his head swathed in bandages, perhaps, lying beneath crisp white sheets. In the event, apart from his shaved head, her brother looked normal.

It had been two days since the scene during the Rite of Scrutiny. Two days in which she'd struggled to deal with her own thoughts, once so firm and now such a jumble. She'd not approached Jenna or Doron and they, thankfully, had been busy with other things. Apart from the Gatherings the only time Arym had exchanged words with them had been at the jetty that morning.

They were there to say goodbye to Emily, Jack and Sarih. The three of them had returned to the mainland on the morning cargo boat. She'd waved until they were only recognisable from their outlines, Emily and Jack seated together in the centre of the boat, Sarih standing up in the prow like a happy figurehead. Arym had wondered whether their families would recognise them, even at close quarters.

It was on the walk back that Jenna had said that she should be able to see Raul soon.

'Doctor Tomas is confident he'll make a full recovery. He'll be cured, Arym!'

'We searched his room,' said Doron. 'We found that journal beneath the floorboards as you said. That forbidden book…' His lips curled in contempt as he forced the words out, 'that Bible, must have been hidden there with it.'

'Didn't he mention it to you, Arym?'

Arym shook her head. If they wanted to assume that, she wasn't going to contradict them. 'No, he didn't mention it,' she said.

And she'd wondered if he ever would have a chance to mention anything again. Now, though, as Jenna ushered her into Raul's room, she thought that he looked normal.

He wasn't in bed. The window was open and he was sitting in his chair, gazing out across the grassy oval. Beyond it, a lukewarm sun shone down on winter-barren trees dappled with the first green buds of spring.

Arym ran to Raul's side. He looked up. Giving him a hug and a kiss, Arym knelt beside his chair.

'How you doing, semi-brother?' she asked brightly.

Raul looked down at her. She saw the familiar hint of a smile at the corners of his mouth. Same old Raul. His brown eyes too, never still, moving now as they scanned her face from top to bottom, tilting his own head as he did so.

Yes, she thought, same old Raul! That is until her brother's eyes stopped moving, his head gave a dull shake, and he asked, 'Who are you?'

When, finally, Raul was left alone, he returned to gazing out of the window. It had been a very confusing time. The girl who'd been to see him had been very sad. She'd cried a lot. That had made him feel sad and he hadn't liked that. What had she said her name was? A-something. A-rym, that was it. Arym was the one who'd held his hand and talked about being his sister. He hadn't known what a sister was. She'd said it meant they had the same mother. That was the only time she'd smiled, when he'd said he didn't remember their mother. She'd said she didn't either. The smile had been a sad one though. The other person, the one in the uniform, had stopped her then, saying Raul is a bit tired, come again and see him tomorrow. The Arym girl had told him she would and said they'd talk about the boat trip he'd be going on as soon as he was better.

246

That had made some sense. As he gazed out of the window, Raul thought he remembered a boat trip not so long ago. Or it might have been years ago. He couldn't tell. His thoughts were a jumble, bits mixing with other bits. He'd felt that a few times as the Arym girl had talked. When she'd used certain words – nurture-house, Guardian, Celebreon – it had felt briefly as though a light was trying to shine through the darkness in his mind. Then the light had gone out.

In the distance he could see water, and land beyond. Was that where the boat would take him, across that water? Raul closed his eyes suddenly, as the sensation of light shining in the darkness came to him again. More water. He'd been on water another time. No, not on the water – *in* water. He fought, trying to hold on to the memory. There was a girl – yes, the Arym girl! – and they were in the water. But not all the time. They were on rocks, too. Rocks with water all round them. The light faded, then came on again in a different place. More rocks. They were climbing them. Now stopping beside a wall of rock. No, there was a gap in it. He was going through the gap. He could hear something. A cough. And he could see a light. But this was a real light, not one in his head. There was a man in the light. A coughing man. Now they were talking. Without his cough he had a soft voice. Soft like the girl who'd come in with the Arym-girl earlier. Who was he? Who? Remember…

Raul's eyes opened. There was a dull, throbbing ache in his head. Remembering things was so hard. Remembering things made his head ache all the more. It was easier not to try remembering things.

247

On the far side of the grassy oval there were birds, encouraged by the returning warmth of sun, fluttering from branch to branch. Nice birds, thought Raul. Pretty birds. Clever. Good to watch. Watching didn't make his head ache.

He leaned forward. He gazed out across the sun-streaked island at the trees and the birds and the water. He smiled a simple smile. He felt happy now.

'Why, Arym?' said Doron.

'To give me some experience at supervising a group,' said Arym. 'To see if I'm any good at it.'

'You'll be wonderful,' said Jenna. 'You helped with your own group. With Emily and Jack. You were good with Sarih, too.'

Arym appeared doubtful. 'But they were all getting better. I'd like to try with some new guests. To see if they're any different.'

Doron weighed things over. 'Well…if Jenna's happy you could take a couple from her new group. They've only been with us for a week.'

'That would be wonderful,' said Arym.

'And you want to have them clear some more of the garden, yes?' said Jenna.

'Yes, that's right,' said Arym. 'I thought I'd take Raul out there to watch.'

Doron gave a nod of approval. 'Yes, that's a good idea. So long as he doesn't join in. Doctor Tomas says Raul mustn't over-exert himself. He's doing well but there is still the slight risk of a haemorrhage.'

'He'll be doing nothing. Just watching.'

'Very well, then,' said Doron.

'And I'll come over every now and then to see how you're doing,' said Jenna. 'Where did you say you thought you'd have them working?'

'Alongside the sanitarium wall,' said Arym.

'How are you, Raul?' asked Arym.

'I'm good, Arym,' smiled Raul. 'Sister.'

'Well done!' She wiped a tear away quickly. Raul had already said how her being sad stopped him being happy. 'Keep doing as well as this and they'll soon be letting you leave.'

Raul frowned. 'What was wrong with me?'

'You were having...' Arym appeared to be searching for the right word, '...different thoughts. Different to other people.'

'What sort of thoughts? I can't remember them. There's so much I can't remember.'

'Later,' said Arym. She took Raul by the hand. 'Come on, I'm taking you outside this morning. It'll do you good.'

Raul got to his feet a little unsteadily. The throbbing behind his eyes had eased a little but it was still there.

He walked alongside Arym, down the stone stairs to the vestibule. A couple of guests were there waiting for them, kitted out and all ready for garden work. A light flickered in Raul's memory, then faded to be replaced by the thought that the two workers didn't look happy. They looked a bit angry and a bit sleepy. Perhaps they hadn't been made well yet.

Arym led the way out into the cloister garth. As they walked round Raul pointed at the statue of Charles Darwin.

'The Saviour, right?'

Arym nodded. 'That's what we call him, Raul.'

'The Saviour is a good man. He saved us from…something.'

'Superstition,' said Arym. 'Well done, Raul.'

Outside, the garden felt fresh. Before spring arrived properly there would still be cold winds and sharp frosts to blacken tender buds, but on that day it seemed as if the season had arrived already. Even when Arym led them through the archway into the jungle of brambles and undergrowth, Raul still felt as if he was in some kind of wonderland.

Arym instructed her two charges, then sat him on a bench seat. Raul looked around. So many colours. So many shades. Dark and light. Light and dark…dark in a cave…light in a cave…an old man…hair white in the light…

Raul snatched at Arym's arm as the memory tried to fade. 'An old man. I keep seeing an old man. It's dark and it's light and he's there and I'm there and…' He looked up, saw Arym framed in the archway of trees just as she had been framed in the entrance to the cave before she left, '…and you. You were there, Arym, sister.'

'Yes, I was,' said Arym quietly.

'Who was the man?'

Beyond Arym the two new guests were looking lost. Raul's sister went to turn away, saying, 'I'll tell you later.'

Raul felt the moment fading, as if he was walking into a morning mist. 'Now! Tell me now!' he shouted, snatching at her arm, only to let go again as a pain shot deep into his temple.

'Easy,' said Arym quietly. 'His name was Mark – Brother Mark.'

'Will I see him again?'

'No, Raul. He's dead.'

The coughing. Yes, he remembered thinking the coughing was bad. But there was more. 'He told me things, didn't he?'

'Yes, he did.'

Raul closed his eyes, trying to recapture the moment. It was too much effort. He gave up, letting the memory float away. The pain in his head slowly eased. When he opened his eyes again, Arym had gone.

He could hear her, though. Raul stood up, took a few steps towards the big wall to his left. Then he saw her. She was with the helpers. They were deep in the dead brambles and sprouting new growth that was clawing at the old stones. He watched for a moment, then went back to slump on his seat. Again, unreachable memories seemed to be bobbing just beneath the surface of his mind.

This place...garden...bonfire...cutting branches...not like them, though... I was making a nice shape...they're just cutting, hacking, pulling...

The effort wearied him. He gave up and fell asleep, his cowl wrapped warmly round him like a blanket. When he woke, it was to find Arym tugging at his sleeve. A bell was tolling loudly nearby.

'Gathering of Sext, Raul,' said Arym.

He walked slowly with her, back to the cloister garth. The service was nice. He couldn't remember all the words of the Lyrene Promise, but he joined in where he could.

The chanting sounded nice. Arym seemed to know exactly when the notes fell and when they soared. She had a nice voice. The statue of the Saviour looked like he was listening to her, so Raul settled for listening too.

'We prom-ise *this* day

To be cheer-ful *and* kind

And cur-i-ous and brave *and pat-ient*

To study and think *and* work hard

All of us in our diff-*er-ent* ways.'

They had a meal afterwards. The healers – Doron? Jenna? – were there. They talked with Arym about how the work was going. Raul didn't listen, not to them. The final sentence of the Lyrene Promise was still lingering in his head:

All of us in our diff-er-ent ways.

The words were still there when Arym took him out again for the afternoon. He sat and watched them do more clearing. One of the helpers was left-handed, noticed Raul. The other was right-handed. Arym used both hands as she pointed and directed.

All of us in our diff-er-ent ways.

They were doing well. He could see all the way alongside the big building now, right up as far as the point where it seemed to fall over the edge of the cliff.

Now Arym was coming back to him, leaving her helpers to drag the shorn branches and roots and tendrils of vine to the fire they'd got under way.

'Raul,' she said quietly. 'Remember the man?'

'The man?' echoed Raul.

'The man in the cave.'

'Mark. Brother. Not sister. Brother Mark.'

'That's right. Do you remember asking me what he told you?'

The man. The dark and the light. Raul tried to claw the memory close. The man was saying things. Many things.

'I remember. What did he say?'

'He talked about a window. In a chapel.'

Chapel. The word resonated in Raul's head. Cha-pel. He felt a sudden sadness. The man was crying.

'The man wasn't happy, was he? Why wasn't he happy, Arym, sister?'

'He was remembering his friends, Raul. From long ago. Their names were Romuald and Conor and Liam – and Stefan.'

As she said this it seemed to Raul as if two separate pieces had floated together in his mind. Those names. And…

…in our diff-er-ent ways.

'They were – something. Something different to other people. That's why he was sad. They'd been…' The link to what he was looking for wasn't there.

'The man's friends had been trapped in the chapel you asked him about, Raul.'

'No!'

'Yes, Raul.'

'No, that's not why he was crying! He was crying because— '

Raul squeezed his eyes together, trying to shut out the pounding in his head, trying to find the link.

…diff-er-ent ways.

'—because he knew of a different way! He knew and he didn't tell them. That's why he was sad!'

Arym hugged him, made him sit down as she knelt beside him. 'Well done, Raul. Oh, well done.'

She looked around. Her two charges were looking her way. Arym realised that the Gathering bell would soon be tolling for Vespers. She waved them off, but didn't follow. Instead she eased Raul to his feet.

The area they'd spent the day clearing was like a corridor through time. On one side, the aged stones that had once been a monastery. On the other, new growth summoning energy for the future months. Arym led Raul along it as quickly as she could, talking as they moved, trying to keep the memories firm in his mind.

'He *did* say there was a different way, Raul. He said it was beside the wall. He said it looked like a round drain.'

She stopped then, and pointed at the ground. Raul looked down. He saw roots and thin stumps projecting from the dark earth like – like – rocks from water…like the rocks they'd gone across to find the man, the Brother. He saw a patch swept clean of leaf mould and soil. And in the centre of the patch he saw a round thing, a circle defined by a radius and a universal constant, and in that moment more links connected in his head and he knew that down beneath that circle was a place he had to see before he could be truly happy.

'Chapel,' he smiled. 'Stefan's window.'

'That's right, Raul. You want to go down there, don't you?'

Raul nodded. 'Yes.'

Arym led him away. 'Then do it, Raul. Don't tell anybody, not me, not Doron or Jenna. Just wait till nobody's around and do it.'

They walked, arm-in-arm, back through the garden and into the cloister garth. In the fading light the statue of Charles Darwin looked downcast, unhappy. A good man, thought Raul. Like the man in the cave. Both good in their different ways.

...*diff-er-ent*...

His head ached, badly. But the memory was still there, and growing. Flickering thoughts of other times he'd heard – no, read – that word were trying to crowd in on him. A book. Two books. One faded. One wrinkled and water-stained. Both taken away by Arym's friends. Unhappy friends.

'If I go to the chapel your Doron and your Jenna will be unhappy,' he said. 'And the other lady. The one who looks at my head every morning.'

'Doctor Tomas,' said Arym.

The name meant nothing. Only the eyes came to Raul, looking down at him from above while he was helpless. 'If I make them unhappy, will they do things to me again?'

Arym stopped. She shook her head, blinking back the tears. 'Raul, there's nothing they can do to you that's worse than what they've done already.'

Thoughts kept coming and going, like creatures of the night. One would enter into the light of his mind, stay for a while, then dart away into the shadows. Raul lay back on his pillow, breathing deeply, waiting for the throbbing behind his eyes to ease. Finally it did, though not completely. Since the Gathering of Compline a hint of it had been ever-present, a dull echo of pain. Raul eased himself out of bed.

The flashlight lay where he'd left it, on the table. Arym had slipped it into his fingers during the Gathering of Compline. She said nothing, for nothing was needed. If he didn't understand why she'd given it to him then words wouldn't help. But he *had* understood. Hard as it was, he *had* remembered.

He turned on the flashlight, angling it so that it shone across the square of paper beside it. Raul's scratchy, wavering diagram was lit up. He'd drawn it earlier, worried that he'd forget what Arym had shown him and where it was. Now he realised he wouldn't need to take it with him. The picture of the garden wasn't melting from his mind, nor what he was going out there to do. Those links at least were holding firm.

Flashlight turned off again, Raul eased open his door. The dull night lights glowing in the corridor and on down the stone staircase were enough to guide him out into the cloister garth. Outside there was a wan moon above, its face scarred by wispy cloud. Raul shivered in spite of the warmth of his cowl. Slowly, almost plodding, he made it to the garden and on through the archway to where he'd sat watching Arym's clearance work. Now he turned the flashlight back on again, playing it over the sanitarium wall as he felt his way alongside it. Further...further... until his feet left the softness of nature and landed on metal.

Briefly Raul wondered what he was supposed to do next. Then he was bending down, forcing his fingers beneath one edge of the rusted plate. He heaved it upwards. It didn't move. He heaved again, pulling upwards with all his might. The cover came free with a groan. Earth and twigs clattered gently down into the hole. Raul played the light down after them, bouncing it off the dry brickwork and the curved rungs embedded in it.

Leaning over the edge of the hole, he placed one hand on the top rung. He was surprised to find how much his hands were shaking. His legs too. He had to steady them on the lower rungs before he could think of moving. Slowly, with the torch jammed between one arm and his side, Raul finally began the short descent to the bottom.

When his feet touched earth he almost overbalanced. The pain behind his eyes returned, as if the effort of wrenching the metal plate aside had torn them free from their sockets. He paused, catching his breath and playing the flashlight into a passage ahead. He edged forward, one hand stretched in front of him as he pointed the flashlight down at the uneven ground.

Thus it was that Raul touched the lever before he saw it. Recessed into the stonework, his fingers caught it as he reached the end of the passageway. Before he'd even brought the light up to eye level he'd felt another contrast. First it had been cold metal instead of rough stone, now it was smooth wood – for that was what faced him. From ground to head-height, the passageway ended in a wall of stained but smooth wood.

When you pulled that lever, a false part of the chapel's wood panelling sprung loose.

Where the voice in his head came from, how the links in his memory had mysteriously connected, Raul didn't know. But they had, and so with a juddering hand he did what the voice had said. The lever resisted no more than necessary for the spring-loaded catch it controlled to be released. The snap as the panel sprang free echoed around the walls like the crack from a whip. And then Raul inserted his fingers into the gap between wood and stone…he slid the panel to one side…and walked forward, sensing the change from rough earth to smooth tile…was at the end of his journey.

The panel brought him out beside a row of eight dusty and cobwebbed wooden seats, high-backed and topped by carved canopies. Raul slumped into the nearest before his legs gave out. From somewhere beneath his feet came the sounds of small claws scurrying away. He played the beam downwards. A padded rail, perhaps for kneeling on, ran the length of the row. Beneath it, a layer of dust on the floor was littered with black droppings.

As he pulled himself up, the flashlight struck something solid. A long shelf, also row-length, was in front of him at waist height. It still had a book on it, open. Raul leaned forward, shining the beam on the pages. As he turned them they crackled with dust and age. A shaft of memory – of another book he'd seen that had felt the same – came and went. But in this book, the words he was reading sounded new, not old; familiar, yet strange. *Lauds, Matins, Vespers, Compline.* He read through some chants and responses. They were different. There were no mentions of Darwin the Saviour. No Lyrene Promise. Some unknown region of his mind formulated an explanation. These versions were here first, the others had followed.

Other questions arose. Why the changes? Were wrongs being made right? Or were these right and the later versions all wrong? Could they both be right? But, as quickly as they arose, the questions faded and were gone.

Raul stood up, holding on to the shelf for support with one hand as he held the flashlight with the other. In the wider arc of light he saw that an identical set of seats were ranged opposite. Separating them was a scuffed and dusty aisle. He turned the light to one side, directing its beam along this aisle. It ended at a closed door. Raul edged out, shuffling slowly through the dust and droppings.

The door was barred and bolted. Thick iron bolts were rammed into the stone arch above and the flagstoned floor below. Reinforcing them, at head-and-knee-height, two powerful cross beams sat wedged defiantly in unbreakable iron clasps. And, as he looked at it, Raul knew what lay on the other side of this door. Scarred woodwork, from frustrated battering and chopping. Stairs leading upwards, hollowed by the feet of many. But stairs now buried beneath layers of rubble and cement...and a mask of flagstones.

Yet again Raul's fractured mind tried to heal itself, tried to rejoin links that had been torn apart. Again the man in the cave, Mark, brother, was there, still crying. Why? What for? No, no – *who* for? His friends. He was crying for his friends. Names gushed in, as if a pipe had burst. Romuald, Liam, Conor. The brothers of Mark, just as Arym was his sister. But not together like him and Arym. Separated. Telling him to go while they stayed...

He turned then, too quickly, almost losing his already unsteady balance. Gripping the flashlight in both hands to stop it shaking, Raul moved back along the dusty aisle, back the way he'd come, unsteadily, his head throbbing, not looking up but playing the beam back and forth just beyond his feet, as a blind man would a stick. Forward, forward…to stop as the fading beam revealed something other than dust and droppings: the flat sole of a sandal.

Raul shifted the light slowly to one side. A second sandal was beside the first, in the same upturned position, as though the wearer was laying face down. For the sandals were not empty. Jutting out from beneath the fastened straps were two white ankle bones. Raul played the beam upwards, knowing in both his heart and his mind what it would reveal: two pairs of leg bones, fibula and tibula, gnawed clean and white by rats; bones which eventually disappeared beneath the layers of a tattered brown cowl. Further over the cowl now, beyond its rope belt, above its unnaturally flattened back, to light the figure's outstretched arms, their skeletal fingers level with the hooded and hidden skull.

Slowly, still gripping the flashlight with both hands, Raul now moved the light to the side. It revealed a second figure, in an identical position. Beside it lay the third.

Romuald, Conor, Liam.

In death each of them prostrate, as though the three monks had deliberately arranged their bodies in this position before their final moments.

Raul suddenly found himself unable to stand any longer. As his legs gave way he threw out a hand towards the shelf in front of the seats nearest to him. His grip was devoid of strength. Stumbling, he landed on his knees then slumped to one side, his back against the shelf. The flashlight landed some way away. He couldn't summon the strength to reach for it. All he could do was look at what its fading light now revealed: at what the three monks had prostrated themselves before.

Beyond their heads lay a square of wooden flooring. Here and there, where scuffling claws had disturbed the dust of the years, some of the polished wood block still glinted faintly. The floor led on to a carved marble table. Vaguely Raul was reminded of another table, the one in the Celebreon. Except that, whereas the Celebreon's table was surmounted by its statue of the Saviour, garishly garlanded and surrounded by birds and beasts, this table bore nothing more than a simple wooden...what was it? ...cross...the shape he'd found in the garden...the shadow on the wall of his room...

Desperately Raul made another lunge for the flashlight; for there was something else, something beyond the cross that he couldn't see and that a dark part of his mind was telling him should be there. A window. A special window. A window that melted hearts. The window that would have let in the light, against which that cross would have been the last living sight of the three men.

His fingers landed tantalisingly close. He stretched again, breathing heavily with the effort, until with a final stretch and a needle of pain behind his eyes, he managed to drag the flashlight to him. He sat up as best he could, and pointed the stuttering beam towards the very end of the chapel.

Set in the rugged stone of the wall was a circle. Raul traced its outline with the beam of light. A circle, maybe two metres in diameter. A circle of dull, dark nothingness. A circle filled with glass which seemed to absorb the little light shining on it and reflect only gloom in return.

Raul's head was burning. But already the deep-down memory that had spurred him towards this place was turning cold and ashen; as cold and ashen as the bleak circle of darkness that was Brother Stefan's window.

At the tolling of the gathering bell for Lauds, Arym had dressed quickly. She'd then walked – not down the stairs towards the cloister garth as usual – but up, to Raul's room. The door was ajar.

She'd gone in and felt his bed. The cool of the sheets told her that he'd been gone for a while. She sat, waiting, listening to the footsteps shuffling along the corridor outside, then to the silence they left behind. The Gathering bell stopped. Arym remained where she was.

Outside, the first fingers of dawn were lightening the sky.

She saw the square of paper on the small table beneath the window. She picked it up, smoothing it on her lap. Raul's diagram was just about readable. She smiled. She didn't move.

They would be in the refectory now. Raul's absence wouldn't cause them any concern. They would wonder about her, though.

Outside, dawn had broken. The sky was clear. The sun was cresting the horizon.

Arym stood up. They could do no more harm to Raul. But she could possibly do some harm to them.

With Raul's scrawled plan between her fingers, she went in search of Jenna and Doron.

Raul squeezed his fingers against his right temple. The pressure did little to ease the pain behind his eyes. And nothing could help the pain in his heart. He burst into tears.

Tears, like the man in the cave. His memory of him was becoming hazier, like a shadow in winter. But he'd talked about a window, this window, of that he was sure. He'd said that it was special. Deep in some hidden place Raul's mind had kept that hope burning. Now, like the flashlight he'd been holding, that hope had flickered and died. He'd not known what to expect, what to look for, even. But it had to be more than the iron-grey nothing he'd found.

Exhausted, Raul slumped back. Sometime later – it could have been seconds or minutes – he became vaguely aware of scratching and scuffling near by. The sound caused Raul to flick his eyes open again. A rat was creeping close, snout twitching. Raul kicked out with his foot, and watched it scurry away to a gap in the panelling beside the marble table – panelling that he could now see, where once there'd been only darkness.

He wondered briefly if it was because his eyes had become adjusted to the gloom. He realised that had to be part of the reason, but only part. It was getting lighter. Dawn was breaking. For confirmation, Raul looked again at the window.

It had changed, almost imperceptibly, but changed it had. The top part had lightened fractionally. It was still a dull grey. And yet – there was more. It was a subtly different greyness. Unless the pain in his head was causing his eyes to play tricks on him, some of the upper fragments of the circle had taken on hues of the palest green. He looked harder, trying to focus. Had other greys become the faintest of yellows? The weakest of blues?

Raul closed his eyes again, trying to work out what might be happening. And a memory came to him. He was back in the nurture-house. At his seat beneath the window, watching the stars and moon disappear as if being melted by the first rays of the sun – rays that would strike the top part of any window before they trickled down towards its bottom.

Now he began to use his eyes in synchrony with his breathing: twenty breaths with them closed, twenty breaths with them open. And each time he opened his eyes the window had changed. Out of the darkest, most forbidding areas emerged scarlets and purples. Slowly these took on subtle variations, melting into cerise, maroon, amethyst, cyan. The lighter colours acted as counterpoint. Yellows melted into gold and amber, ochre and citron; blues shaded through azure to turquoise; reds varied from carmine to pink. As the sun rose further, each colour seemed to blossom and swell to take on a unique brilliance of its own. It was as if the window was coming alive before Raul's eyes.

Slowly, too, the shape became clear. At first it seemed to be no more than a circle with an irregular perimeter. It stayed that way through many cycles of on–off looking until, finally, he saw it plainly.

The window was the earth itself, set in a universe of star-studded black. Raul could make out the delineations of the oceans and the continents. But this globe was not

264

like that of his class atlas, a globe of dull brown and green lands surrounded by oceans of unlikely blue. It was a kaleidoscope of colour. No land was in one colour. Every land was in many colours. And with every moment that passed, every fraction further that the sun rose, these colours were spilling out from this globe, casting their light into the darkest corners of the chapel. They were flooding across the dark wood of the choir stalls; over the tattered cloth on the altar table; over the trails of cobwebs and the clouds of dust and the filthy rat-droppings; over the symbol of the cross; over the cowled and prostrate skeletons.

Over him, too.

Shakily, Raul tried to struggle to his feet. He couldn't move. His head was throbbing, throbbing. As he looked up, the colours of the window seemed to merge and separate, swell and fade, then swell again. Now he became vaguely aware of noises from somewhere close by. Earlier he'd thought he'd heard a bell chime, but these were different noises. Of scuffling feet. Of voices.

'Raul!'

Somebody was calling his name. More than one person. They sounded distant and close at the same time. He heard a scream, the sound of running, feet slapping against the floor, kicking up dust that swirled and danced in the rays of colour. Then there were hands reaching for him, helping him sit up, hands bathed in the same myriad colours.

God said, let there be light.

Arym was there, weeping, like the Brother had.

He looked up at her, shook his head at the futility of her

265

tears, just as the Brother had done. 'Don't be sad. I am happy, Arym, sister.'

'Raul!' A shout, panic and irritation mixing to form fear.

It was Doron. Jenna was kneeling beside him. They were shouting at him, urging him, but their words seemed to do no more than mingle with the motes of dust in the air. What remained of Raul's mind was concentrated solely on the sight of their heads framed in the window, each surrounded by a penumbra of colour – colour from Brother Stefan's resurrected world, washing over them.

Raul smiled his final question.

'Why did there have to be colour, Doron?'

And then he was falling, falling, even though their hands were firmly supporting him, and everything was slipping away as if he was floating and the pain in his head was easing and his heart was singing and the one, blissful thought in his fractured mind was that he was finally going to discover the truth.

They entombed Raul where he'd died, alongside Abbot Romuald and Brother Conor and Brother Liam.

Before then the chapel was gutted. The choir stalls were ripped out and burnt. The wooden cross joined them in the flames.

The chapel's stained-glass window was disposed of in moments, shattered by a Duty team with hammers and whoops of delight. The shards of coloured glass flew out, tumbling down the sheer cliff face and back into the swirling sea from which they'd come. The gaping hole was plugged with brick and stone, then sealed with grey concrete.

The secret entrance was sealed in the same way, the shaft and corridor filled like the cavity in a troublesome tooth, and the metal plate buried beneath a crown of dirt.

The formalities were completed swiftly. Doctor Tomas sent a note informing the Guardian that Raul had sadly failed to recover from essential treatment. The Guardian adjusted her records accordingly and passed the information on. Shortly after, somewhere in the bureaucratic layers supporting the Republic, a keyboard was tapped and Raul's file was deleted.

Standing at the window of her brother's silent room, Arym had seen the cargo boat leave the mainland as a speck and grow to a large dot. She picked up her nurture-house sack and turned to leave. Jenna was standing in the doorway.

'Are you sure about this, Arym?'

Arym smiled, nodded.

'Really sure? You would make a wonderful healer.'

'I don't think so, Jenna. I don't have the...' Arym paused, wanting to choose the right word, one that would have them parting on the right terms. '...dedication,' she added.

Jenna walked with her, down the stairs and through the vestibule. 'Is that all it is?' she asked as they passed out into the fresh air. The healer's voice sank to a murmur. 'If it's any help, I'm ashamed of what happened to those monks.'

'And my brother?'

Jenna shrugged. 'We were trying to help him, Arym. All of us.'

'Like I say, I don't think I'm dedicated enough to offer that sort of help,' said Arym guardedly.

At another time she might have said more, but Doron had hurried to catch them up. He was slightly breathless. *The Writings* were gripped firmly in his left hand.

'I see Jenna has failed to persuade you to stay with us,' he said to Arym. 'A pity. There is a growing need for healers.'

They passed the grassy oval and entered the corridor of trees. Then they emerged and the jetty was in sight. Nearing it, the cargo boat swung to catch the swell that would bring it smoothly into berth. Even from that distance, Arym could see that the two youngsters huddled in its stern looked fearful of what faced them.

Doron pointed with his book. 'Such a need, Arym,' he repeated. 'For as it is written, "the harvest is plenteous but the labourers are few."'

They paused then, Jenna and Doron holding back at the top of the incline, watching, just as they had the day Raul and Arym arrived. Arym put down her sack.

'Why do you think that is, Doron?' Now she too pointed at the new guests approaching the jetty. 'Why do they keep coming?'

'Because they are misguided. Unwell. Like – Raul,' said Doron firmly. 'Even at the end. What were his last words?'

It was a poor act. Arym could see that Doron knew full well what Raul had asked; that he would never be able to forget his question. That knowledge made it easier for her to repeat it to them: '"Why did there have to be colour?"'

'Yes,' nodded Doron. 'And so simply explained by Science. The properties of electromagnetic radiation, the visible spectrum, the constituents of white light – all these have been known for many—'

It was Jenna who interrupted him. 'Raul didn't ask how colour was made. He asked *why*. Why are humans the only creatures known to appreciate its beauty?'

Doron again brandished *The Writings*. 'Not every question has been answered, Jenna. "For now we see through a glass darkly,"' he quoted, '"but in days to come Science will reveal all things. Then shall we understand fully." *That* is the vision that wonderful people like Doctor Tomas are leading us towards!'

The cargo boat was close to its berth. Doron strode on ahead, leaving Jenna and Arym to follow behind.

'He's a true believer,' murmured Jenna.

'Is he?' said Arym.

'What do you mean?'

At the jetty Doron was winding the boat's rope round a bollard. In the stern, the two youngsters hadn't moved.

'Maybe he's not being honest with himself. Maybe the harvest is plenteous because nature is filling a gap. Just like his lemurs in Madagascar.'

Jenna frowned, shook her head. 'I don't understand.'

'He said lemurs evolved because there was a source of food that no other creatures had found. Well, if there is a God, wouldn't nature have filled that gap too? By evolving creatures capable of knowing him?'

Jenna smiled – then laughed, an unthinking laugh. 'Arym, that would only make sense if God exists! And he doesn't!'

But Arym had gone, her sack over her shoulder, down towards the bobbing cargo boat. Tossing her sack lightly aboard, she jumped down onto the weathered seating. She sat in the same spot that Raul had occupied the day they'd

269

come to Parens Island. On the jetty Jenna was still staring at her, leaving Doron to welcome the new arrivals.

The boat's engine thundered into life. Arym turned to face the mainland. She was going back – but to what?

As Jenna had pointed out in her vain attempts at persuasion, 'You'll be sixteen soon, Arym. The Republic won't support you any longer. You'll have to leave the nurture-house. Here you'd be warm and safe and doing so much good. What are you going to do?'

She'd murmured something vague, about knowing people who'd take her in and give her work.

She'd been lying. The people she knew about didn't know her. And she herself knew little more than their names: Glyn and Ruti, Brother Mark's family. She was going to try and seek them out, tell them her story, hope that they would come to her aid just as they'd come to his – and Brother Mark had come to hers.

As the boat angled away from the stone jetty she seemed to hear the old monk's voice on the salt-filled wind:

'...one day you might see something, hear something...experience something; something that tells you you're wrong. It might be a breath of wind, a snatch of music, the love of another person, a cry of fear...'

She hadn't believed him. Far more than that, she hadn't expected it to happen so quickly afterwards. But it had.

The cry of fear.

The cry of fear as she'd struggled in the water after being washed from the reef, as she'd thought she was going to drown; that had burst from her unbidden, springing from a source deep inside that she hadn't known existed.

270

The inexplicable cry that had influenced her actions ever since, its very mystery forcing her to recall what the dying monk had said to her next.

'That's when you'll have to be honest with yourself. That's when you'll have to follow, like I did.'

As the boat turned away, Arym leaned over the gunwale and looked down into the cream-topped water: the same water that had delivered the glass for the window that had been her brother's dying sight; the water that had forced her to cry out as she felt it sucking her under.

And now she whispered, rather than cried, those same words, hoping that they would be heard in some way she didn't begin to understand.

'God, help me.'

MORE ORCHARD BLACK APPLES

Ten Days to Zero	Bernard Ashley	978 1 84362 649 7
Down to the Wire	Bernard Ashley	978 1 84616 059 2
Flashpoint	Bernard Ashley	978 1 84616 060 8
Little Soldier	Bernard Ashley	978 1 86039 879 7
Tag	Michael Coleman	978 1 84362 182 9
Weirdo's War	Michael Coleman	978 1 84362 183 6
The Hollow People	Brian Keaney	978 1 84616 225 1
The Gallow Glass	Brian Keaney	978 1 84616 087 5
Jacob's Ladder	Brian Keaney	978 1 84362 721 0
A Crack in the Line	Michael Lawrence	978 1 84362 283 1
Small Eternities	Michael Lawrence	978 1 84362 870 5
The Underwood See	Michael Lawrence	978 1 84121 170 1
Milkweed	Jerry Spinelli	978 1 84362 485 1
Stargirl	Jerry Spinelli	978 1 84616 600 6

Orchard Black Apples are available from all good bookshops,
or can be ordered direct from the publisher:
Orchard Books, PO BOX 29, Douglas IM99 1BQ
Credit card orders please telephone 01624 836000
or fax 01624 837033 or visit our website: www.orchardbooks.co.uk
or e-mail: bookshop@enterprise.net for details.

To order please quote title, author and ISBN
and your full name and address.
Cheques and postal orders should be made payable to 'Bookpost plc.'
Postage and packing is FREE within the UK
(overseas customers should add £1.00 per book).

Prices and availability are subject to change.